Dance with Me on New Year's Eve

Alana Highbury

Copyright © 2024 Alana Highbury

All rights reserved

The characters and events portrayed in this book are fictitious. Any similarity to real persons, living or dead, is coincidental and not intended by the author.

No part of this book may be reproduced, or stored in a retrieval system, or transmitted in any form or by any means, electronic, mechanical, photocopying, recording, or otherwise, without express written permission of the publisher.

ISBN-13: 979-8-9900284-2-5

Cover design by: Beetiful Book Covers

Printed in the United States of America

To my wonderful children,
May you never doubt how amazing and worthy you are.
I love you, always.

Chapter 1

As I arranged my hair over my cheeks to curtain my face as much as possible, I spotted his form through the corner of my eye, even through the thick, dark strands.

Jeff Chamberlain.

The bane of my existence.

Now it all made sense … Jeff's terse email requesting that I meet with Hazel on Monday morning. Given that *I'm* her assistant, not Jeff, I'd found it peculiar to hear this from him, but I tried not to worry about it. Because thinking about him was bound to ruin my weekend, and I'd resolved on New Year's Day to make every weekend a *great* one. Reading. Watching *Cast Afar* reruns. Maybe even sipping a little wine or making strawberry shortcake if I felt adventurous. Like I said, a great weekend by any standards, right? OK, maybe only by mine.

"Roxanne," he said briskly as he came to a stop several feet in front of me, nodding slightly as his face formed his trademark frown.

A flash of long, shiny black hair caught my attention. My boss rounded the corner into the floral-themed waiting area where we stood, and she eyed my nemesis curiously. "No one calls her Roxanne."

I rolled my eyes. "It's fine." Roxanne was better than Ms. Swan, which he'd called me for the first two years after we met. I was 99% sure he was mocking me because my short, thick neck was nothing like a swan's. After all, he'd decided to dislike me from our very first meeting years ago.

Jeff shook his head. "Nicknames are for family. We are

hardly even colleagues, barely acquaintances."

Flustered, I felt my cheeks redden. Still, he was right that we were barely colleagues—although we both worked for an elite lakeside resort on the edge of town, my event planning role was rather distant from his finance role within the broader corporate structure. And unlike Jeff, I also worked for Hazel.

Hazel's eyes danced in amusement. "I suppose you shouldn't take offense, Roxy, as he insists on calling Mari 'Mariana' too, many years after she hired you two at the resort." She laughed, although neither Jeff nor I was smiling. "Well, anyway, you're about to become much more than acquaintances. You're going to be close colleagues."

My heart rate doubled, and I glanced at him in confusion. I doubt it was possible for his face to become stonier and his posture stiffer as he spoke. "Pardon?"

"Follow me," Hazel said with a wave of her hand as she turned toward the dining room. "I got us the best table."

I glared at Jeff, whose jaw clenched as we followed her past the vacant hostess station. When we stopped behind her at a dark, polished wood table by the floor-to-ceiling window overlooking the icy lake, he muttered, "Hardly."

Hazel whirled around. "You don't like it?"

She scooted into the booth and placed her oversized red handbag on the seat next to her. After Jeff sat across from Hazel, I reluctantly sat next to him. He scooted closer to the window, and I tried to sit as far from him as possible.

"This is a business meeting, is it not?" he asked, folding his hands in front of him. When Hazel nodded, he added, "The glare and the draft near a large window are not ideal. Plus, the view may be distracting for some of us." He shot a sideways glance at me.

Hazel's dark eyebrows rose as she looked between us. "A distracting view? Jeff, I had no idea—"

"The *lake*." He waved his hand briefly in my direction. "It's an objectively appealing view, and some people are easily distracted."

I inhaled sharply as my face heated again. He was accusing me of being easily distracted? "Ah—I—" I attempted to clear my throat. "I have an excellent attention span. A neurologist once told me I—that is, I once heard ... um."

Stop, just stop talking.

Why, why would you mention a neurologist? As if they need another reason to think you're weird!

I clutched the water glass on the table, wondering when it had gotten there as I took a long swig. I tried to think of something else to say, but I managed only a few more awkward vocal-like sounds.

"Jeff, that was unfair. I've known Roxy for years now—we both have! She's not flighty or constantly distracted." Hazel shook her head, frowning at him. "I don't know where you got that idea."

But I knew.

Sometimes I got flustered, or anxious, or I just ... froze. Often all of the above, basically any time I was with any other person. It wasn't distraction exactly, but I got stuck in my head, battling with my anxiety and nerves ... it wasn't that ludicrous to assume I was daydreaming.

In fact, *that* assumption was better than the reality, which I tried so hard to hide: the social anxiety that was debilitating at worst and humiliating at best. I sometimes feared my pitiful attempts at concealment only made it more obvious.

So this idea of me being prone to distraction? Maybe it wasn't the worst thing. Nope, the truth was the worst thing. Sure, let them think I'm just a daydreamer.

I forced the corners of my lips into what I hoped was a polite smile and glanced at Jeff briefly, summoning my calmest voice. "It's all right. You're probably right, Jeff."

His light-brown eyes settled on me, his face unreadable for a moment. I held my breath until he turned to pick up the menu in front of him.

I watched as Hazel studied the menu too. "I can never decide what to have here! So many great options. Even the steamed broccoli here is divine here, somehow." Her gaze swung to me. "Aren't you going to order anything, Rox?"

I nodded. "I've been here before, so I know what to order."

Her head tilted as she eyed me questioningly. "You always order the same thing?"

I nodded more slowly, feeling hesitant about my answer now because she was giving me that look. The one I *hated*. The one that said *There's something odd about you*.

But I had to be honest. "I do."

Hazel's mouth opened and then closed. Finally, with a quick glance at Jeff, she turned back to me and shrugged. "OK, I kind of envy you. It's so hard for me to decide because everything sounds so good. Jeff, is it the same for you?"

He snapped his menu closed. "No."

What a strange man. Infuriating most of the time, confusing at other times. For whatever reason, neither Hazel nor my other boss, Mariana, seemed to mind his off-putting demeanor. But our dislike for one another had only worsened after we met. He was cold, rude, abrupt ... and I couldn't read him. Ever.

And that was *terrible* for me because my overactive brain constantly tried to read people, trying to see if I was making a good impression or making an idiot of myself or acting weird or ... you know, resembling a normal, social human. If I couldn't read a person, then I couldn't assess how I was doing, how soon I needed to escape, whether people noticed how nervous I was. All the thoughts of a chronically shy and socially anxious woman, unfortunately.

When the waiter came to take orders, I was barely aware of Hazel placing an order, and then my eyes came back into focus as Jeff held up the menu and pointed to the pasta section. "Is there raw egg in the cream sauce?"

The waiter looked at the menu and then at him. "I don't think so?"

Jeff's angular face hardened. "If you don't know, please find out. If there are no undercooked eggs, I'll order that dish.

Otherwise, I'll have the grilled salmon with a Caesar salad."

The waiter swallowed visibly and then nodded before turning to me quickly. "And you, miss?"

"I'm—uh—" I looked desperately at Hazel, who looked at me with sympathy. *Pity.* The worst.

I forced myself to focus on the waiter. "Salmon."

"Soup or—"

"Salad," I spit out as my eyes avoided the waiter's and instead landed on a bowl of greens on a nearby table. "I mean, no, soup. Yes, soup. I want soup."

"The soup of the day is chicken and—"

"Yeah, that." With trembling hands, I busied myself gathering up the menus and nearly shoved them at the waiter as I felt my cheeks burn. "Thanks."

I knew the two of them were probably staring at me because I was acting so odd. But then again, surely they'd seen me act really awkward in public before. That thought certainly didn't make me feel better.

Quick, think of something to say. Anything to distract them from your awkwardness.

"The lake is so nice to … to see."

I nearly face-palmed right there on the table but forced myself to look at Hazel as she smiled and attempted to rescue me. "The lake is beautiful, even when frozen. Hence my desire to sit here."

I forced myself to take some slow, deep (but not too obvious) breaths as Hazel looked between us again and said, "So you both heard the good news about the investor for the new counseling center. Well, Jeff's the one who shared the exciting news." She laughed. "So, I wanted to meet with you both and start making some plans."

I nodded, still not sure why we were *both* here together but trying to be open-minded. I knew how much this new counseling center meant to Hazel. She was fairly well known in the self-help world as a crusader for women with body image issues through her frequent international speaking arrangements and writing, among other things. She'd recently decided to open her own counseling center to expand her local and regional impact and to meet people face to face, which she vastly preferred as an extrovert. Before she even told me this news, she'd already enrolled in an online master's program and spent hours researching how to become a licensed counselor. I was proud to work for her and, honestly, admired her even more now than before.

"So the first agenda item is to set up a project team or at least hire some people to set up the project team. I know the two of you aren't project managers exactly, but you have a lot of the necessary skills." She paused and smoothed her already smooth hair over her left shoulder, probably for effect because that was a very Hazel thing to do. "I want you to be co-project managers on this."

I gasped, and Jeff made some kind of hoarse sound that I only vaguely heard through the tunnel of disbelief as I stared at its source. "You—what?"

Jeff crossed his arms and said calmly, "I work for Mariana, not for you, Hazel."

I nodded vigorously, hoping his characteristic bluntness would actually be a benefit in this case.

Leveling her shrewd, dark eyes at him, Hazel replied, "I'm aware."

I saw the tiniest muscle flex in his square jaw before he spoke again. It was basically the only sign of emotion his face ever showed, besides his usual frown. I'd certainly heard the frustration and arrogance in his voice a million times. Usually directed at me though.

"I'm not sure I can fit in both—" he started.

"Oh, I already talked to Mari about it. She's cool with the plan." Hazel smiled and took a sip of water, as though she hadn't just delivered the worst news.

"The ... *plan*? I—we—" I sputtered and looked at Jeff helplessly. "We can't—"

"What Roxanne is ineptly trying to say is that this would

never work. And for once, I agree with her."

Silence settled over the table as we both stared defiantly at Hazel. Well, Jeff did anyway. I probably looked frightened and meek.

She stared at us with a blank expression before a small smile teased the corner of her mouth. "Why not? You are both very capable and focused, and you'll have an ample budget to hire contractors."

I took a deep breath to summon my dignity. "With all due respect, Hazel, I'm not as capable as you think. I—"

Jeff scoffed but didn't look in my direction. "It has nothing to do with capability, and you know it."

"Then what is it?" Her eyes held a challenge, and I had a sinking feeling that my boss wasn't going to give up easily. She never did. It was something I admired about her. Most days. Not today.

I swallowed with some effort, trying to think of a professional way to say that Jeff and I ... well, we hated each other. "Hazel, I genuinely care about you and your career. I'm only concerned about the future of the project if I'm working with him. I want the best for you, and I ... well, you see ..." I looked at Jeff, who was peering at me with an unreadable expression, as always. "We wouldn't ... *he* wouldn't—"

"Speak for yourself, Roxanne," he said curtly as he turned back to Hazel and sighed audibly. "I accept the role. It's business, not personal. If she's not up to the task, that's fine. Better, even. I can handle it myself and hire out when needed. I am perfectly capable of working successfully with anyone. It's called being a professional," he added with a side glance at me.

The ire rose suddenly within me, replacing the anxiety of a moment ago, and I almost stood up in protest. Hazel looked as though she was about to speak—hopefully to defend me—but then paused, eyeing me with interest.

I attempted to calm my rapid breathing, trying to ignore the sweat beading on my forehead and in many other places beneath my starchy blue business suit, which I obviously regretted wearing. I turned to Jeff, my voice shaking as I said, "Your unkind implication isn't professional at all, *Jeffrey*." I glanced over at my boss, who'd made a noise that sounded suspiciously like a choked laugh. "Hazel, I'm definitely up for a challenge. I do wonder, though, if hiring a more experienced project manager might be helpful. I could be very successful working with someone whose background and skills complement my own. Jeff could just ... do the bookkeeping or whatever it is he does."

I couldn't believe my mouth was producing all these words, like I was possessed. By indignation, I suppose. I was pretty sure every inch of my skin was covered in sweat now and flushed blotchy red from exertion—not to mention the itchy suit—but for once, I didn't care. I *had* to put Jeff in his place and try by any means necessary to escape Hazel's awful idea that we'd be able to work together. I looked at her with pleading eyes while attempting a wobbly smile.

She merely sighed. "You're both perfectly capable. Jeff's expertise and experience combined with yours ... it will be great, Rox, and I *need* this to be great. If you can learn to get along. So far, I see no evidence that you've even tried. You seemed to dislike each other from the moment you were introduced years ago, and you've made zero effort to get along since then. Am I right?"

My mouth couldn't manage to form any words, and Hazel looked exasperated as she turned to him. "Jeff?"

For once, he didn't seem to have a response at first and slowly rubbed the sleeve of his shirt. Finally, he said, "As you wish, Hazel. I will call Mariana after this to discuss an interim solution for handling my resort finance responsibilities. I'll submit the proposed project plans to you within two weeks."

"You mean *we* will submit the plans, right?" I said, nearly breathless from irritation and overexertion.

Who am I right now?

I never exerted myself this much in conversations. Never. But I couldn't let his swipes at me go unanswered.

He merely crossed his arms and eyed me as his jaw clenched.

"Jeff, I get it," Hazel said, her tone soothing. "You like working alone, and your collaboration skills—"

"My skills are just fine, Hazel," he barked.

She shook her head slightly. "I was going to say that your collaboration skills might be a bit rusty, but I have every confidence you'll rise to meet the challenge."

I couldn't resist a smirk as I glanced at him sitting there even more rigid than usual. It was exhilarating to see him taken down a peg.

"The good news is, Roxy is in a similar boat." She turned to me and patted my hand resting on the table. "You have so much talent and skill, but you're used to working alone a lot. Or only with me."

"That's the way I like it." The words rushed out before I realized I probably wasn't selling myself as someone who could meet this challenge. And normally, I wouldn't *want* to. But seeing the challenge in Jeff's eyes …

Oh yes, I would meet this challenge. "Don't worry, Hazel." My voice was shaky, but I was too incensed to feel embarrassed. "I'm going to do an amazing job for you. You deserve to see your vision become a success."

She smiled warmly. "Thank you. Both of you. Where is our food? I'm famished." Then she laughed in a peculiar way that made me nervous. "By the way, I'd like to open the center by the end of the year. Nine months might be challenging, but I'm sure you can handle it, right?"

Chapter 2

The frigid March air felt wonderful as I strode down the lightly snow-covered sidewalk an hour later. Stress and anxiety tended to make my body heat up a million degrees. But within a minute, I was putting on my mittens and thick knit hat.

My phone buzzed in the pocket of my thick coat, but I wasn't about to take off my mittens to check it. I could wait one more minute until I got home. At least I lived near the restaurant where I'd met Hazel and Jeff. I was basically within walking distance of everything in downtown Shipsvold, a tiny, charming town in southeastern Minnesota. Downtown was less than a mile long and only a couple of blocks wide. And that was pretty much the town.

Sure, some Shipsvold residents—including Hazel and her new boyfriend, Peter—lived a distance away off the country roads. And there was the fancy resort across the lake, which was a bit of a distance to walk uphill. But thank goodness for that, because I wasn't exactly great at committing to organized "exercise." I did own a car, but it sat in my apartment building's underground garage most of the time. I couldn't remember the last time I'd driven anywhere. Like most residents, I could walk or bike almost anywhere, even in the harsh winters, though I preferred to stay home as much as humanly possible.

When the icy two-minute walk was over, I slumped against the wall inside the foyer of my apartment building. I didn't remember today's weather forecast being *this* brutal. I'd grown up in the South but had lived in Minnesota for the last decade, so I should be used to this. Winter here consisted of Christmas, New Year's, and then at least three months of icy misery.

Maybe you never get used to it.

Too late, I spotted a tall, curvy blonde woman starting to open the door into the foyer, where the mailboxes were located, and I cringed under my heavy knit scarf.

Jenna Stirling was the most extroverted person I'd ever encountered, I was certain.

Before I could dash off in the other direction, she was in my face, squinting at me through her thick black lashes. "Is that ... Roxy, is that you?"

I nodded reluctantly, pulling my scarf off my face and immediately regretted it as her rich amber perfume assaulted my senses. "Uh, hi—"

"I am *so* glad I caught you. We need to talk, like, yesterday."

My brows furrowed. What could be so urgent?

Doesn't matter.

Get out of there.

But before I could even begin to utter an excuse to run off, she put a hand on my right shoulder. "Did you *see* that new guy who just moved in?" I shook my head, knowing she wasn't really looking for an answer. "His name is Roberto, and he's freaking gorgeous, Roxy. You would not believe what he was wearing when I bumped into him this morning in the gym. These shorts that barely covered—"

"Jenna, I really can't—"

"Believe me, you're going to want to hear this, hon. He didn't just have a physique to die for, but his *voice*, like velvet, was the most sensual thing I've ever heard. I couldn't resist asking what he was doing tonight." She raised her eyebrows.

"Uh, probably unpacking? You said he just moved in."

She elbowed me sharply and giggled. "Oh no, he has sons who will do all that. Yes, *two sons!* Can you believe it? A single dad. I mean, this is *perfect* for you, Rox. I made sure to tell him you're single, and he—"

"Wait, you said *what*? What … why me?" My brows furrowed as I frantically tried to process her words. Why would a single dad be perfect for me? Granted, I did enjoy children. Still, I wasn't even sure if I wanted kids at all, considering my, er, deficiencies as a human being; I definitely wasn't interested in some random guy's kids.

"Well, I … I just assumed you might …" For once, Jenna seemed to struggle for words. Then she clapped her hands together as her full lips curved into a smile. "You know what? It doesn't matter. If you're not interested, I know someone else who is."

Was she implying I was desperate? I mean …

I swallowed, wishing I could end this conversation immediately but knowing she'd just follow me. "You?"

She erupted into giggles, making her long earrings shake. "You know me too well. He's almost young enough to be my son, but that's never stopped me before, has it?"

I nodded weakly, unsure how to respond.

Think. Think fast.

"Well, that's great for you. So, I need to go—"

Her long, thin eyebrows peaked with interest. "Oh, where are you off to? I'm not busy, so I could come along—"

Nope. Just no.

"I—work. I have to work. And then wax. In the, uh, all the places. I also have to clean out my—"

Jenna's expression soured as she put her hand up to silence me. "OK, not right now. I'll stop by later, all right?"

I opened my mouth to object. Then, just as fast as she'd appeared, she took off down the hall toward her apartment.

I let out a long exhale.

Way to go, you're a sweaty mess again.

I groaned while trudging down the hall to my apartment. After entering and dropping my keys on the antique front entry table, I peeled off all the extra winter layers now sticking to me, sniffing them to discover that they did indeed need a wash now.

Just as the phone slipped from my pocket, I lunged forward and caught it inches before it hit the ground. Remembering I had a text or other notification, I brought it closer to my face and unlocked the screen.

Unknown number: Give me your email address. I'll send my initial plans by tomorrow.

Ugh, the rude tone. It had to be Jeff. How'd he get my number? I couldn't remember texting him before.

Oh, probably Hazel. I caught myself clenching my teeth while I added his number to my contacts and resisted the urge to reply, "Who is this?"

Roxy: YOUR initial plans? We're supposed to be partners.

I waited a moment for him to respond, but when he didn't, I abandoned the phone to the couch and took the four or five short steps to my bedroom to change. My one-bedroom apartment wasn't large by any means, but it was cozy and comfortable and just right for me. Well, except for the bland white and tan walls—I should really get around to painting those.

After shedding my suffocating work clothes, taking a two-minute shower, and donning my favorite blue fuzzy pajama pants and top, I grabbed my laptop from my desk and sank into the couch. Briefly, I considered doing some online shopping to look for a new couch because, let's face it, this one was a bit worn from all the time I spent on it. Especially this spot on the left side. The best side.

But before I could fire up an online search for furniture, my eye caught the red message indicator in the corner of the blue and green icon on the taskbar. The furniture search already abandoned, I clicked eagerly on the icon and waited for the fan forum app to open.

I hummed impatiently and brushed my thick, wet hair

behind my ears as the app slowly started. Five new notifications and a private message indicator appeared. I smiled and licked my lips. This was the perfect way to blow off steam from this awful day. I mean, it wasn't the worst day I'd ever had, but I felt drained and stressed out just thinking about what the coming months would bring. And somehow, she expected it done by New Year's!

But not tonight, no more.

I'd had enough stress for one day.

Instead, I'd get lost in my favorite world.

Cast Afar had been my favorite show since it debuted two years ago. At first I'd been skeptical that any show could be better than *Lost*—a similar but older show about strangers being stranded on a mysterious island—but I'd been dead wrong. *Cast Afar* had all the great things about *Lost* and so much more. The plot was intriguing and mysterious and made *sense*. Don't get me wrong; I absolutely loved *Lost* and its plot, but that series finale—ugh. *Cast Afar* was nowhere near finished, and I fully expected several more seasons, all the way to an ending that wouldn't make me want to scream at the TV. OK, maybe not scream. Even when by myself, I was too quiet and reserved to do such a thing. Mostly.

A flicker of disappointment swept through my mind as my eyes scanned the lone private message. A forum member named IslandedHere wanted to ask, yet again, if I'd join the weekly virtual discussion group.

Instead of turning her down again, I ignored the message and clicked over to the discussion board. I scrolled through the five new comments on my post about Mel's shocking disappearance on the show and shook my head as I read. The commenters were missing the point, I thought with gritted teeth, and then my eyes landed on the comment from CastGamer55 containing a detailed answer and partial agreement with my theory.

A grin stretched across my face as I set my fingertips on the keyboard. *He gets it.* My hands flew over the keys as I typed an enthusiastic response. Five paragraphs later, I sat back with satisfaction after posting the comment without hesitation.

Just as I rose to grab a drink from the kitchen, my phone buzzed, and I groaned. Fearing it was Jeff, I unlocked it reluctantly as I ambled over to the kitchen. But it wasn't him.

> **Julia:** Rox, how are you?! You better text me back this time!
> **Roxy:** Hi. What do you mean??
> **Julia:** You never replied to my text last weekend
> **Roxy:** I distinctly remember texting with you for at least an hour last Saturday.
> **Julia:** Yeah, but then you just went quiet

I leaned against the counter near the fridge and scanned my text history with her. Before today, the last text from her was Saturday night when she said goodnight. I started typing a response and then halted. I'd forgotten this aspect of my friend Julia. My only friend, really. She also had social anxiety, but it manifested differently than mine. Quite different, actually. She became very anxious when someone didn't reply to a communication of *any* kind.

> **Roxy:** I'm sorry, I must have been tired
> **Julia:** It's OK ... how are ya?
> **Roxy:** I'm fine. Ish.
> **Roxy:** Actually, no. I'm not fine. Hazel just dropped the bomb that I have to work with Jeff the Jerk on a huge project!
> **Julia:** Ohhhh, that accountant guy?
> **Roxy:** Financial advisor, but yeah. Him. He's the worst
> **Julia:** Ugh, Rox, well you can vent to me anytime <3
> **Julia:** Do anything fun today?
> **Roxy:** Does banging out a 5-paragraph essay on *Cast Afar* on a casual discussion forum count?
> **Julia:** LOL! For us, yes
> **Roxy:** Why oh why can't I have that kind of ease and

confidence communicating with people in real life? It's like I'm not even shy on the internet

Julia: Preaching to the choir, girl. I remember that first message board I introduced you to in college. If I didn't know better, I would've thought you were a really outgoing person...

Roxy: Right? NO ONE from real life would ever believe SawyerRox4 is the shy mouse who can barely hold even an easy conversation with someone she knows.

Why was I this way? I had considered a million theories, such as genetics, parental influence, and even ADHD. Bad choices, even. But they never quite added up.

You'd think that I, as a former therapist, would be able to easily pin down the source of something as relatively common as social anxiety. But self-assessment wasn't easy—even for the experts. And honestly, I hadn't lasted long in the counseling field. It was hard to believe I'd ever thought I could work as a mental health professional. Not only did the profession require strong people skills, but the emotional fortitude and resilience necessary were far beyond what I possessed.

I sat back on the couch with my water bottle and a blueberry muffin and wondered why Julia was taking so long to respond. Letting out a long exhale, I propped my feet up on the coffee table and leaned my head back. What a day. Leaving my house to interact with people was nearly always exhausting, but today was brutal.

Julia: Sorry, gtg

Weird, she didn't usually drop from conversations abruptly like that. Oh well. My eyes veered over to the open laptop next to me on the couch, but before I hauled it onto my lap, I remembered I should fire off a goodbye text to Julia, lest she worry about our friendship.

I finished the last of my muffin and brushed the sticky

crumbs off my lap. My eyes lazily scanned over the new topics posted today, and a ping sounded from my laptop speakers. Eager to avoid this restless feeling creeping in, I clicked over to see the new message.

IslandedHere: Hello? I saw you posting something on the board. Didn't you see my message?
Roxy: Sorry, no thanks. I'm not really into online meetings.

A strange response, for sure, but what else could I say? I'd already tried using the excuses that I didn't like Zoom, that my speakers didn't work, that I was busy at the meeting time, and a few others. Yet she still kept asking, apparently determined to have me join the discussion group. And if it were a text chat thing, I probably would've. Gladly. But I can't do video chats. I *won't*. At least not willingly. The one time I'd joined an online event that IslandedHere hosted a few months ago, she hassled everyone to turn on their cameras, and I'd had to bail early.

It wasn't really a physical insecurity that I could pin down. I mean, sure, I have physical flaws like anyone, surely more than most people, but it wasn't the reason for my debilitating shyness. I wasn't entirely sure why, as it didn't seem genetic in my family. In any case, my anxiety wasn't about appearance so much as ... well, I just didn't want people to see me talk. Audio-only chat wasn't my favorite either, but it was better than being on camera.

You're really messed up.

I clenched my jaw, wishing I could silence the inner doubts that plagued me constantly. At least I'd managed to arrange my life so I could mostly avoid social interactions or, really, almost all in-person interactions. It worked for me.

Well, it *used to* work for me. Until Hazel dropped the bomb today. Now I was going to have to somehow work with the most difficult man I'd ever met. Hopefully *he* preferred text chat over other kinds of communication too.

Chapter 3

As I settled into my evening routine on the couch the next night, I wished I'd retrieved an ice pack for my sore jaw. I often wasn't aware of clenching or grinding my teeth when stressed—despite my recent New Year's resolution to stop clenching—but even I noticed it today, a day that turned out to be even worse than yesterday. Putting my feet with pink and blue slippers up on the couch as I opened my laptop, I decided not to grab the ice pack from the kitchen. It seemed like too much effort, along with closing the blinds to the darkness of the town square outside my window. Maybe later.

Just as I was poised to click on my favorite app, I realized I hadn't had time to check my personal email all day.

I should.

I didn't want to.

But what if it's important?

A heavy sigh escaped me as I reluctantly opened the email tab in my browser. Nothing but newsletters I'd probably never get around to reading. Following another one of my recent New Year's goals—resolutions were kind of my thing—I spent a few minutes mostly deleting emails even though they looked interesting. I wouldn't read them anyway. I should probably unsubscribe, but … what if I changed my mind and wanted to read them later?

I shook my head, trying to clear out all the mental junk, and then my phone pinged with a text.

Jeff: Should I assume from your silence that you are busy reading over the plan?

I stretched out my jaw before I could tighten it and cause more pain. The nerve of that man! He'd sent an email this morning with a list of links to project management courses and books and asked when I'd be able to finish them all. I'd promptly reminded him he was not my boss. And I already knew the basics of project management; I'd taken an online course after getting hired as the resort's event planner. Jeff didn't respond to my message until later in the day, when he sent a ten-page project plan document. Shock and outrage warred within me, and eventually I gave up and decided I was done putting out fires today—and I wouldn't read his plan tonight. Work was over. Time to relax.

Roxy: I'm off the clock.

I typed "sorry, not sorry" but then deleted it reluctantly. I wanted to tell him off, reminding him we were supposed to be collaborating. But even more than that, I wanted to *not* engage with him tonight—to not think about work at all. I sighed and turned my phone on silent.

The *Cast Afar* online forum beckoned, and I bit my lip while waiting for it to load. Sometimes the internet was slow here in Shipsvold, one of the hillier parts of the state. When the forum loaded, I eagerly clicked over to my notifications. Only one comment and three reactions, and one was a thumbs down emoji! How could that be? I'd posted such a great, well-supported analysis last night. Nothing from CastGamer55 either. I frowned while reading the sole reply to my monologue; it was from some smug guy who seemed more interested in the character's appearance than the events and emotions surrounding what happened to her.

My fingers hovered above the keys just long enough for me to stop and remind myself to take a breath. I should give myself some space before firing off my hot take on Mr. Mansplainer's comment.

Reluctantly, I clicked away from the post and skimmed over the other conversations.

Thirty minutes later, restlessness crept in. My mind cycled through all the things I could do tonight—because I wasn't the early-in-bed type—but nothing sounded appealing.

I sighed.

The trouble with my life was that although I *loved* staying home and being on my own with my various interests and my job ... every now and then, it felt stale. I was reluctant to call it boredom or loneliness because I didn't like to think of myself as experiencing those feelings. It would mean something was *wrong* with my life. Something like ...

Fine. I can face facts. There was plenty wrong with my life. But it's the best I could do. I had plenty of comforts that others didn't. A decent job, an apartment, parents who weren't divorced, enough money for food and clothes, fairly good health, and all that. That should be enough, right? Not to mention my beloved show and fan forum, which I'd been fairly obsessed with since the pilot two years ago.

Something nagged in the corner of my brain though.

Something I didn't want to think about.

Something silent, but it was there, stronger at some times than others.

I closed my eyes briefly, and there it was. That nagging feeling or whisper or ... something. I couldn't even—

My eyes flew open as the new message ping sounded on my computer.

A message from CastGamer55.

I clicked so eagerly that I almost accidentally selected the button to start a video chat. Whew, that was a close one. It frustrated me to no end that a user couldn't just turn off that feature altogether. Still, I smiled while reading his message.

CastGamer55: Your analysis yesterday was spot on. I just don't have the energy to reply again tonight, sorry. It was

a long day.
SawyerRox4: Not a good day?

His green availability dot was visible, so maybe he would respond soon. To avoid staring at the screen, I set the computer aside, leaving it open as I rose to my feet and stretched my limbs. I should grab a snack at least, since I missed dinner. The whole day had been a train wreck from start to finish.

When I returned with a handful of snacks to quiet my growling stomach, my eyes landed on the screen. Finally, a reply.

CastGamer55: No. A long workday with a frustrating colleague, among other things.
SawyerRox4: I can definitely relate, if it makes you feel better
CastGamer55: It doesn't.

I reared back. *Oh.* He tended to be pretty direct but had always been kind in the past. I bit my lower lip, unsure how to respond.

SawyerRox4: Oh, ok. I didn't mean to offend you
CastGamer55: You didn't.
CastGamer55: I mean it doesn't make me feel better that you also had a bad day.
CastGamer55: I'm not that much of a jerk. Not like your man Sawyer.

I threw my head back and laughed. We had only been chatting one-on-one for a month or two, but he'd sometimes teased me about my obsession with Sawyer, one of the most controversial but handsome characters on *Lost*.

SawyerRox4: Oh! lol. Sorry, totally misunderstood. And you're not a jerk. I'm hypersensitive sometimes
SawyerRox4: Well, more like all the time
CastGamer55: It's all right.

SawyerRox4: So your bad day was work related?

CastGamer55: I also had a minor accident in the kitchen tonight. How about you?

SawyerRox4: I didn't have any kitchen accidents. Dinner is a hard-boiled egg and some sugary cereal, so not much chance for danger there

CastGamer55: That isn't much of a dinner.

CastGamer55: But I meant more generally, why was your day bad?

SawyerRox4: Oh *blush* Of course. Uh ... I too had a frustrating colleague to deal with. But the worst part is, I disappointed a sweet old lady. I still feel terrible.

CastGamer55: I'm sure it was an accident.

SawyerRox4: Haha, I see what you did there. Yes, I certainly didn't let anyone down on purpose. I would never. But the look on her face ... I just keep seeing it in my mind, over and over.

CastGamer55: Don't do that.

SawyerRox4: ?

CastGamer55: Don't do that to yourself. Listen, I don't know you that well, but I'm certain you tried your best to fix whatever the situation was.

He was right about that, at least. I spent nearly all day trying to figure out how to fix the scheduling mess caused by Frieda, the resort's social media manager, but in the end, we had to cancel the book signing for this weekend. The author was a 92-year-old, recently widowed woman with the sweetest smile and the biggest heart who lived right here in Shipsvold. Mrs. Jennings was crushed, though she tried to hide it. Even though I kind of blamed Frieda, I blamed myself more. I double- and triple-checked every booking, but I could've done more. When things went wrong with resort events, I always took it to heart.

SawyerRox4: I won't bore you with all the details, but yes, I did try my best ... It was too late

CastGamer55: Sorry to hear it.
SawyerRox4: It's so nice to chat with you though!

As soon as I hit Send, doubt set in. Was that a weird thing to say? I didn't know much about him, but we agreed often enough. And he didn't seem to hate talking to me. I couldn't say that about most people. I was not the kind of person who was sought out for socializing with.

Crap. I shouldn't have said that to him. He probably thought I was reading way too much into things. It wasn't like we were really *friends*. We were just online acquaintances in a fan forum. And barely even acquainted, at that. I didn't know his name, his location, his age ... or whether he had a family.

Still, chatting with him always put a smile on my face, so I wouldn't mind being friends. Friendship was a little easier online because I wasn't so painfully shy on the web.

I wished I could delete the message, but that would look even weirder, probably. He probably already saw it, so—

My hands stilled on the keyboard.

CastGamer55: You too. Sorry, I stepped away for a moment.
SawyerRox4: No worries. I didn't mean that to sound weird, by the way...
CastGamer55: What sounded weird?

Oh great, maybe he *didn't* think it was weird, but now I've *made* it weird. I cradled my face in my palms. Such a Roxy thing to do, unfortunately. I didn't usually feel *this* awkward when talking to people online. I shook my head, wondering why my weirdness couldn't at least be consistent from one day to the next.

SawyerRox4: Nothing.
SawyerRox4: Did you see that new preview of next week's episode? I think Ali is finally going to find Percy in the

west fort!

CastGamer55: I did not. I avoid spoilers.

SawyerRox4: Well, it's a preview or teaser, not a spoiler

CastGamer55: All the same to me. I like to be surprised.

SawyerRox4: OK, OK. Next week we'll see if I'm right then

CastGamer55: I actually was thinking Emily would find Percy first, but now I'm not so sure. See, you ruined the surprise.

SawyerRox4: Ah, you'll just have to deal

CastGamer55: *arms crossed*

SawyerRox4: Is that you being petulant?

SawyerRox4: I could be wrong anyway. :(I often am.

CastGamer55: Stop. Nearly every theory you've shared on the boards has proven true or almost true.

SawyerRox4: So you're basically saying I'm a *Cast Afar* fandom legend?

CastGamer55: It's true though.

SawyerRox4: That's what I like about you. You're so direct. But you also think deeply about all the intricacies just like I do. For a fandom, some of the other fans are shockingly naïve or shallow when it comes to the show.

Oh. No.

I just put my foot in my mouth again. Ugh, I just told him I *like* him. Not like *that*. Surely he wouldn't think—

CastGamer55: I couldn't agree more.

A flutter in my chest drew my attention away from the screen, and my hand reached up to touch my chest. What was that? I'd never really experienced heartburn, but I guess there was a first time for everything. I grabbed my water bottle from the coffee table and chugged down as much as I could. That would help with indigestion, I hoped.

He still hadn't replied, and his status was now idle. Frowning, I started typing a reply, my fingers hesitant on the keys.

SawyerRox4: Well, I'm sure you'd like to kick back and relax tonight after your long day. I don't want to keep you ...

I waited another minute, and my brows furrowed more deeply as I realized our chat was already over. I didn't *think* I scared him away, but who could tell? He probably just had better things to do. Better people to talk to.

Anybody but you.

I bit my lip, knowing it was true.

But when I'd almost given up and decided to log off, the three dots appeared, indicating he was typing a response.

CastGamer55: I have an off-topic question for you, if that's OK.
SawyerRox4: I love off-topic questions
CastGamer55: Do you like board games?
SawyerRox4: No, I don't like them.
SawyerRox4: I *love* them!
CastGamer55: Ha-ha.
SawyerRox4: Juvenile, I know. But I like the adult games
SawyerRox4: I mean, games for adults!
SawyerRox4: Not "adult" like THAT. I just mean, not kids games
SawyerRox4: Sorry for being the most awkward person on the planet
CastGamer55: Surely not *the* most awkward. That would be hard. There has to be someone out there who's more awkward than you.
SawyerRox4: gasp :0
CastGamer55: I was joking. You're probably not as awkward as you think.
SawyerRox4: I am just going to go hide in the basement storage closet for the rest of my life now. Thanks.

CastGamer55: You might be the most dramatic person on the planet though.

SawyerRox4: OK, you got me. I am terrible at giving good impressions…

CastGamer55: Joking again.

CastGamer55: I might not be very good at joking around. So I've been told. I've been called harsh.

SawyerRox4: *shrug*

CastGamer55: Sorry.

SawyerRox4: You've nothing to be sorry for. Anyway, back to safer territory … yes, I love board games. Do you?

CastGamer55: Yes, particularly complex strategy games.

SawyerRox4: Oh, same! I'm not that picky, but the more strategy involved, the better. I don't have a lot of people to play with though. Most of my friends aren't into games.

Of course, I didn't really have friends, but he didn't need to know that. It was true, anyway, that I loved board games but rarely got to play. Hazel once invited me over, but I declined because it was likely just a pity invite.

CastGamer55: Have you ever thought about creating a game?

SawyerRox4: You mean an online game? Like a website or app? I don't have coding skills, unfortunately.

CastGamer55: I'm referring to a tabletop game.

SawyerRox4: I always thought it must be really fun for the people who design board games. But no, I've never seriously considered it.

CastGamer55: I have.

SawyerRox4: Oh, wow! What games have you designed?

SawyerRox4: If you don't mind my asking …

CastGamer55: No, I haven't created any games. I have seriously considered it though. I've been thinking a lot about our show, and it would be a great premise for a board game.

SawyerRox4: Ooooh, what kind of game?

CastGamer55: Maybe a world-building game or survival game. Both.

SawyerRox4: That sounds really fun. I'd definitely play that!

CastGamer55: Would you design it?

SawyerRox4: Uh, what? ME?

CastGamer55: Yes.

SawyerRox4: Well, I don't know the first thing about developing a game.

CastGamer55: You could learn.

SawyerRox4: I suppose … maybe. Why don't you design a game like that? It is your idea. And a great one.

CastGamer55: I'd like to.

SawyerRox4: Oh, do you mean

I stopped typing but didn't press Send. Was he hoping I would design a board game with him? Seriously? That couldn't be right. He couldn't mean that. Could he? But before I could finish my message, he sent another.

CastGamer55: I was thinking we could work together.

CastGamer55: If you're not interested, that's fine.

SawyerRox4: No, yeah, I might be. I just need a moment. It's just a surprise, that's all.

CastGamer55: Have you heard of Game Acres?

SawyerRox4: No, is that a gamer site?

CastGamer55: It's a community of game designers. Game Acres sounds like Game Makers, right?

SawyerRox4: Oh, neat. You're part of the community?

CastGamer55: I just joined fairly recently.

SawyerRox4: That sounds interesting

CastGamer55: It's open to all experience levels, even complete novices.

SawyerRox4: It sounds great

CastGamer55: So you'll join?

My breath caught in my throat. He was asking me to create a game with him and join this game developer group? We knew virtually nothing about each other than our opinions about the show.

And yet, as my heart raced, I realized it was excitement, not fear. Not nerves. Well, maybe some nerves.

I wanted to say yes.

I could admit life had become stale lately. I'd known deep down for a while that I needed something new, something to stimulate my mind and my creativity … maybe even friendship. But *this* …

This could be both. I could connect with another person *and* do something intellectually stimulating.

Would it be ludicrous to say yes? He wasn't asking to meet up in person. I didn't even know where on earth he lived. It was just a different form of online interaction, channeled into something more creative. More fun. More … everything.

I had every reason to say yes.

CastGamer55: You still there?

But also every reason to say no. Because I wasn't a person who just tried new things and chased excitement. Just the opposite, in fact. Sure, maybe I was kind of a different person on the internet … not in a deceitful way, but without the extreme shyness, I could be myself more. But I wasn't *so* different that I'd easily jump into something big and different with a near stranger.

Or maybe … maybe I was boxing myself into some stupid "type" of person. Maybe I didn't need to. I could try this.

SawyerRox4: I'm intrigued. But honestly, we don't know each other well. What if we clash constantly? What if I'm a pain in the … you know.

As soon as the words were out, I winced.

Way to sound really anxious and insecure. Guys love that.

I took a deep breath in and out and then started typing, but a new message appeared.

CastGamer55: I think we'd figure that out relatively early on, before we've invested much time or anything else.
SawyerRox4: True.
CastGamer55: Most likely if we were really unsuitable as partners, we'd have already clashed.
SawyerRox4: True…
CastGamer55: You're probably overthinking this.
SawyerRox4: Also true, lol … OK, I'm in!
CastGamer55: Excellent. I'll share the link, just a moment.

My toes curled as a familiar mix of anxiety and curiosity swept through me. Had I really just agreed to this? I knew nothing about creating games—or about this man. We hadn't even shared our names. Should we?

SawyerRox4: I don't even know your first name. Should we share that?
CastGamer55: We could use fake but real-sounding names if that would make you comfortable. I could be, like, Danny or something.
SawyerRox4: Yeah, that's a good idea. Uh, my name is Mindy, and it's nice to meet you, Danny.
CastGamer55: Any significance in the name Mindy?
SawyerRox4: I *loved* the show *The Mindy Project*. Do you know it?
CastGamer55: Can't say I do.
SawyerRox4: Mindy Kaling? Well, it ended years ago anyway. It was a comedy/rom-com that borrowed from a lot of classic rom-coms in really fun ways. There was a character named Danny …
CastGamer55: Ah, I'm more into drama, as you might guess from our shared TV interest.

SawyerRox4: Interests plural … you liked *Lost* too!
CastGamer55: I did. Are you ready to join the server?

I chuckled a bit to myself. He could be somewhat abrupt sometimes, but still friendly. I kind of liked how direct he was, so I didn't have to wonder what he meant by his words, as I so often do with others.

But what server was he talking about?

Oh. He just sent the signup link for Game Acres.

That was … fast. He must really want to do this. But my brow furrowed as negative thoughts started flooding my poor brain. Thoughts about how I'd probably disappoint him, mainly. I shook my head, trying to clear them out and forcing a smile.

I'd read somewhere that just the physical act of smiling can make you feel better. In my experience, it didn't usually work. But worth a shot, right?

Then again, maybe I wouldn't have to force a smile all the time because this might actually be fun. I loved board games, and game design was intriguing. And I had a chance to try it with this guy online who must think I'm interesting.

The next thing I knew, I was grinning without even trying.

Chapter 4

I nearly slipped on the slick, icy sidewalk before I noticed him and slowed my steps. Jeff beat me to the site again. This was the third building we'd checked out this week in our hunt for the perfect site for Hazel's new counseling center. I'd tried to arrive early because the last two times, I was convinced he'd used the extra face time with Hazel to complain about me, so of course I wanted to prevent that today.

What he'd complain about, I don't know—I'm not usually considered difficult to work with. Of all my flaws, I knew *that* wasn't one of them. At least it had never been an issue before. If anything, I was too accommodating in most situations. But he'd called me an obstacle to progress yesterday after only two weeks of working together, and I'd been fuming ever since.

To make matters worse, I'd only had one opportunity to talk to CastGamer55 about our ideas for the new game because we'd both been busy. Well, he more so than I. Even when busy with work, I usually made time in the evenings or late nights to unwind on the couch with my laptop—in fact, sometimes it was the only thing keeping me going on a stressful day. Apparently, he didn't feel the same, as he said he was extra busy with work and a family thing. Vague, but that's OK. We didn't even know each other's real names. Heck, I was still finding it hard to call him Danny in my mind, as I'd grown used to CastGamer55, as awkward as it sounded.

I slowed my steps as much as possible without attracting attention from other brave wintertime pedestrians, so I assumed Jeff would be well ahead of me and into the narrow brick building by the time I reached it. But inexplicably, he was just inside the door.

I groaned as I followed him silently inside. The last thing I wanted to do was walk with him down that dim, super narrow hallway ahead of us.

"Hello, Roxanne."

"Hello, Jeffrey," I said with a mocking undertone. I didn't even know if Jeffrey was really his name, but I didn't care.

He narrowed his eyes but said nothing and turned to walk down the hall.

"The lighting in here leaves much to be desired," I said. "And when was this walkway built? In the Middle Ages? It's so narrow. I'm half expecting to see a spiral staircase death trap up ahead. Or a maze of narrow corridors and some tiny alcoves next to window slits. At least they could've—"

My mouth snapped shut when he halted and turned, right there in the hallway. "Are you all right, Roxanne? Too much caffeine today?"

Inhaling sharply, I put my hands on my hips—or where I imagined my hips would be if I weren't wearing such a thick winter coat. "Hilarious, Jeffrey."

One time. *One* time. He was mocking me for the one time I'd become sick at a staff meeting from chugging coffee all morning after a sleepless night. He'd never let me forget it.

My face flushed and my mouth clamped shut as I realized I had, in fact, been talking a mile a minute. And even Jeff knew me well enough to know that wasn't normal for me. Well, it wasn't rare—it was a bad habit when nervous to either be silent or ramble—but it was obviously not my default state. I didn't even know what my default state was, honestly. I rarely felt like I could be myself with anyone, and I wasn't one to talk to myself when alone.

Jeff raised an eyebrow ever so slightly but turned back to walk more briskly down the hall. We entered a medium-sized room with overhead lighting that I knew would give me a headache within minutes.

"I hope this isn't the new office, Jeff. It's a little small. And what is that smell?" I looked around, aware I sounded like a master complainer but unable to stop myself. Before he could reply, I looked at him pointedly. "Where's Hazel?"

"I assume she's on her way," he said before pointing to his left. "This is just the foyer. It could be a waiting room, maybe. But come this way."

Following him reluctantly, I passed through a doorway that seemed oddly short. He had to duck his head, as he was tallish, probably close to six feet. Still, most doorways were at least seven to eight feet high. I made a mental note to add doorway height to this old building's growing list of shortcomings.

Jeff led me into a more open area with hallways, closed doors on both sides, and a large central desk. "Receptionist?" I asked.

"Maybe. Or the reception desk could be back in the foyer, and this desk could be for the office manager." He shrugged. "Let's look into the offices."

We entered the first room on the left, and I wrinkled my nose at the musty smell probably baked into the faded, crinkly wallpaper. "This looks more like a conference room."

He surveyed the area with a critical eye, but then his phone beeped, and he picked it up.

I exhaled loudly, annoyed, and walked past him out the door. The next closed room looked more like an office, with empty shelving on one side of the room. I brushed my fingers across the shelves, heedless of the dust, as I allowed myself to imagine having a professional office like this again, with my reference books filling the shelves. I smiled as I picked up an antique bookend that someone had left on one of the shelves.

"Roxanne."

I jerked to attention and dropped the bookend. "Ugh, Jeff! You startled me."

His eyebrow rising slightly, he shook his head as I glared at him and then bent to pick up the bookend.

"Are you finished with your urgent business on your phone?" I asked, pasting a tight smile onto my face. At least I hoped it was a smile, but it probably resembled the face one makes when being strangled.

He sighed. "I am. It was Hazel. She can't make it today."

My eyes widened. "Hazel just contacted you?"

"Yes, to tell me she couldn't make it. She's stuck at the Sheraton by the Minneapolis airport for the night. They're getting a lot of snow again, apparently, but it's going to miss us here—"

"Wait, what's she doing in the Cities?"

"She went away with Peter for a few days. I forgot the name of the place, but it's that town in California where she grew up."

"She … I …"

My breaths came faster, and I couldn't speak. I was Hazel's assistant. Why didn't I know she'd gone away? And why had she contacted Jeff about this today, not me?

"She didn't tell you?"

"Uh, you know, I probably just forgot. My attention was somewhere—" The second the words were out, I wanted to take them back. So much for not looking flighty all the time.

He rolled his eyes. "Figures. I just hope you can maintain your focus throughout this project."

"I can, and I am," I said through clenched teeth.

But I was dying inside as I pivoted to face the window. Why didn't Hazel tell *me* such things? It wasn't just this instance either—this had become a pattern with her. When she'd been stuck in Peter's house during a blizzard for four days, I didn't even hear from her once. When he'd been in the hospital a few weeks later, I had to hear it from Mari. And those were just the very recent examples.

Why would you expect any different? You're just not the kind of person people share things with. You're not friends with her.

Taking a long but shaky breath, I tried to block out the

devastation pouring over me.

This was nothing new. It was the story of my life. I took another slow breath and raised my chin. Determined not to show any weakness in front of Jeff, I spun around with a resolute expression—

OUCH.

I slammed into a hard, unforgiving surface and bounced back, landing on my heels as a larger hand reached out to clasp my upper arm.

We stood frozen for a moment before I hastily walked back two more steps, and he let my arm go. I stared at him and opened my mouth, but no words came.

"Are you all right?" He looked genuinely concerned, his brow furrowing deeper than usual. "Your chin—I think it collided with my shoulder."

My hand flew to my chin, and a gasp escaped my mouth. "Uh, yeah, that really hurts. But I think it was *you* who ran into me."

His concern evaporated, and he shook his head. "You may have a nice big bruise tomorrow."

I scowled. "You'd love that, wouldn't you?"

His face twisted into an expression I didn't recognize, and then he shook his head again. "Well, it seems like you're OK."

"No thanks to you," I muttered, lightly patting my sore chin, which hurt to even touch.

"I heard that," he said, having already turned back toward the door.

I reluctantly followed him out of the room. "We should head out and reschedule this visit after Hazel's back. Or just tell her it's not worth seeing. There's a reason this building hasn't been used in years."

He turned back to me briefly before marching toward the other side of the central admin desk. "No need. We can send her notes."

I wanted to object, but he was walking so fast I could barely keep up.

We entered the first office on the other side, and my eyes were immediately drawn to the large window with a view of the town square.

"What is it with you and windows?" Jeff said, eyeing me quickly before unlocking his phone.

I took a long moment to savor the surprisingly nice view and then replied, "Most people appreciate a nice view, Jeffrey. If you don't, you're the odd one."

Who are you?

Where is Roxy?

Shaking my head in disbelief, I watched as he typed away on his phone. Finally, I walked over to join him. "So you're the one who's easily distracted today."

As soon as I started speaking, he froze. Finally, he took a few steps away and turned toward me. "I'm taking notes, Roxanne, ever heard of it? You should be doing it too."

My mouth tightened as I stepped toward him. "Let me see."

He held his phone against his chest. "No."

"We're supposed to be partners, Jeffrey." I don't know where I got these weird flashes of bravado around him ... he brought out the worst in me, and I couldn't resist arguing with him. "Are you hiding something? Are you writing something you don't want me to see?"

His jaw tightened. "I'm not *hiding* anything. I doubt you'd need to see my notes, as you seem content with a small role in this project."

I saw red. "I seem content ... what? You—" I stopped, taking a deep breath and another step in his direction. "You have been bullishly doing and deciding everything from day one, giving me little to no opportunity to contribute. If I have a small role, it's because you're not letting me *do anything*!"

He walked backward a couple of steps and nearly collided with a small bookcase visibly covered in dust.

"I thought I was the clumsy one. Apparently you can't even handle me being anywhere near you," I accused him, trying to channel the anger instead of acknowledging that it ... hurt. Was I that bad that even an odious person like Jeff who *had* to work with me couldn't stand being near me?

My warring emotions must have been obvious, as the frustration melted off his face, replaced by a neutral expression. "I don't like people in my personal space."

My eyes shifted downward to the right as I tried to play it off as inconsequential. Shrugging, I said, "Sure."

"It's true, Roxanne." He started to take a small step sideways but then apparently thought better of it. "It's not you."

I inhaled and exhaled slowly before meeting his eyes. "I don't like people in my personal space either. But I try not to be rude about it."

We locked eyes for a long moment before he swallowed and nodded.

"Fair enough," he said at last.

My eyes went wide as I'm sure my mouth hung open. "Is that ... it's like almost an apology, right? The closest I'll ever get, I'm sure."

I shifted my gaze to his right hand, which was smoothing the long sleeve over his left forearm. That must be some kind of fidgeting habit. Maybe this was how he dealt with frustration or people he didn't like. I sighed and looked him in the eye again.

"Let's just get this done so we can go home," I said. "Or back to the resort office, or wherever it is you spend your time."

He nodded curtly and turned to leave, so I followed him out into the next office.

But he abruptly turned around before taking two steps into the room, and I bumped into his chest, but more softly this time. Just enough to feel a zap ...

What *was* that?

I couldn't even describe it if I tried, but it was not an entirely unpleasant feeling. It was ... electric. My breath was coming a bit quickly, and I had no idea why.

"Sorry," he said, looking down at me before abruptly sidestepping to cross the room.

"You've got to stop doing that, Jeff," I called out, slumping onto a brown plastic chair someone had left in this office.

He merely turned and gave me an odd expression while pulling out his phone. His fingers started flying across the keys for a few seconds before halting abruptly. His head swiveled toward me. "I'll email you the notes later, and you can add your own observations."

"Oh. Uh-huh," I said, like an idiot. "Thanks," I added, and I meant it.

That was unexpectedly nice. My brows scrunched together as I tried to wrap my brain around all the weird interactions in the past hour. He was rude and insufferable, but occasionally … not. Or maybe I was just tired and not thinking straight. That was more likely. In fact, he—

My thoughts were cut short by my phone vibrating with a text from Hazel, informing me of the weather keeping them stuck in MSP. I sighed, turning off the phone screen. Better late than never, I guess.

∞∞∞

SawyerRox4: Hey Danny.
CastGamer55: Hey Minnie.
SawyerRox4: Mindy. You know, like Mindy Kaling?
CastGamer55: Oh, right. I'm deeply sorry for getting your fake name wrong.
SawyerRox4: lol, well, when you put it that way …
SawyerRox4: How was your day?
CastGamer55: I survived it. You?
SawyerRox4: About the same.
CastGamer55: More of the same with the rude coworker?
SawyerRox4: Yeah, but I want to get my mind off it.
CastGamer55: Same, actually.
SawyerRox4: So, I just finished reading that short book on

game design you recommended last week. I learned a lot, though it was really basic stuff.

CastGamer55: Yeah, it's just an introduction. I can send you a list of further reading if you'd like. For both of us – it's not like I'm an expert yet either.

SawyerRox4: "Yet" ... love your confidence.

CastGamer55: *shrug*

SawyerRox4: Something the book touched on was this issue of the game's theme vs. mechanics and experience. Is that something you've thought about?

CastGamer55: Yes.

SawyerRox4: Oh, am I way behind then?

CastGamer55: No. I thought about this before I suggested we partner up. I actually haven't had a ton of time since then, with work and other things occupying my time.

SawyerRox4: Oh, don't worry about it. I've been busy too

CastGamer55: We should definitely be on the same page even this early though, while we're still brainstorming. I apologize for being a bit behind on doing my part. I saw that you'd already added a bunch of ideas to our shared doc, thanks.

SawyerRox4: Oh, I thought I was the one behind. Dealing with this annoying person from work has been consuming so much of my energy, ugh

CastGamer55: Again, same. Hard to get your mind off it, eh? I guess I'm not so great at putting work aside either, especially with troublesome colleagues.

SawyerRox4: Especially if you have to work with them every day ...

CastGamer55: Indeed, especially then. Is it a long-term situation?

SawyerRox4: Kind of medium term. Not permanent, I hope! If it were, I'd have to find a new job

CastGamer55: I understand. Long term, it wouldn't be good for you.

SawyerRox4: Exactly. You get it!

CastGamer55: Have you tried confronting them?
SawyerRox4: Yes and no ... I avoid conflict. And definitely confrontations. Yet, I find myself more combative with him than I usually am with people. It's weird – he brings out the absolute worst in me, I guess.
CastGamer55: I see.

What did that mean? Was I oversharing? I waited a few minutes for another text. Nope.

Great, he's probably realizing he made a mistake by befriending you.

Or by partnering up on this game project. Maybe he wouldn't even consider me a friend in the first place.

I took a deep breath inward and then slowly let it out. I needed to stop this toxic thinking. I *knew* that—I was a trained therapist, after all—but *knowing* it wasn't the same as *doing* it.

SawyerRox4: Danny, are you still there?
CastGamer55: Yes, just pondering your dilemma. I wish I could suggest a solution to your problem, but I'm in a similar situation that's hard to navigate.
SawyerRox4: Well, when you figure out what to do, can you let me know too?
SawyerRox4: I mean, if you want to ... if not, that's cool
CastGamer55: You'll be the first to know.

An unexpected surge of warmth shot through me, starting in the chest and spreading outward. He ... he would share that with *me* first? Before anyone else in his life?

I forced myself to breathe in and out. Maybe he didn't mean that literally. It was just something people often said, right?

You're making things weird again. Change the subject. Think fast.

SawyerRox4: Do you have animals?

When he didn't respond right away, I reread my text and face-palmed.

> **SawyerRox4:** Sorry, I mean pets. Not, like, farm animals or zoo animals or something.
> **SawyerRox4:** I mean, not that I favor animals in captivity. I definitely don't! Wild animals are pretty neat.
> **SawyerRox4:** I just meant pets like cats, dogs, birds, fish. Though if you have farm animals or wild animals or something, that's awesome too.

I watched the three dots appear a few times, indicating that he was having difficulty formulating his reply. Was it that hard of a question? I mean, sure I asked it in kind of a confusing way, but surely it wasn't that bad?

I rubbed my tired eyes and scanned over my messages. It was that bad. Worse.

I blinked rapidly, feeling unlike myself. Sure, it was totally normal for me to bungle a typical conversation in person, but I usually did fine via texting or the like. I wasn't even too bad with phones. Why was I struggling to sound normal in the context I was usually most comfortable?

> **SawyerRox4:** I'm sorry. So sorry. I sometimes ramble and get awkward. You should know that if we're going to work together …
> **SawyerRox4:** I mean, you probably already know that, but just in case …
> **SawyerRox4:** You still there?
> **CastGamer55:** Yes. I was just waiting for you to finish, as you seem to often hit Send before you're finished typing your thought.
> **SawyerRox4:** Guilty as charged.
> **CastGamer55:** It's fine. And I have no pets or animals in my home.

SawyerRox4: Me neither.
CastGamer55: I like cats and dogs though.
SawyerRox4: Same! Have you thought about getting a pet?
CastGamer55: I have, but I work so much that I fear the pets would be bored or destroy my couch.
SawyerRox4: Cats are better for people who aren't home as much.
CastGamer55: Why don't you have a pet then?
SawyerRox4: Ah it's a little more complicated than that.
CastGamer55: OK.
SawyerRox4: It's just ... I can't even keep plants alive. Maybe I'm just not cut out for keeping other living beings alive.
CastGamer55: That's probably nonsense.
SawyerRox4: lol, is that so?
CastGamer55: You sell yourself short, most likely. But what do I know? Just some random guy on the internet.
SawyerRox4: I mean, that's true. I was kind of hoping you'd have pets actually for that reason :D
CastGamer55: ??
SawyerRox4: People with pets are less likely to be crazy, weird internet stalkers.
CastGamer55: Anecdotal or scientific conclusion?
SawyerRox4: Um ... neither? Just a hunch. Pets humanize people, you know?
CastGamer55: I have no idea if that's true. But in any case, I do like cats and dogs. Does that make you feel better?
SawyerRox4: lol, yes actually. Some day maybe?
CastGamer55: Sure.

I sat back, oddly pleased by this. Instead of seeming turned off by my weirdness in this meandering conversation, he was playing along!

SawyerRox4: So, uh, we should probably talk about the

game. Sorry I got sidetracked.
CastGamer55: I think you mean *we* got sidetracked. I was in the conversation too.
SawyerRox4: Nonetheless, sorry for distracting us from the game project.
CastGamer55: No need to apologize. I like chatting with you.

My heart thumped hard in my chest. Why did this make me so happy? It wasn't *that* unusual for me to find it easier to talk to people online than in person. But there was something about his words that made me feel warm inside. Because I needed a friend, right? That must be why. I only had one friend, after all, and I hadn't heard from Julia much lately.

Against my will, my mind wandered to the woman in real life who obviously didn't see me as a friend. I mean, sure, Hazel was my boss. But she struck me as the kind of person who was friends with everyone, regardless of work relationship or status. Everyone except me. I furrowed my brow, only just now realizing how much this was *still* bothering me.

Was I just not friend material?

And worse yet: Why did I need to care?

CastGamer55: Are you still there?
SawyerRox4: Sorry, sorry! I just got distracted. Again. Thanks, I like talking to you too.
CastGamer55: Well, that's a relief, because we have a great deal of work ahead of us designing this game.
SawyerRox4: You make it sound so fun.
CastGamer55: Well, work can be fun.
SawyerRox4: It can? just kidding, I know. Maybe my real job just isn't that fun. Especially lately …
CastGamer55: I hear you. I normally enjoy my work, though others find it boring. But it's been harder to enjoy lately.
SawyerRox4: Because of the guy at work that you're stuck

with?
CastGamer55: She's not a guy, but yes, that colleague. She's difficult and frustrating. But also unsettling in this way I don't fully understand.

I felt a slight pang in my chest but shook it off. Who cared if he was working closely with a woman? He and I weren't ... I wouldn't even say it. Ridiculous. We barely knew each other, and we were barely even friends yet. Danny could have a girlfriend, a wife, or even a husband. He could live thousands of miles away. He could be 17 years old, or 90. I knew so little. I had long feared the 55 in his handle might be his age. He did kind of talk like a middle-aged man—not that there was anything wrong with that. I sort of liked it, actually. I mean, as a quality of a *friend*.

A friend who likes cats and dogs, like you.
A friend who has excellent taste in TV.
A friend who likes chatting with you.

SawyerRox4: So regarding the reason we're here ... what are your favorite board games? I'm curious what you might be thinking about as inspo
CastGamer55: How many favorites do you want?
SawyerRox4: Um, as many as you have?
CastGamer55: This will take a while then.

A laugh bubbled up from my chest.
A friend who loves board games even more than you do.
Hmm.

Chapter 5

I nearly fell flat on my face as I raced through the elegant lobby of Grantham Resort, waving slightly at the pair of women behind the reception desk. Or maybe they were men—I didn't get a good look.

I really didn't like being late, but writing a message to CastGamer55 had taken far too long this morning. And then Jenna had briefly delayed me on the way out. And *then* I forgot we were meeting at the resort today instead of the new office because Jeff had a meeting with Mari and Hazel earlier. At least the last of the snow had finally melted last week, just before May Day, so walking uphill hadn't been as treacherous as it was when we'd last met with Hazel to sign the paperwork for the new office building. The new *old* office building that she'd fallen in love with immediately, for reasons I'd never understand.

Finally, I rounded the corner and swept into the conference room to the right of Mari's husband's office.

I nearly slipped again on my ill-advised high heels as I gripped the wooden door frame and my eyes took in the scene. Not a conference room but an office. The familiar hazel-eyed man behind the large marble-covered desk lifted his eyes before they widened slightly. His hand slammed the cover of his laptop down, and I could almost swear a look of guilt flitted across his face for the briefest moment. Maybe not guilt … panic? Embarrassment? Something I'd never seen from him before.

I fought to keep my voice steady and my breathing quieter. I was in decent shape, but running wasn't my forte. I took a slow breath in and out and stood up as straight as I could. "Are you all right, sir?"

Any tiny lingering awkwardness on his face vanished, and he raised his right eyebrow. "Sir?"

I didn't know why I called him that. I wanted to annoy him, but it was an odd choice. He probably preferred it. Great, the opposite of my intent. "I was born in Tennessee," I blurted out. His left eyebrow joined the right, climbing up his forehead. "OK?"

"We use 'sir' a lot in the South," I said, again failing to think or say anything rational. "I mean, when I lived there—"

"Oh? What state did you live in? How long?" His arms were crossed now as he cross-examined me.

"Tennessee. I was … it was a couple years," I mumbled, hoping he didn't hear me. "So anyway—"

"A couple of years, as in two? You were already saying 'sir'—"

"Yes, I was saying 'sir' before I was two years old," I said through gritted teeth, refusing to meet his eyes as I sat in the cushioned leather chair in front of the desk.

But I looked up when a faintly strangled sound met my ears. If I didn't know better … well, it sounded almost like a laugh. Not quite, but almost. When I scanned Jeff's face, though, I saw no sign of humor. I shrugged and set my handbag next to me on the wide chair.

When I sat and glanced up at him, he hadn't moved. His hands were still flat on the closed laptop, and his usual grim expression was staring back at me. It was sad that he always looked grumpy because he was actually a good-looking guy. Objectively. Not that I would *ever* be into him. But I supposed some women would. Glancing quickly at his left hand, I noticed his ring finger was bare. Not surprising—not that I was in any position to judge though.

Before I could open my mouth to ask about the laptop thing, he rose abruptly, briefly tensing his hands before they fell to his side. "Right, thanks for coming, albeit late. We need to review the latest quotes from the subcontractors." He paused, pressing his lips together. "Well, I've already reviewed them, but I figured you would want input."

"Yeah, it's called being a partner." I was so tired of this attitude from him—so beyond tired. "Not like you'd understand," I muttered while examining the polished hunter-green floor tiles.

When I looked up, he was now standing only a couple feet away, leaning against the front of the desk. "Are you implying I don't know how a partnership works?"

My eyes must have been golf balls by then. My heart raced as I took in his scent. Wait, what? He never wore cologne.

Or did he?

Maybe I'd never been close enough to notice.

My heart raced as I considered that, my eyes slowly rising to meet his.

And he ... he saw me. He watched me as my eyes swept slowly over his surprisingly fine form.

He saw you checking him out. This is rock bottom for you, Roxy.

My face heated and my knuckles whitened as I gripped the sides of the chair. I was about to combust into flames. Flames of awkwardness, of something else I couldn't define.

Closing my eyes for a moment, I took a slow breath and then met his eyes. "Never mind," I said coolly, raising my chin.

He shook his head slightly and sighed as he picked up a water bottle from the other side of his desk. "So, are you ready to get started?"

"Started on ..." I tilted my head, looking at him curiously but oddly a bit dazed.

"On work! What is wrong with you?"

I gasped indignantly. "Wow, that is rude, even for you, Jeffrey."

He exhaled loudly and fought to keep the irritation off his face, only partially succeeding. My eyes followed the direction of his, pointed at some interesting spot on the floor.

At this time during a conversation with virtually any

other person, I'd usually try to make amends, keep the peace, and all that. But I was tired of always meekly avoiding conflict, and Jeff didn't truly intimidate me. He probably should, but he didn't.

So I stubbornly remained silent as we both studied the floor tiles.

Finally, his voice jarred me out of my incessant thinking. "Fine. Forget I said anything. Can we move on? I'd like to—"

"Yes, I know. You want to get on with the important thing: work." I smirked, annoyed at his non-apology and the irritable way he'd delivered it.

"Well, yes. This is a work meeting, Roxanne," he reminded me in a condescending tone.

Oh ... well, he had a point. It's not like Jeff and I were two friends meeting to chat, or two lovers—woah, where did that come from—we were colleagues, and not by choice.

Wait.

Oh my—does he think ...

No.

He wouldn't think I was implying that we were on a date or something, right? *Right?*

Damage control. Now!

"You do know that most colleagues actually do talk about things other than work, right? Or were you unaware?" I forced a smile. "Are you the exception?"

"I believe in efficiency. Water cooler chat just wastes time."

I nodded. "Well, I sometimes agree. Small talk sucks. But when you say that, it makes it sound like you value productivity over human beings. Which makes you sound like ... well ..."

"What do I sound like? Don't spare my feelings now," he said dryly.

"Like a jerk," I blurted out.

The briefest moment of bravery was quickly eclipsed by regret. Dread. Panic.

Was I breaking some rule in employment law by ... name-calling? Wow, that sounded more childish than I realized.

"Sorry, I—I shouldn't have called you that." My face flamed

as I tried to hide behind my long hair, one of my go-to avoidance strategies. It was part of the reason I'd always kept my thick, wavy hair long, at least shoulder length

He looked at me earnestly for what seemed like hours before finally saying softly, "Maybe we were both being jerks, Roxanne. I apologize."

My eyes nearly popped out of my head as I took this in. *He actually apologized for something?* That's never happened—I didn't think he was capable of it. I picked up my jaw from the floor and bobbed my head up and down jerkily.

"So, this is your office?" I heard myself asking the obvious question.

"Yes. I've laid out the files we need to review over there." He pointed to a large round table I hadn't noticed. This was quite a decent-sized office, I realized. Almost as big as Mari's, in fact. It surprised me that he'd be valued enough to have one of the biggest offices here.

"Wait, you have files? I thought we were just reviewing a couple of quotes or contracts. Not entire files ..." My voice was uncertain as I sat at one of the black leather chairs circling the table.

He sat in the other chair and scooted closer. I had to restrain myself from moving my chair back.

"Files are good for organizing, Roxanne."

"Yes, but this looks like ... a lot." I eyed the thick file folders and sighed. "OK, let's get this over with."

"OK, this first one is for a contractor right here in Shipsvold. You might have even heard of him—"

"I haven't," I said after reading the name in large letters on the file. "But I like the idea of hiring locally."

He nodded briskly. "Yes, when possible."

After what seemed like hours, we finally closed the last file. I rubbed my eyes, which had started blurring after reading so much fine print.

"All right, let's review the notes. Or would you like to wait until tomorrow? You look tired."

I bit my lip. I *was* tired, but the last thing I wanted to do was show any weakness, even a reasonable amount of fatigue. "I'm fine," I managed with what I hoped was enthusiasm.

He raised an eyebrow and studied me for a moment before shrugging and turning his attention to his notebook. "Well, I think Jonson is an obvious choice for design."

"It's not obvious to me. Why should we go with his company?"

"He's got more experience than the others combined."

"Maybe," I said doubtfully, "but Sanders Design has a lot of potential. Jill Sanders has already won some state and national awards, yet her quote was very reasonable."

Jeff sighed. "I guess we can meet with her too. But I think experience and a long record of success are key, and Jonson is unmatched in that regard."

"And he's a man. That's another plus, right?" I asked, sarcasm dripping from my voice.

Jeff gave me a side-eye and shook his head. "It has nothing to do with gender. And I think you know that. Are you arguing with me just to argue?"

Do I know that Jeff isn't a chauvinist? Not really. I didn't even know him that well. But I had to admit, he didn't seem like the type. He might be a jerk in many ways, but I doubted he was a misogynist too. Finally, I just shrugged. "No. I want to make sure we're considering this from different angles."

"Fine, we'll meet with them both. Separately, of course. Do you have any schedule blockers for the rest of this week or next?"

I opened my mouth and then closed it. "Potentially," I fibbed.

"Would tomorrow or Friday work? Say, mid-morning?" He glanced at me quickly before returning his eyes to his calendar on his phone.

"Afternoon would be better." Not because I had a real conflict but because I wasn't a fan of early mornings. Especially lately, with the longer workdays and late nights chatting with CastGamer55. Not for the first time, I wondered what he did for a living. I could just ask, but something held me back. Honestly, I was afraid that the more we got to know each other, the less he'd like me. It's not like that hadn't happened with many other people in my life.

"Roxanne?" Jeff said, interrupting my thoughts. "Did you hear me?"

"Ah, what? No, sorry," I mumbled.

"I said let's do 2 p.m. tomorrow. It's the only time Jonson has open this week."

"Wait, how do you know that? Are you guys, like, buddies or something?"

He flashed me an irritated look. "No, we're not, like, buddies. I just emailed him, and his assistant responded right away."

"Fine. Tomorrow at two works, I guess." I narrowed my eyes. "What about Sanders? Don't think I forgot—"

"Calm down. I was just going to email her next."

I sulked for a moment and examined my nails while he typed out a quick email.

His phone rang, and I nearly jumped out of my chair. He didn't seem to notice as he frowned down at his phone and sighed. "A moment, please."

I watched him walk to the other side of the room and speak quietly. His posture was stiff, and at one point, I saw his hand clench at his side. Finally, he swiped to end the call and palmed his forehead for a moment before returning to the table where I still sat.

"What was that all about?"

"I need to pick up my daughter from school tomorrow afternoon to go to the dentist." His voice was tinged with frustration, and his jaw was tense.

My eyes widened. "You—*you* have a daughter?" I shook my head as I stared at this man I thought I sort of knew. "How can that be?"

His brow furrowed as his eyes met mine. "Well, Roxanne, you see, when two people—"

"Stop. That's not—I mean, you ..." I bit my lip and flinched at the pain. "You really have a child?"

His eyes swept the room from left to right and back. "Yes. Is this hard to believe?"

"Yes—I mean no. Well, I-I just didn't know," I stammered. "You never mentioned her before. No one did."

He shrugged. "I try not to mix personal and professional." He exhaled heavily. "Unfortunately, this time couldn't be helped."

I breathed in and out a few times, trying to take in this new information. "OK. What's her name? And why did you seem upset after talking to her?"

"That was her mother."

"Oh, your ... wife? Girlfriend? Or—"

"Ex-wife," he said with a frown as he distractedly looked at his phone.

I frantically searched my memory, trying to remember if I'd heard he was divorced. A comment once or twice from Mari came to mind, but it hadn't really registered at the time. Wow, Jeff had been *married*?

"What?" he asked, confusion etched onto his face.

"I just ..." My mouth clamped shut. Even though I didn't like him, I couldn't be as rude as to say that—

"Did you not know I was divorced?" His head was still tilted in confusion before a frown resurfaced. "Or are you just shocked that I was ever married?"

I averted my eyes to prevent him from seeing the guilt I'm sure was evident in my features. I pretended to look down at one of the documents in the top file. "No, of course not."

After a long moment, he said, "Roxanne, you're not a good liar."

I gasped and then studied his expression. He didn't look furious, nor did his frown look severe. He looked almost relaxed ... no, he couldn't possibly be. The man didn't know how to relax. Especially not around me. It was always business first, middle, and last. Nothing but business.

Not that I should complain. Small talk and other kinds of discussions that weren't directly work related tended to make me anxious and self-conscious. So Jeff's all-business style kind of worked for me.

Of course, that didn't mean I liked him.

When I finally started to reply, my voice sounded hoarse, so I coughed for a moment and drank from the water bottle I'd stuffed in my bag this morning. Breathing out steadily through the awkwardness consuming me, I resumed eye contact and tried to change the subject. "Anyway, so, the meetings with the contractors. Do you have to reschedule?"

Jeff looked at me thoughtfully and then shook his head.

"Oh, I thought you had to bring your daughter to the doctor or something."

His mouth twisted to the side in a shape that was only a little less foreboding than his frown. "The dentist. Yes, I will need to miss the meeting. You can handle it without me, right?"

My eyebrows rose at the challenge in his eyes. "Since when do you trust me with anything in this project?"

"Consider it a trial run," he said without a trace of humor in his tone.

I scoffed. "Seriously?"

"Yes, Roxanne. Seriously." He crossed his arms. "You *can* handle this, right?"

I wanted to scream *no* because even though my event planning work required a lot of communication with other professionals, I was a lot less confident about this project.

But I could never admit that to him. Obviously. "Of course."

He eyed me warily. "All right, I'll forward you the email with the address."

"The email address? Do you mean to send the meeting invite?"

"No, I'm talking about his business address. It's not that far, and you have a car, right?"

I felt my pulse jump as panic set in. "Uh ... oh. He wants to meet in person?"

"Yeah, that's pretty typical for a meeting like this."

I didn't even know if he said it condescendingly or not, as I couldn't pay attention with my mind racing frantically. Why, oh why, hadn't I asked for details before agreeing to this?

You need to get out of this.

Think, Roxy. Think!

After forcing myself to take a slow breath in and out, I managed to speak. "Oh, darn, I just remembered. I have a conflict tomorrow. It's ... uh, it's for my neighbor ... Janice. She's having an engagement party, and I totally forgot."

Jeff's eyebrows rose. "Your *neighbor* is having an engagement party on a *Thursday* afternoon?"

I tried to keep my voice steady ... even polite. "I'm helping her with the setup."

He stared at me for a few more seconds before shaking his head slightly and looking back at his phone. "If we don't take this meeting time, his next open meeting slot is June 10, over a month away. We can't afford to lose that much time."

"If he's that busy, he won't have time for our project anyway," I snapped.

"He is probably booked out on appointments with new clients, but when I mentioned Mariana's name, they offered the earlier time. She's an important figure in the region now, you know."

"I know that," I said, feeling irritated. "But maybe this is a good reason to meet with Jill Sanders first."

"We'll meet with her next week," Jeff said firmly, as though I had no say in it. "Are you serious about the neighbor's engagement stuff though? I don't want to reschedule this meeting unless we absolutely have to. I kind of think Hazel would agree with me on this one."

I scowled at him. He was probably right.

And he knew it.

"Fine."

"Fine?"

"You want me to reschedule with Jenna so I can meet with *your* pick? Fine."

Jeff frowned for the hundredth time that day. "Jenna?"

"My neighbor." I smirked. "Keep up."

"Thought you said you were planning an engagement thing for *Janice*."

"I ... what?"

"Maybe *you* should keep up." He paused and then spoke slowly, "Is Janice marrying Jenna then? Odd how similar their names sound." I could almost swear he was trying not to smile.

"Oh, uh, yeah. They are married. I mean, engaged."

He stared at me a moment. "Your face gives you away, you know. Your cheeks are pink when you lie."

My jaw dropped. "They do not."

"Oh?" He crossed his arms and continued to stare with an unreadable expression. "Why are your cheeks pink then?"

"They're not," I retorted. When he raised an eyebrow, my hands flew up to my cheeks against my will. "OK, maybe they are. Well, it's hot in here. The heat's turned up too high."

This time, both his eyebrows rose.

If it were possible, my cheeks would have heated even more. As things stood though, I was already starting to sweat. I wanted to avert my eyes, but something in his held my attention. "Um. I mean—"

What did I mean? It was late springtime in Minnesota, so it was far from sweltering. Today's weather was actually a pleasant seventy degrees, so I doubted the heat was on in the building. And I couldn't admit to him the real reason I'd turned red ...

Obviously.

"Believe what you want," I managed to say as casually as I could—which meant not casually at all.

He looked like he was considering a response, but his phone buzzed. His keen eyes shifted to the phone, and a severe frown overtook his entire face as his eyes scanned whatever message was on his phone.

"Is something wrong?" I asked, trying to sound polite when I was actually just nosy.

His jaw tensed, but he didn't look up.

"Jeff?"

Finally, he set the phone down slowly as he turned to me. "Nothing is wrong. Just an email from Hazel about an accounting issue I thought was already resolved."

My eyes moved from his still tense jaw to his forearm, where his other hand was smoothing the light blue fabric. "But you seem—" I halted when he dropped his hand abruptly. It was none of my business if something was bothering him. I didn't care. And surely he didn't care to tell me anything anyway. "Never mind."

His sigh was long and pained. "I'm fine. But I need to go call Hazel." Then, like an afterthought, he muttered, "I should never have let Hazel's boyfriend assist with the books."

My brow was furrowed as I studied his face. "Wait, you're working with Peter?"

"Yes."

"Since when?"

Yet another thing I didn't know about my boss's life. I tried to ignore the hurt creeping over me like an enveloping fog. "I thought Peter was great with financial stuff. He used to run a big company, you know."

"I'm aware," Jeff said dryly. "But this business is different. He doesn't—" He stopped, running his hands through his short dark hair. I'd never seen him do that before. It actually made him seem ... human. A little bit. After a slow inhale and exhale, he said quietly, "It's fine. Don't worry about it, Roxanne."

I opened my mouth to object and then closed it. Why would I worry about him or the finances? I didn't need to care about that. Despite not caring though, I said, "Hazel's been leaning on you a lot more, hasn't she? You are busier than I thought." I briefly considered asking if I could do more to help. If it were anyone else, I would in a heartbeat.

"I told you it's fine," he barked.

Well then. He didn't deserve my offer of help. Not that he'd even take it anyway.

"Anyway, I'll just reschedule with the contractors. I have to go now," he said, with both his voice and his face seeming more neutral now.

I nodded curtly and dug my phone out of my pocket. "OK, bye."

He stood for a moment, a few seconds probably, before I heard a soft exhalation and footsteps as he gathered his things and then closed the door behind him.

How was I going to survive the coming months?

Chapter 6

I picked at the grass in front of me, searching for the longest, softest blade while trying to ignore the prickly ones biting at my bare ankles and calves beneath me. I had stupidly forgotten to bring a blanket or even a chair. Going back to the apartment to retrieve a blanket sounded like too much work, especially in this heat. And, of course, every bench and picnic table in the square block that Shipsvold called a park was either occupied or nowhere near the shade. So here I was, pretending to enjoy nature at midday on a sweltering July day.

Suddenly a voice—the last one I wanted to hear—shattered the blissful peace and humming of nature. "Roxanne. Where have you been all summer? I never see you in the offices."

I glanced up briefly, and Jeff was staring down at me with hands on his hips.

"Why do you care?" I snapped.

The silence was thick as I refused to meet his eyes, looking instead at his feet, which shuffled a bit.

"I do care. Because we're supposed to be working together, but you're apparently taking an extended vacation."

"I'm not!" I protested, seething. "Have I not been as responsive as usual over email and text?"

He ignored my question, instead probing further, "Why haven't you come into the new office? Or even the resort office?"

Why would he care? "It's called working from home, Jeffrey. You should try it. It wouldn't kill you to loosen that tie once in a while."

His eyes widened slightly. Honestly, I was as shocked as

he was. I was the sort of person who always thought of the best comebacks long, long after a conversation was over.

He cleared his throat. "My work attire is just fine. But thank you for noticing."

I felt my face heat up even more than before. "I didn't—"

"Do you want some ice water?"

"What?"

"It's a simple question, Roxanne." He held out a water bottle that was still sealed.

I gripped the bottle as my fingertips briefly brushed the side of his hand, causing a tiny shiver that was totally at odds with the heat today. "Thank you," I said softly, unsure what was going on.

"Where's your laptop?" he demanded after watching me take a long drink.

"What?"

"You said you're working from home."

"Oh, I do work from home often. But I'm not home. I don't live in the park, Jeffrey."

"So you're on vacation?"

I let out a sigh of exasperation. "No, I'm just taking a break. Not that it's *any* of your business, but my apartment's A/C isn't working. It's so unbearably hot and humid in there that I had to get out of there."

"Your apartment is even warmer than it is out here?"

"Believe it or not, yes." I sighed, uncrossing my stiff legs in front of me. "I don't even know why I'm telling you any of this. You'll probably try to find a way to use it against me."

His brows furrowed as he shook his head slowly. If I didn't know him better, I'd almost think he was hurt by my remark. But I *did* know him, and there was no way he'd be hurt by anything I said. One had to care a little before they could be hurt. One had to *have* feelings before they could be hurt.

I shook my head, trying to clear the awful thoughts from my mind. I was being uncharitable, and it didn't feel right. Even to Jeff. Even if he deserved it. I bit my lip before finally saying,

"Sorry, my filter sometimes malfunctions." I flashed a half-smile because for some reason, it seemed important to remind him that I was actually a nice person. "I live across that street over there. What about you? What are you doing here?" I resisted the urge to say, *Extended vacation?*

"I live on that block," he said, pointing to the large apartment complex kitty-corner from my building. "I did go into my office at the resort today, but it was distracting because everyone around me was obsessing over wedding decorations for the resort. Some rockstar is getting married tomorrow."

I laughed. "I'm aware. Sam Solstice is not just 'some rockstar.' His wedding is the biggest event of the year so far. I've spent months helping to coordinate with their wedding planner."

He gave me a blank look. "Oh. Right, you're the event planner. I guess I assumed you'd given up those duties to work on Hazel's projects."

"No, at least not yet."

"So you've been quite busy after all."

"Hard to believe, isn't it?"

He narrowed his eyes. "I'm not falling for that."

I shook my head and looked away. "Are we done here then?"

After a long silence, I finally resumed eye contact. His brows were lowered as though he were conflicted. "Are you all right, Roxanne?"

"Just peachy, Jeffrey."

"You just seem … less peachy than usual."

I opened my mouth to dispute his observation, but then it fell shut. He was right, after all. What was the point of denying it? "Well, I'm not a fan of ninety-five-degree weather. Plus, I'm a human. Sometimes I have bad days.."

"Sorry to hear it," he said in a hesitant tone I'd rarely heard from him. "Do you—"

"I don't want to talk about it."

I didn't even want to *think* about the call that had stolen the joy from this day. I'd woken up to quite a few messages from CastGamer55 since I'd fallen asleep early last night. The wedding planning tasks, on top of my other work, had been exhausting lately, and I'd taken advantage of the cool breeze through my window to get some sleep during this midsummer heat wave. The messages from CastGamer55—Danny, I reminded myself—had been fairly brief, but it felt good to be missed. I'd started the morning with a smile.

And then my parents called.

Feeling agitated as usual after talking to them, I'd tried to take an early nap after that—one of my few successful forms of self-soothing—but it was already so hot at 10 a.m. that I couldn't sleep. And then off to the park I went. At least there was some wind, even if it was a warm wind.

He was still just standing there with his hands in his pockets.

I exhaled slowly. "You know, I had a difficult phone call first thing, and my apartment was unbearably hot. Topping off a really busy week, honestly. I work a lot, you know, even though you don't see me in the office," I added, my tone defensive though I tried to be casual.

He ignored most of what I said, asking instead about the one thing I definitely didn't want to explain. "A difficult work call?"

"No. It wasn't work." He was still looking at me as though expecting more, so I conceded. "Fine, it was family."

He nodded and spoke quietly. "Ah. That kind of call can definitely ruin a person's day."

My eyes flew up to meet his as I drew in a breath sharply. "Are you actually empathizing with me?"

Whatever human-like emotion I saw in his eyes quickly vanished, replaced by a hard expression.

OK, I guess I was rude, but so was he, most of the time.

Why on earth was I telling him anything anyway? There was no purpose. I didn't need to talk to people just for the sake of talking—I wasn't my mother.

It was perfectly fine to be shy, to minimize talking to others, to just ... be *me*.

You know you'll never believe that.

Why couldn't I be someone else? A normal person who doesn't deal with the pain of social anxiety every day of their life? Someone who doesn't ruminate on every interaction? Why?

I took a deep breath, trying to banish the thoughts threatening to spiral into an anxiety attack.

Yet I felt a twinge of shame. More than a twinge. I clenched my fists. Wasn't I old enough to stop worrying what my parents thought? But this was a familiar feeling after talking to my mom, or sometimes even my dad.

"I'll just leave you alone," said a voice that sounded far away.

I spoke without thinking, my voice quiet as I looked at a distant oak tree across the lush lawn. "My parents—well, mainly my mom—asked if I'd booked my flight for Thanksgiving yet, but I probably won't be traveling because there's so much to do to meet Hazel's goal of opening the new center by the New Year. And, well ... my mom didn't like that."

I left out the part about how *both* my parents asked whether I was dating anyone or making friends here yet ... and the subsequent lecture about being more outgoing and not wanting to end up alone. Despite how many times we'd had those kind of talks, they crushed me every single time. I didn't even know why I was explaining anything at all to him, but I *definitely* wasn't going to go even further than I had.

He remained silent for a long moment and then shifted on his feet. "Believe it or not, I can sympathize."

I aimed my eyes directly at his, but I couldn't read him. "You can?"

"Not the Thanksgiving thing, but the unnecessary drama, guilt ... the works."

I nodded slowly, searching his face but finding only a tiny muscle in his cheek flexing. "Thanks, Jeff."

I wouldn't beg him to say more. If he wanted to, he would.

And why would he? We weren't friends.

He cleared his throat. "Anyway, I do need to get back soon. I'm planning to email you the new design brief from Sanders along with my notes this afternoon. Can you review it this evening?"

I rubbed my neck, which was getting sore, and finally realized I was still sitting in the grass, alternating between looking up at him and gazing at our surroundings. I stood slowly and looked up at him, but I noticed his eyes were elsewhere.

Looking at my legs?

He couldn't be checking me out.

He wouldn't …

Oh.

I was a mess. Literally.

"Oops." Most likely flushing from head to toe, I bent down to wipe off the small pieces of dirt and grass stuck to my legs. "I forgot to bring a chair or blanket."

Great, now I look like a total space cadet. I should've just said I enjoyed connecting physically with the earth.

As if that sounded better.

You are hopeless, Roxy.

I frowned as our eyes met. "Uh, I …" Crap, what was the question again? Oh! The brief. "I can review it today, sure."

He nodded once and opened his mouth to reply.

"Wait, no. I can't!" I chewed my bottom lip. "I'm busy tonight."

Jeff's eyebrows were furrowed. "This is important, Roxanne. We told Jill that—"

Glaring at him, I pasted on a tight smile. "I know that. But you can't expect me to drop my plans."

"What plans?"

"That's none of your business!" I wasn't about to tell him that I wanted to clear my evening so I could catch up with my fan forum buddy. Since we hadn't talked last night, I needed my CastGamer55 fix, as stupid as it sounded. Jeff would probably burst into condescending laughter—if he were capable of laughing, that is. I hadn't even seen him smile before.

His eyes narrowed as he studied my posture, with my hands on my hips. "Fine. Can you send your notes by tomorrow, say early afternoon?"

"Hmm…" I placed my index finger on my chin, pretending to think for a long moment just to annoy him. "Yes, that should work."

"Fine." His voice sounded like a hiss as he spoke through clenched teeth. "I'll still fulfill my part and send you the document later this afternoon."

"OK." I chewed on one side of my lip. Did I cross a line? I deliberately unclenched my hands, which were getting even sweatier than the rest of me. "Well, I—"

"We'll speak tomorrow," he said curtly with a brief nod before abruptly turning and walking away.

I stood with my lips slightly parted, unsure if I should call out goodbye.

Unsure why … something felt off.

Unsure why I felt a whisper of disappointment.

Chapter 7

SawyerRox4: Summer is so overrated, don't you think? I hate the heat!
CastGamer55: I don't love summer, but I don't hate it either.
SawyerRox4: July was miserable here, so glad it's over now. You couldn't step outside without sweating instantly.
CastGamer55: Yeah, it was brutal here too.
SawyerRox4: Then winters are the complete opposite. You step outside, and it's instant frostbite!
CastGamer55: Even with gloves.
SawyerRox4: Yep. Are you my next-door neighbor? :D
SawyerRox4: J/k of course

I lifted my fluffy blue slipper-clad feet up onto the couch and bit my bottom lip. We hadn't revealed many real-life details. Should I ask him where he lived? Or mention where I lived? Would that be too forward?

Did I even want to know? Sometimes the fantasy was better than the reality. I'm picturing him somewhere in New England, or maybe even actual England.

And then there's always the chance that he could be a serial killer.

No. He couldn't be.

He might worry that *I'm* a serial killer—or at least a stalker—if I asked him where he was located. We hadn't even exchanged real names. I sighed, deleting the words I'd started typing.

> **CastGamer55:** I am also not a beach type of guy. You won't find me at a pool party or amusement park or anything like that. Crowds aren't my thing, especially when everyone's sweating and intoxicated.
> **SawyerRox4:** Oh, same! I nearly threw up this morning after a meeting when I realized I'd forgotten to decline a coworker's bachelorette party ... so she was expecting me to go. Fortunately, I must've actually looked sick, pale, or green or something, so she suggested I stay home.
> **SawyerRox4:** Sorry if that's TMI
> **CastGamer55:** Was she not a friend? Or why did you feel sick about it?
> **SawyerRox4:** Oh it was a pool party at some swanky house. And no, not really a friend ... just, it's hard to explain, you don't want to hear about it.

I bit my lip harder this time, wanting to erase everything I'd just said. What was I thinking? Danny didn't need to know about my mortifying social anxiety. I always went to great efforts to hide it from people. Apart from wanting to avoid further embarrassment for myself, I didn't want to burden anyone with my problems.

> **SawyerRox4:** Anyway, we should start discussing the player profiles tonight, right? I wrote down a few ideas ...
> **CastGamer55:** Yes, we should. But I do want to hear about your rough morning; that's why I asked. Still, if you don't want to talk about it, that's fine.
> **SawyerRox4:** Oh, trust me, you don't
> **CastGamer55:** Mindy, I do trust you. As much as I can trust someone I've never met, of course. But *you* can trust *me* too.

My fingers stilled over the keyboard. I couldn't really tell him, could I? I never, ever talked to anyone about this. It was bad enough that most people probably guessed I suffered from debilitating shyness and social anxiety; I wasn't in the habit of confirming it by admitting my shame.

Then again, we were basically anonymous. We knew very little about each other outside of our *Cast Afar* interests. What harm could it do?

A lot of harm! Don't be stupid and lose one of your only "friends."

But what was the point of having friends if one couldn't confide in them?

> **CastGamer55:** Mindy, still there? I didn't mean to pressure you. Sorry.
>
> **SawyerRox4:** No, it's OK. You have nothing to apologize for...
>
> **SawyerRox4:** It's just not easy to talk about. You see, I'm very shy.
>
> **CastGamer55:** Oh, really? I wouldn't have guessed it. You don't seem shy to me. But there's nothing wrong with being shy either. My sister used to be a little shy.
>
> **SawyerRox4:** No, you don't understand. I'm extremely shy. Like, I go out of my way to avoid social situations because I'm terrified of them. I always decline invites. The few I've actually gone to have been a disaster.
>
> **CastGamer55:** Ah, I see. But I wonder if they were *really* a disaster or if that was just your perception.
>
> **SawyerRox4:** I think they were, but you're right. It's hard to say, but either way I end up feeling terrible and regretting even trying :(
>
> **CastGamer55:** I think I understand. My sister struggled a bit in school at first, kind of like you describe. But eventually she seemed to get more comfortable around people. Now, you'd never know that she used to struggle with that.
>
> **SawyerRox4:** Wow.

CastGamer55: Honestly, you seem socially adept too. I wouldn't have guessed that interacting with people is so hard for you. If I've ever put pressure on you to talk more than you'd feel comfortable, I am sorry.

SawyerRox4: No, no, you've never done that. And I'm actually not that shy online. Sometimes quite the opposite ... it's weird

SawyerRox4: So anyway, that's why I felt physically ill this morning. I almost had to actually GO to a party and interact. Thank goodness I looked as sick as I felt, I guess.

CastGamer55: Sorry to hear your morning was so rough. I can't imagine how hard that must be.

SawyerRox4: So you're not shy then. Outgoing?

CastGamer55: I wouldn't say I'm outgoing. I don't really like talking to people that much, especially not small talk, but it doesn't scare me. Perhaps I'm just impatient. In any case though, you're fine as you are, Mindy. You don't need to be outgoing, and it's OK if you're shy.

SawyerRox4: Ah. I wish I believed that ...

CastGamer55: Why don't you?

CastGamer55: Wait, let me guess. Family or friends pressuring you or not accepting you?

SawyerRox4: Yeah. Being shy isn't OK in my family. It's seen as rude or weak or something.

CastGamer55: Rude? Hardly. Weak? The exact opposite – you have to be so brave to fight anxiety every day. And being shy or not is like being tall or short. Not better or worse than any other trait.

SawyerRox4: Well, trying telling that to my parents. "Shy" was a bad word in our house ... it was like the *worst* thing I could be

CastGamer55: So, you never felt accepted as you are?

SawyerRox4: No. Far from it.

CastGamer55: I'm so sorry. You deserve better. I hope you know that.

The tears were streaming down my face now, and I had to grab a tissue from the end table to blow my nose.

I felt seen.

I never, ever felt that way.

The intensity of feelings coursing through me was overwhelming, and I tried to swallow the thick lump in my throat.

SawyerRox4: I know it ... in theory. Not sure I truly believe it though
CastGamer55: I can understand that.
SawyerRox4: Thank you. You have no idea how much this means, your understanding. Your acceptance.
CastGamer55: You're welcome, Mindy.
CastGamer55: So, your parents: have they lightened up at all on the criticism over the years? I'm assuming you're an adult now.
SawyerRox4: I'm an adult, yes, lol. Probably something we should've established months ago, haha
SawyerRox4: Anyway, my parents ... my dad is OK, but he rarely communicates his thoughts and feelings, so I have no idea what he's thinking usually. Really passive-aggressive. Mom, on the other hand, is still really hard on me all the time.
SawyerRox4: I actually had a really bad call with her a week or two ago, and she gave me a hard time about lots of things
CastGamer55: Sorry to hear that. Do you want to talk about it?
SawyerRox4: Not really. I'm trying to tell myself I'm over it ... I don't or *shouldn't* need my parents' approval for anything. But again, it's one of those things I believe in theory but maybe not in practice, you know?
CastGamer55: I get it. More than you know.

Should I ask him what that meant? I set the laptop on the couch and padded over to the kitchen to get the half-eaten sandwich I'd stored in the fridge and then refilled my water bottle.

Why did you ask something so personal? Now he'll probably balk and shut down the chat.

Then again, I just revealed something *super* personal.

Ah, worth a shot.

I ignored the doubting voice in my head as I returned to my computer and typed the question before I could think about it too much.

SawyerRox4: Care to swap depressing stories then?
CastGamer55: Well, that sounds like fun.
SawyerRox4: That's me, always a riot!
CastGamer55: I don't like self-deprecating on you, Mindy. You often do that. I wonder if you think people don't notice?
SawyerRox4: Eh, maybe … but you're deflecting. Please, tell me a story about your troubled past, if you have one, so I'm not feeling weird being the only one…

I watched as the three dots indicating he was typing appeared and disappeared several times. Was I being too pushy? I stuffed a large bite of the sandwich in my mouth and started chewing, only to nearly spit it out when I saw his next message.

CastGamer55: My father left when I was young. Left my mom, all of us. He went on a trip with friends and then called to say he wasn't coming back.
SawyerRox4: Oh my :0 … That's heartbreaking. I'm so sorry, Danny.
CastGamer55: Well, it felt awful at the time. But we were better off without him. He was totally irresponsible, not fit to be a parent or a spouse. He only cared about himself

and living wild and free as he called it. In other words, living irresponsibly and selfishly and recklessly.

SawyerRox4: Wow, I can't even imagine. My parents made a lot of mistakes, but nothing so bad as that. I knew they weren't going anywhere, and they were pretty responsible. But your situation must have been so hard :(: (:(

CastGamer55: Don't discount your own experiences. Sometimes we're better off when a toxic person leaves us.

SawyerRox4: True, but that couldn't have been easy to understand as a child

CastGamer55: No, not at first. My sister took it harder, I think, but I did my best to take care of her because Mom had to start working extra jobs to pay the bills. She meant well, but she was never around.

SawyerRox4: Dare I ask, do you have a decent relationship with your dad now?

CastGamer55: No.

SawyerRox4: A bad one then?

CastGamer55: We've had NO relationship since he left. He's tried calling a few times over the years, but I refuse to engage. I have no desire to know him.

SawyerRox4: Do you think he's changed?

CastGamer55: I doubt it, but I don't care.

SawyerRox4: That's understandable. Well, thank you for sharing that. It's probably not an easy story to tell

CastGamer55: It used to be hard. I'd be embarrassed or even try to hide it from the kids at school, teachers, etc. But over time, it got easier, as most things do.

SawyerRox4: Do you talk to your mom and sis often?

CastGamer55: I don't talk to my mother that often, outside of the major holidays. I remember her being a loving mother when I was really little, but when my father left, it changed her. She was always working, kind of emotionally distant. We knew she loved us, but there was just this distance and strain. It's still there but kind of hard to explain.

SawyerRox4: I can see that. So it's almost like you lost two parents :*(

CastGamer55: I suppose so. My sister and I were always close though. Still are. How about you, any siblings?

SawyerRox4: Nope. I always wished for one, but I think they had fertility issues. I'm not sure because they've never been very open about it.

SawyerRox4: Look at us, a couple of fan forum addicts discussing our depressing family history

SawyerRox4: I mean, not a *couple*. A pair. Two people. Friends? You know what I mean.

CastGamer55: Relax, Mindy. Of course we're friends. I don't talk about personal things or my family with most people.

SawyerRox4: <3

CastGamer55: So, it's getting kind of late, do you still want to talk about the player profiles for the game?

SawyerRox4: I'm kind of tired, but we can if you want to.

CastGamer55: No, I don't want to keep you up. If you're tired, you should sleep.

SawyerRox4: You're a kind person, Danny-o.

CastGamer55: Well, *that*'s not something I hear very often.

SawyerRox4: People don't think you're kind?? Are they idiots?

CastGamer55: LOL, sometimes they're idiots. But no, kind isn't the first thing that comes to people's minds when they think of me. But I'm OK with that.

SawyerRox4: Oh, so you reserve your sweet side for me?

CastGamer55: First I'm kind, now I'm sweet? Trust me when I say no one's ever called me sweet before. At least not since I was a toddler.

SawyerRox4: Aww, well, as you said, they're idiots

CastGamer55: Sure, Mindy. And thank you.

SawyerRox4: No, thank you, Danny. You have no idea how

much your words meant to me tonight.

Ah, was that over the top? It was the absolute truth, but maybe I was admitting too much. I sounded pathetic, probably. I frowned, wishing there was a delete button.

I blinked a few times when my eyes settled on my unfinished sandwich I'd throw on the end table. My appetite had vanished.

CastGamer55: You're welcome. And back at you.
SawyerRox4: <3 <3 <3

Chapter 8

I grinned to myself as I marched down the sidewalk and reached the new office building. Summer was finally ending, and I couldn't be happier about the light breeze today. Plus, I was early to work for once, and Jeff was going to be shocked.

You shouldn't care what he thinks.

My smile faltered just a bit, but then I shook my head and ignored the stupid voice.

When I walked into the half-circle office area, my grin faded as I widened my eyes.

Who was *that*?

My jaw dropped and my heart raced as I took in the sight of a short, bleach-blonde woman wearing a sun hat, her tiny wrist—adorned with at least five bracelets—resting on the receptionist's desk where she sat. She started turning toward me, and I reminded myself to keep walking and try to act normal. She had dark, shiny sunglasses and large, dangly earrings and—

Wait a minute. That face …

"Welcome to the office! How can I help you?" the high-pitched voice called out as this woman—no, a young girl!—removed her sunglasses and smiled a toothy grin. She had the most adorable gap between her teeth, and her face was covered in bright makeup that most people would call gaudy, but on her, it looked cute.

"Hi, I'm Roxy. I work here." I pointed my hand vaguely in the direction of my temporary office. "And you are?"

"I work here too. I'm Ms. Lila, the new receptionist. I just turned eight this year."

I fought to keep the smile off my face. "Oh, I didn't realize we'd hired someone. Pleased to meet you, Ms. Lila."

"Honey, we talked about this," Jeff's voice called out as he walked up to the girl and put an arm around her. "You're not the receptionist. Leave poor Roxanne alone." Despite the serious words, he nuzzled her head and kissed her forehead.

"Oh, are you … is that …" I trailed off, at a loss.

"This is my daughter, Lila." He turned to the girl. "Roxanne is someone I work with here." His eyes shifted back to me and slowly moved down to my feet and then back up to my face. I immediately felt self-conscious about the long, yellow floral dress I'd chosen to wear. I couldn't recall another time he'd paid any attention to what I wore. It wasn't a bad feeling exactly, but definitely a strange one.

My shock was evidently still obvious as the girl laughed and said, "It's OK, we won't bite. Very often."

I chuckled, feeling some of the tension drain from my body. "Whew, good to know. It's nice to meet you, Lila." I took a slow breath before my eyes shifted back to Jeff's. "I didn't realize it was Bring Your Daughter to Work Day."

His expression clouded over. "It's not. But sometimes she accompanies me to work when her mother drops her off unexpectedly. I didn't expect you this early. I hope this won't be a problem for you."

"Oh, no, not a problem at all!" I said quickly while smiling as serenely as I could. "I'm happy you're here, Lila. I was just surprised. But it's a pleasant surprise."

Now I wouldn't have to be alone with Jeff! That was a relief.

"OK, are you sure you don't mind?" Jeff asked cautiously. "I know we decided to work in the office a few days a week to meet with the consultants. But if you have a problem—"

"I don't. It's fine." I smiled, but it was a wobbly one.

What did he think of me anyway? That I hated children?

Just because I didn't plan to *have* children myself didn't mean I didn't like them. And the only reason I didn't want kids myself was something I rarely admitted: Parenting would just be another thing I'd fail at—and, even worse, I'd probably pass along my worst traits to innocent children. It seemed immoral.

"She's so pretty, Daddy."

My eyes flew back to the girl, but before I could respond, Jeff said gruffly, "That's not really appropriate in a workplace, Lila."

I made a dismissive motion with my hands. "Thank you, Lila. You're very kind. And *you* look gorgeous, I must say."

Her eyes lit up. "You like my look today? Dad rolled his eyes when I was putting on the makeup in his car mirror, but I think I look amazing."

"You absolutely do," I said warmly.

The girl had a positive self-image ... during my brief stint as a therapist, I often observed a connection between parenting and self-image. And this very topic was one of the reasons I was so excited to support Hazel in opening a counseling center for women with body image issues and related concerns. So this could mean ... Jeff might be a pretty decent parent. Who knew? I shook my head at the unkind thought. I might not like him very much, but I shouldn't be so shocked that he might be a good dad. I shouldn't be so quick to judge.

I turned to him with a tentative smile. "She is lovely, Jeff. I'm happy you brought her in. Will you both be staying all day, or ...?"

"Mom's picking me up later."

"She should be here any minute, actually," Jeff added.

Lila's face fell as she turned to him. "Oh, I thought we were going to spend most of the day together, Daddy."

His face took on a tender expression I'd never seen on him. "I wish, sweetie. But work is really busy this week, and your mother said she wanted to take you to brunch."

Lila nodded, a flash of disappointment crossing her adorable face before being quickly replaced with an excited smile aimed at me. "Until she comes, can I hang out with you, Roxanne?"

"No, she is busy—"

"I'd love that, Lila," I interrupted him. "And please call me Roxy."

Her smile widened further. "OK, Roxy!" She looked up at her father briefly before running around the desk and darting toward me. Just before reaching me though, she tripped on her high heels, which were obviously too big for her, and fell toward me.

I caught her, which surprised me as I'm not often quick to react to sudden events. "Lila, I've got you. Are you all right?"

Jeff walked over but seemed unconcerned.

She giggled. "NBD. I'm a klutz, Mom always says. It's not a normal day if I don't trip or bump into something at least a few times."

"Oh … well, I'm glad you're all right." My eyes shifted to Jeff briefly, whose arms were crossed over his chest.

"I won't even ask what NBD is," he said.

Lila rolled her eyes dramatically. "It's no big deal, Daddy."

"I know it's not," he said with a shrug as he stuffed his hands in the pockets of his pleated black pants.

Lila burst into laughter, and I couldn't help chuckling with her. "Daddy, you're hopeless. NBD stands for *no big deal*."

The corner of his lips twitched upward as though he was holding back a smile or laughter. Who *was* this guy?

"All right, Lila," I said. "Let's head over toward that side, and I'll show you my office."

It wasn't really my office, just a temporary workspace for now. I still didn't know what kind of role I wanted to assume in Hazel's new business, if any. Yet another to-do: Figure out what to do with my life.

As I took a step in the direction of the office, I felt the lightest hand on my sleeve, just briefly. I stilled. Jeff had never touched me willingly before, and even though this was barely even a touch, I felt my breath hitch.

His voice was gruff as he asked, "Are you sure?"

I stared into his eyes. This close, I realized they were not brown after all. "Hazel," I whispered, unable to look away.

His eyebrows rose ever so slightly as I realized what I'd just said. I'd just admitted to noticing his beautiful eye color.

"Um, Hazel, our boss …" I trailed off, trying to think of something. "I just remembered she—she's going to be out of town tomorrow. Going to meet with Sofia. That's her literary agent in Minneapolis."

Jeff crossed his arms again over his chest, which was far too close and too … wide. Firm. How had I never noticed—

"I know, Roxanne. She emailed us both yesterday."

I couldn't read his expression, so I simply nodded. "Oh, OK. I just wanted to make sure."

He eyed me in a peculiar way. "You—"

"Daddy, stop monopolizing Roxy!" cried an impatient girl standing in my office doorway, making me chuckle.

Jeff shrugged. "OK, sweetie. She's all yours." Then he turned to me with a serious expression. "If she needs me, please just come get me and shout across the hall."

"I'm sure we'll be fine," I said before pivoting toward the office, not looking back to see if he was watching. Then again, why would he be? I shook my head briefly to shake off the weird thought.

"Sorry for the delay, Lila," I said, smiling warmly at her. "Come on in."

She had a skip in her step as she entered the office and dashed around the space, looking at everything, which wasn't much. My desk was currently a folding table with a desk chair, and there was a small bookcase, a plain floor lamp, and one of those motivational posters on the only wall that wasn't covered in 1970s-style flowery wallpaper.

"Well, this is fun. It needs some decorating, right? But I love a good project!" She laughed and waved her hands around.

"It needs a ton of work, yes. It's just my temp workspace until we get the interior designers in here. They were meant to come last month, but we had some scheduling conflicts ..." I noticed her eyes glazing over and then shifting to the lone window, so I stopped. Of course, she's eight and probably didn't care about such details. "Anyway, what brings you to the office today? No school?" I asked brightly.

"Summer break, duh." She plopped down on my desk chair and spun around. The desk chair was the only thing in the room that was nice ... so far. I couldn't work in a terrible chair, I'd told Jeff, and he'd surprisingly relented when I asked to purchase a chair before the other furniture came in.

"This chair is *fun*," she said, dragging out the last word as she spun ever faster and then suddenly stopped, making a goofy face and giggling.

"I bet you're dizzy now," I observed with a grin.

"Last night, my mom had a 'hot date,' so she dropped me off at Dad's to sleep over," she said, while I tried not to wince when hearing "hot date" coming from a child's mouth. "It was so fun, Roxy! We played board games until way later than my usual bedtime."

"Really? With your dad?"

"Oh yeah, he's great at games. I think he loves playing even more than me." She laughed. "And I think he lets me win occasionally."

My head bobbed up and down as I tried to think of anything to say to that. I could hardly believe that Jeff liked to have fun, much less the idea that he and I shared a hobby in common. It was shocking. But in the best way.

"You look shocked. Are you surprised he'd let me win?"

"What—no. I mean, maybe."

"He *is* really competitive. But he's also the best daddy ever, so ..." She shrugged.

I tried but failed to keep the shock from my face. I wouldn't have thought he was a terrible father, but I also wouldn't have expected such a warm, loving one—probably because I'd never seen a hint of that side of him before.

Lila grinned, showing several missing teeth. "What, hard

to believe Daddy's competitive?"

I choked on a laugh. "No, it's ... I can believe that." I bit my tongue lightly and then forced the words. "I'm sure he's also a good father."

This was enough for Lila, apparently, because she just nodded and started humming.

"What song are you humming?" I asked.

I didn't hear her answer because I was suddenly struck by the realization that I was actually carrying on a normal, pleasant conversation with someone *in person*. Sure, she was a child, but I'd had many awkward moments with children in the past. They were a little easier than adults; at least the nice ones were.

I shook my head, focusing again on Lila because she'd started walking toward the open door. She turned back to me. "I have to go," she said with obvious regret on her face.

"What?" I asked, following her through the door. I mean, I did need peace and quiet to work, but I was sort of enjoying having Lila around. Oddly, I liked her.

"Hi, Mom," she called out to a woman standing in the middle of the reception area.

The woman had her arms crossed as she eyed Jeff, who'd emerged from his office.

"What is my daughter doing with *her*?" the short, flame-haired woman hissed. Her pointed high heels clicked on the floor as she walked straight up to Jeff.

He stepped back. "Aileen, don't be rude. That's my colleague, Roxanne."

I widened my eyes, shocked yet again. Was he actually defending me?

In a flash, Lila rushed over to give the woman a hug. "Mommy, I have a new friend! Roxy is legit so nice."

The woman's dark pink lips were set in a firm line as she turned back to Jeff. "I'm going to ask you again, *why* is—"

"You were supposed to pick her up hours ago. What was I supposed to do? I have to work, so I had to bring her to work with me." Jeff sounded exasperated, and his jaw was rigid. "Why were you so late? You know what, never mind. I don't want to know."

The woman shifted her calculating gaze to me, and I swallowed hard as she looked me over. She pasted an obviously false smile on her face. "I'm Aileen Chamberlain, Lila's mother. Jeff's wife."

"Ex-wife," he said, shaking his head in frustration. "Aileen, you really must—"

"And you are?" she asked me, ignoring Jeff with a dismissive flap of her hand. When she took a step toward me, I wrinkled my nose at the strong perfume that assaulted my senses.

"I'm Roxy. I'm working with Jeff, uh, to—to help Hazel open a new business," I said shakily.

Aileen yawned. "One of those alternative health stores where they sell snake oil, right? Isn't Hazel into stuff like that?" She glanced down at her long, orange painted nails.

My eyes swung to Jeff, whose lips were squeezed shut as he glared at her.

Aileen narrowed her eyes. "What? Are you into Hazel now? I heard she hooked up with some rich guy, but then she never stays with any guy very long. Last I heard—"

Jeff's face was red as his jaw tightened. "Aileen!" he snapped, pulling an arm around Lila, who was frowning and twirling her bracelets around her wrist as she eyed the adults anxiously. "Our daughter doesn't need to hear you talk about my *boss* like that. You are wrong anyway."

"Whatever," the woman said under her breath as she took her phone out of her purse and started scrolling. "Let's go, Lila."

The girl looked at everyone again and then shrugged before turning to hug her father fully. I almost had to look away because my brain couldn't process what I was seeing: Jeff being affectionate with someone.

"I'll see you next weekend, sweetie," Jeff said as she pulled away.

"OK, Daddy." She started walking toward her mother but then turned to me. "I'm going hiking with Daddy next weekend.

I'm *so* excited!"

"That's wonderful," I said with a smile, trying to ignore the sound of Aileen tapping her feet impatiently. "Hiking is a lot of fun. You'll have a great time!"

Lila paused in her footsteps and turned more fully toward me. "Wait, I know! You should totally come with us, Roxy! It would be so fun."

My eyes widened as I swallowed. I couldn't have heard right. "What?"

"Come hiking with us, silly!" she said with a smile.

"Oh, I don't know …" I managed.

Aileen put her hands on her hips as she stared down at her daughter. "You didn't invite your own mother. You don't even know this woman, Lila," she whispered loudly. "She's a complete stranger. Haven't I at least taught you to avoid strangers?"

The sweet girl's face fell, and my heart broke for her. She deserved to be happy, and her mother didn't seem to care how she felt.

I swallowed painfully and then said, "It's nice of you to ask —"

She hit me with puppy dog eyes. "Please?"

"I don't—I don't think your dad will want me to come. And you should have some bonding time."

"I'm sure Daddy would be fine with it. Right, Daddy?" She aimed her hopeful face toward him. It would be hard to say no to that sweet face, but I knew he would.

He made eye contact with me briefly before turning back to his daughter. "It's fine. She can come if you want. If *she* wants to. She might have other plans."

My jaw hung open as I shook my head, feeling confused. "No …"

"You don't want to go?" Lila looked like she was going to cry now.

"No, I mean, I don't have plans." My eyes bounced back and forth between her and her dad. Going hiking with a colleague I could barely tolerate on even the best day—and who felt exactly the same about me—was a bad idea for so many reasons. But I couldn't say no to Lila, could I?

I glanced at Aileen, who was rolling her eyes and exhaling loudly. And I knew what I had to do.

"OK, I'll go."

I didn't dare look at Jeff, afraid of what I'd find there. He was surely hoping I'd decline.

Chapter 9

"Maybe I could just make up an excuse not to go," I said over the phone a week later, with a heavy sigh. "I'm good at that."

"Hmm," said Julia.

I leaned forward on the couch to stretch my tight calf muscles, which were a bit sore from walking uphill to the resort more than usual this week. Mariana and her executive assistant were leading a series of staff meetings and professional development sessions that I'd unfortunately had to not only plan but also attend. At least the planning and logistics kept me busy and away from Jeff for the most part.

When Julia didn't say more, I prodded her. "What does 'hmm' mean, Julia?"

"It means ... you could do that."

"But?"

"Do you want to disappoint a little girl?" she asked in a too-casual voice.

I groaned. "Of course I don't. She's so sweet." I ran my palm over my hair and tugged on the ends. "Do you think I haven't thought of that?"

"Of course you have."

"I mean, it's the reason I said yes."

"Right, of course."

"But you understand my hesitation, surely?"

"Of course," Julia said in a voice that sounded a little *too* nonchalant.

She was my best friend—my only friend—but sometimes

she could be maddening. I took a last sip from my wineglass and rose to refill it in the kitchen. "Julia—"

"Are you drinking, Rox?"

Despite being mildly annoyed, I chuckled. "Guilty as charged," I said while opening the red wine bottle and pouring some more. "I feel just a slight bit bubbly."

Julia burst into laughter. "Were you just trying to do an English accent? Because I'm living in England?"

"Guilty again!" I took another sip. "I've only had one glass so far though."

"You never did have *any* tolerance, even during college."

"I know. Or should I say 'I know'?" I donned my horrendous English accent for the last words. "Sorry, I can't help it. CAH-n't help it, that is."

She laughed. "OK, I get it. You're a little tipsy already."

"Just a wee bit," I said, assuming the accent again.

She tsk-tsked. "Just don't have too much. You'll just get sick."

"Yeah, yeah, still acting like my RA, aren't you?" I said, returning to my own voice. "Then again, that Julia was *fun*. Remember how we'd have binge-reading and wine-drinking weekends? It was seriously the best part of college."

"Yeah, I just wish we hadn't met those jerks from the baseball team."

I smiled ruefully to my usual audience of no one at home. "In fairness, it was our breakups that inspired those fun books-and-wine weekends, so maybe we should be grateful to those guys."

"Nah, they were idiots who didn't deserve us, Rox."

"I wish I could be so confident," I heard myself saying.

My chest tightened as the regret poured in. Why did I say that? Sure, I *could* tell Julia almost anything—she was the only person I trusted with the real me—but that didn't mean I *should* admit to everything. After all, I didn't want to drive her away as I'd done with many others in my life.

The real Roxy wasn't someone that people wanted to be

friends with.

"I wish that too," she said quietly. "You are a wonderful person who deserves only the best in life. We both are. *Problems*, like having social anxiety, don't define us. *We* define us."

I took a sip of wine as I settled back onto the couch. I reached for the remote control for the ceiling fan and turned up the fan speed. It was warm and humid, as per usual for early September, and I was determined to reduce my A/C usage. "I know, Julia. I know all that, it's just—harder to internalize it. Like, it applies to you, to anyone else, but somehow not to me."

"I know, Rox." She paused and then spoke hesitantly, "Have you thought about—"

"Oh, hey—" I interrupted her because I knew what she was going to say. It had come up before: She was going to suggest therapy. To me, a former therapist. The idea of it was silly. "I—uh, I just remembered I was going to ask you about your weekend in Bath! What was that like?"

"It was OK."

I gasped. *"Just OK?* You went to see Roman baths, the Abbey, one of the homes where *Jane Austen* lived, and it was only OK?"

She exhaled slowly. "It's just—do you remember how my family and I spent a lot of summers at a lake house up north?"

"Odd change of subject, but yeah, you'd go to your grandma's house, right?"

"That's the one. Well, there was this boy at the lake who was just the *worst*. His family lived next door, and my parents and grandparents were really friendly with his parents, so he was around *a lot*. I swear he was such a moody butthead."

I snorted. "Did you just say 'butthead'? You're showing your age, Julia."

"Very funny. I'm only two years older than you," she said dryly. "But yeah, it was over ten years ago, so I called him a butthead. A lot. To his face. Because he *was*—seriously, Roxy, I swear he lived to torment me with his condescending faces and … and words. And, you know … that sort of thing."

I tried not to giggle. "He made faces at you? He sounds like a real villain."

"Laugh it up, Rox. It's hard to explain, but he was just so frustrating. So difficult, always. But often so aloof at the same time. He thought he could criticize me because I was younger and ... well, I don't know why else. He always had something against me, I think."

"I believe you. What on earth does this have to do with Bath though?"

She breathed in and out audibly. "*He* is here."

I gasped. "No."

"Unfortunately, yes."

"He's on the other side of the world, in *Bath*, on the same day you are? The odds of that have to be miniscule."

"No—well, yes, he was in Bath too, but he's at the university too. He's in the same master's study abroad program."

"What?" I nearly screamed. "How did *that* happen? And how am I just hearing about it now, halfway through your program?"

"It wasn't a big deal," she said.

I snorted again. "Right."

"OK, I was *hoping* it wouldn't be a big deal." She sighed and spoke slowly. "At first, maybe I hoped he'd be different. But he definitely wasn't. He was just the grown-up version of himself. And that's worse."

"How's it worse?"

"It's hard to explain."

"Try?"

"I don't know. He's just more obnoxious, he still treats me like a child, and he's more ..." she trailed off. "I don't want to talk about it, honestly. He already ruined the last few days in Bath, and I'm not giving him a chance to ruin this one too."

"Well, I can't argue with that. Stupid logic."

Julia laughed. "Thanks for listening."

"Always."

"You know you're, like, my platonic soulmate, right?"

I smiled. "Same, you know."

I loved that I could be myself around her, and our conversations didn't feel stilted or forced or awkward like with every other person in my life. She knew me better than anyone ever had.

"What are you doing tonight?" Julia asked. "I'm just studying, as usual."

I bit my lip, unsure how much to say about my current passion project. I'd mentioned him a few times in texts, but Julia and I didn't do *phone* calls very often, so it felt different. "I'll probably work on that board game project I told you about."

"Oh, right. With the online guy." She paused as if thinking. "Danny, was it?"

"Yes. I mean, that's the pretend name I call him," I said sheepishly.

"What does he call you then?"

"Mindy. It's—"

"Danny and Mindy from *The Mindy Project*! That's so perfect. So this is kind of a slow burning more-than-friends thing, then?" Her voice rose, and I winced.

"Oh. No, it's not like that. We're just friends. I mean, I think we are. It feels like we are, despite not knowing our real names. He's great, but it's just friendly between us. Very friendly."

"Really friendly, huh?"

"Yep," I said, popping the *p* sound at the end.

"Interesting," she replied in the tone of voice that usually came with a smirk.

I shook my head, feeling my lips twitch at the corners. "Anyway, I'll leave you to your homework. And your lake boy."

She scoffed. "Not my ... never mind. Not taking the bait, Rox. You have a great night, all right?"

"You too," I said before pressing End Call on my phone and tossing it on the other side of the couch.

My eyes swung over to the empty wineglass on the coffee table. I started to rise to refill it again but then slumped back onto the couch. No, two glasses would be plenty, at least for now. I didn't want to be drunk when Danny came online.

I supposed I cared what he thought. Shrugging off the slightly awkward feeling, I opened my laptop.

My eyes widened when I saw his green dot, indicating he was online. I hadn't expected him for another hour or so. He usually came on fairly late, I assumed because he worked long days. Or late days. I wasn't sure. We knew so little about each other outside of this online community.

I shook off the thought and opened the chat window eagerly.

> **CastGamer55:** When you get online, take a look at this template I made for the player sketches we started last time.
> **SawyerRox4:** Hi!
> **CastGamer55:** Good evening.
> **SawyerRox4:** Wow, the template is great! This will really help us.
> **CastGamer55:** You said you were having trouble seeing how all the info fits together, so I hoped this would help.

He did that for me? I felt something warm and fuzzy float through me. Maybe it was the wine.

> **SawyerRox4:** Thank you, really appreciate it
> **CastGamer55:** You're welcome.
> **SawyerRox4:** So where do we start?
> **CastGamer55:** I figured we'd try to discuss and come to agreement on some basics and then divide up the profiles to work on later.
> **CastGamer55:** To begin with, we should finalize the names. Or at least agree on what we'll use for now in the template.
> **SawyerRox4:** In my notes, we already decided on seven of them.

CastGamer55: Yes, so we need three more. I made a list of suggestions we could start with.
SawyerRox4: OK, shoot
CastGamer55: For the character we're modeling after Abbey, I was thinking about Valentina. Thoughts?
SawyerRox4: I *love* that!
CastGamer55: And just so we have some normal-sounding names in the mix, I was going to propose James, since you're such a big Sawyer fan. And Andrew for the medic guy. We can think of more interesting last names for them—
SawyerRox4: Yes to James. No to Andrew.
CastGamer55: OK. We could also use it as a last name. Like James Andrews or Valentina Andrews.
SawyerRox4: No Andrew in any form, please.
CastGamer55: Oh, OK. You just don't like that name?
SawyerRox4: I don't.
CastGamer55: Should I ask why?
SawyerRox4: Oh no, that isn't *your* name, is it? If so, I'm so sorry...
CastGamer55: LOL, no.

Wow, that was the first time he'd ever laughed in the chat. Not that I could tell if he was really laughing, but I'd never seen him write "lol" or "haha" or any typical text slang.

CastGamer55: Makes me wonder if we should exchange real names.

What? Did he just ... no. I wasn't ready for that. I wasn't sure I'd ever be ready for that. I couldn't even explain why. I knew he wasn't a stalker or catfisher or other dangerous person. I couldn't explain how I knew, but I just did. Yet ... I didn't want to know too much. Distance seemed kind of essential, for reasons I didn't care to examine.

I'd just politely say no. But maybe I should reveal

something else.

> **SawyerRox4:** I don't think so. At least not now.
> **CastGamer55:** OK.
> **SawyerRox4:** But I guess I can tell you ... I dated a guy named Andrew. In college, years ago. He was not a great guy, we'll just say.
> **CastGamer55:** Did he hurt you?
> **SawyerRox4:** Not like physically. Mainly my pride. Gaslighting, probably cheating, you know
> **CastGamer55:** He sounds terrible.
> **SawyerRox4:** Yes. I mean, he seemed nice from the start. And I'd never had a boyfriend before, so I was probably overlooking a lot.

The moment I hit Send, I cringed. Why had I told him that? My scarce romantic history wasn't something I told people about. Other than Julia.

> **CastGamer55:** Ah, I see.
> **SawyerRox4:** I suspected he'd been cheating because I'd often hear girls in the background when he went out of town for games. He was a baseball player. I mean, it's normal for college athletes to party a lot so at first I thought it didn't mean anything. But then every time I offered to travel to his away games, he had some excuse that I shouldn't come.
> **SawyerRox4:** My friend was dating his friend, and when she realized her boyfriend was cheating, I started suspecting Andrew even more.
> **CastGamer55:** And he was indeed cheating?
> **SawyerRox4:** I never found out. When I started asking questions, he tried to turn things around and blame *me* for this lack of trust. I tried to defend myself (which I don't often do, actually, but I was feeling kind of brave that year of college), but he shut it down by saying

some really cruel things about my family :(
CastGamer55: He insulted your family?
SawyerRox4: No, he criticized the way I grieved my grandpa.
CastGamer55: WHAT?
SawyerRox4: My grandpa had died a few months before. He was my best friend, so of course I grieved. Just too quietly, I guess...
CastGamer55: I'm so sorry, Mindy. That must have been devastating.
SawyerRox4: It was. I never got a chance to ask Andrew if he was cheating because he ended it then and there.
CastGamer55: Well, he didn't deserve you.
SawyerRox4: *blush* Thanks, that's sweet

My eyes bulged as I reread what I'd just typed. Did I sound like I was flirting? Was he going to think ...

I bit my lip. *No.* I'm just a little tipsy. Right?

SawyerRox4: Um, anyway, there's my boring college love story. What's new with you, Danny?
CastGamer55: Your story wasn't boring. You can keep talking about it, if you'd like.
SawyerRox4: Oh, no, that's OK. I don't want to waste any more time thinking about that jerk. I'd prefer to never think about him or see him ever again.
CastGamer55: Understandable.
SawyerRox4: So how've you been? I feel like you should share something really personal since I just did.
CastGamer55: Oh?
SawyerRox4: I mean, you don't have to. Sorry, silly idea.
CastGamer55: Oh, I see. You think I owe you.
SawyerRox4: No! You don't owe me anything. I was mostly kidding
CastGamer55: I do owe you though. I don't mind. Let me just think of something.

SawyerRox4: It's OK. You really don't have to.
CastGamer55: Mindy.
SawyerRox4: Danny.
CastGamer55: Oh, do you remember the colleague I've been clashing with lately?
SawyerRox4: Yes, how could I forget?
SawyerRox4: I mean, because I really identified with it.

Because you, Roxy, are obsessed with Danny's colleague, who's a woman.

That would be ridiculous. I'd never given it a thought.

Or had I? I probably just hadn't admitted it to myself.

But I had no business thinking that way. None. He was a buddy. An online friend I didn't even know very well.

CastGamer55: You know me pretty well now. You know I don't spend much time talking about other people. But she's my nemesis, or I thought she was.
SawyerRox4: What's been going on?
CastGamer55: She's just been different.
SawyerRox4: What, like she had a glow-up? She's suddenly nicer? Harsher? Depressed?
CastGamer55: None of those. It's hard to pin down. Maybe she's a little depressed, I don't know.
SawyerRox4: What has changed?
CastGamer55: Maybe I'm just discovering that she's much more complicated than I expected.
SawyerRox4: Is that a good thing?
CastGamer55: Yes.
CastGamer55: No. I don't know.
SawyerRox4: I see.
CastGamer55: It doesn't make sense, I know. I shouldn't have brought it up.
SawyerRox4: It's totally fine. I like hearing about you.
SawyerRox4: Gotta go. Goodbye.
CastGamer55: Oh, I didn't realize we were concluding.

CastGamer55: Bye.
SawyerRox4: Goodbye again.
CastGamer55: :) Bye, Mindy.

I started typing, but then I slowly pulled my hands from the keyboard. That was a little childish ... he was probably wondering what was wrong with me.

What *was* wrong with me anyway? Yes, I'd been drinking, but did that explain my perplexing, uncomfortable feelings when he talked about another woman?

Nope. Nope. Nope.

Not going to overanalyze this.

I'm *done* with overanalyzing everything.

Chapter 10

After a week of overanalyzing my options for declining the weekend hike, I still hadn't come up with an empathetic way to decline without hurting Lila's feelings. It was this thought that had me mentally kicking myself as I sat quietly in Jeff's immaculate living room, avoiding eye contact with him. We were waiting for Lila to finish packing. Apparently packing is one of the most fun things in the world at her age.

"Does she think we're going camping? We're just walking, right?" I asked in a half-joking way in an attempt to slice through the awkwardness of sitting in Jeff's townhouse.

His eyes rose to meet mine as his elbows remained on his knees, and he leaned forward on the small couch across from mine. "This is just a day trip, Roxanne. An hour or so, hopefully, but it's up to Lila."

I frowned as I took in his implication. He wanted this to be over as fast as possible, probably because of me. He didn't want to spend time with me, and he wasn't even going to try to hide it.

I mean, this wasn't a surprise. I didn't want to be here anyway. Yet, his words stung a bit.

My lips stayed tightly closed as we waited for Lila. I avoided his eyes and instead looked around the room. It was tidy and sparsely decorated with tasteful navy blue and dark brown accented furniture and matching lampshades flanking both sides of a small, clean fireplace. A few small photos of Lila, including one with the two of them together, lined the mantle.

So this was where Jeff the Jerk lived. It sort of humanized him a little.

When my eyes accidentally landed on him, I stopped short. The sunlight streaming through the open bay window had shifted closer to him, and I noticed how different he looked here at home. He was wearing shorts, a tech shirt, and a baseball hat. I'd never seen him in anything but dress slacks, button-downs, and neckties.

Did I think he was going to wear business attire while hiking in the woods? I hadn't thought about it, actually. I didn't usually notice or think about how he looked. But there was something about seeing him in casual clothes that made him more attractive. And I already knew he was attractive; I wasn't blind. It just hadn't mattered. And it still didn't.

Crap, I'm staring at him.

I jerked my eyes away. They landed on Lila, who was just coming in, walking a bit lopsided with a giant backpack on her back. Her eyes lit up when they met mine. "Roxy! You came!"

"Of course," I said, pasting on a bright smile. "Wouldn't miss it!"

"Well, Daddy told me you might not come," she said, rolling her eyes. "But he's wrong a lot."

"I heard that," came his cross voice. We looked at him as he rose and grabbed his smaller pack. "I packed the sunscreen and bug spray. You can put it on in the car," he said as he looked her over.

"Yay! Did you pack all the snacks I asked for?"

"Yes," he said with a sigh. "Sweetie, I'm going to have to carry that overstuffed bag of yours, aren't I?"

"As if! I'm strong, Dad." She turned to me and rolled her eyes. "He's so cringe sometimes."

"Right?" I winked at her. "Bets."

Lila's eyebrows quirked up. Shoot, did I use that wrong? I'd spent an hour last night trying to learn the latest slang that kids use.

"I think you mean 'bet.' No one says 'bets.' Well, except maybe Dad." She gave me a conspiratorial look and giggled.

"Heard that too," he said, crossing his arms over his chest

and looking between us. "Are you ready to go, or do you two want to have a gab-fest?"

Lila grinned. "What's a gab-fest? Let me guess, it's a thing from your generation, Dad?"

"It is," I said, unable to resist poking the bear.

His eyes rose in my direction. "And you only know that because you're from the same generation as I am."

"It's not worth it, Roxy. He never lets anyone win an argument. Trust me, I've tried." She had a sparkle in her eye, so I knew she was still teasing him. It was so strange; I hadn't known he was capable of being teased.

The corners of his mouth twitched up slightly. "Well, the apple doesn't fall far from the tree, sweetie. There's another old expression for you."

Lila just grinned and shook her head before abruptly turning around and wobbling toward the kitchen. We followed as she headed to the door to the garage.

I hadn't even realized he was so close when suddenly he whispered, "Sorry you got dragged into this. I'll do my best to keep it short."

Just to be contrary, I shrugged and said, "I'm cool with whatever." As though I was some kind of cool girl.

I opened the backseat of the SUV and realized I wouldn't be sitting there. One seat back was down to accommodate the length of … "Tiki torches? Why are we bringing those?"

Lila popped her head into the other side of the backseat. "They're for decorating."

"Decorating what?" I asked as I climbed into the front seat at the same time Jeff slid into the driver's seat.

"It's a mystery," he said dryly. Then he shrugged and turned the car on. "She wanted to bring them."

Who was this man? He looked almost relaxed as he backed out of the garage and down the driveway. He was gruff most of the time, but it was an affectionate kind of gruff.

He … he'd do anything for Lila.

It floored me.

I stayed quiet as Lila chattered, with occasional short replies from Jeff. I just couldn't wrap my mind around this Jeff.

Had I been totally wrong about him?

"Roxanne," he said sharply.

I blinked a few times.

Nope, I wasn't wrong about him. He was still a jerk.

"Are you going to answer Lila?"

"I—what?" I swung my head around toward the backseat. "Sorry, what did you ask?"

"I asked what your favorite season and holiday are! Dad says he hates choosing favorites, so he's no fun."

I heard him sigh next to me as I gazed out the window at the array of trees beginning to show autumn colors. "Sometimes it *is* hard to choose. I mean, this early fall is so beautiful. Watching the glistening white landscape after a long snow can be so serene. Spring is lovely because everything comes back to life, and the days get longer. And summer is … my favorite, I guess. I don't even know why! I don't particularly enjoy the humid Midwest heat, the mosquitoes, pool parties … but there's just something about summer."

"Wow, you sound like a poet. The kind that doesn't rhyme."

"Thank you … I think?" I don't even know what came over me.

I snuck a glance at Jeff, and he was obviously wondering the same thing. I never said stuff like that. And if I did, it wasn't spontaneous.

It must be Lila.

Even a person with strong social anxiety symptoms can sometimes benefit from being around a person like that: someone who puts everyone at ease and yet draws them out. Not just fellow extraverts, but *everyone*.

Hazel was like that when we first met. But something changed in our dynamic over time, and I don't know what happened. Apart from Hazel, I couldn't recall meeting many people like that since I moved here.

Lila was only a child, yet she possessed that special quality. It definitely wasn't hereditary in her case.

She prodded both of us with some more questions, and Jeff eventually convinced her to listen to some music.

Not long after, a bump jarred me upright. "What?"

Jeff's cheeks were sucked in. "Wake up, we're almost here."

I pulled down the sun visor as I licked my lips. "Oh, I wasn't sleeping—"

"You so were," Lila chimed in. "You were kind of snoring."

Jeff raised both his eyebrows a bit, but he said nothing.

"Lightly!" she added. "Not like all loud and gross."

Her father cleared his throat. "Snoring isn't gross. It's not something people do on purpose. Besides, she—"

"*Fine*, fine, maybe I had a slight doze," I said, irritation lacing my tone. "It's been a long week."

"Actually, all weeks are the same length unless there's a time change," Lila pronounced.

"It's just an expression, sweetie," Jeff said.

"Oh, grown-up speak? Blah."

I bit my lip to keep from laughing, and Jeff pulled into a small parking lot surrounded by trees in every direction, a few nearly bare and several shedding leaves as we arrived.

As they retrieved the bags from the back, I stood outside the car and yawned as my eyes swept the area, landing back on Jeff.

"Are you really tired, Roxanne?" he asked.

"A little. But it's no big deal, just—"

"Do you like 'Roxy' or 'Roxanne'? I thought you liked 'Roxy,' but Dad calls you 'Roxanne.' You have to tell us which one of us is right, OK?" Her expression was gleeful as she snuck a glance at her father.

"I really prefer Roxy." I paused, watching him spray bug spray on everything.

She laughed. "Dad, see, I was right!"

"Oh, your dad knows I prefer 'Roxy.'"

Her eyes widened as she looked between us. "Then why do

you call her that, Daddy?"

"This isn't relevant. Do you girls want to hike or not?"

Lila and I frowned at each other.

"Sorry, I don't mean to be grumpy, sweetie. I just want to be on our way. You know, not to miss the midday sun."

The girl shrugged and started walking toward the trail entrance, marked by a sign I couldn't read from here.

"Don't be so slow!" she called back, laughing as I was trailing her, with Jeff a few steps behind me. She stayed within sight but ahead of us for the first few minutes but slowed down so we could catch her.

Jeff sighed and held out his arm. "Give me your bag."

Lila grinned sheepishly. "OK, fine, I'll let you carry it."

"Aww, what a thoughtful daughter you have," I chimed in. Her playfulness around Jeff was apparently catchy, as I couldn't imagine any time I'd ever felt comfortable joking around in front of him. Quite the opposite, in fact.

Apart from occasional exclamations about random sightings in nature, we were all fairly quiet as we hiked for the first half hour and then came to a clearing that revealed a pond, peaceful and bright as the water reflected the sunlight.

I raised a hand to shade my eyes as I scanned the scene. The lake was surrounded by maple and willow trees, my favorite kinds. I could just barely see a couple of lonely docks on the far side.

"This is beautiful," I said to no one in particular.

Jeff merely nodded next to me. It's a good thing we weren't working, as he'd probably accuse me of being distracted by the scenery.

"Yeah, it's pretty," Lila said nonchalantly from a few feet behind us. We turned to see her sitting at a picnic table and smiling up at us. "Come on! I need the bags, Daddy."

"Are you hungry?" he asked.

"Starving. This place is *perfect*!"

"For what?" he asked, setting their two packs on the bench next to his daughter.

She rolled her eyes. "Duh, for a picnic. And other things."

He simply lifted his eyebrow but didn't respond, instead pulling his water bottle out of his waist pack.

"I didn't even know you could buy, like, harnesses for your water bottles," I said. "Are you two hardcore hikers?"

Lila's laughter sounded louder than usual against the peaceful calm surrounding us. "Um, no. Dad usually wears that thing when he runs."

"Oh, cool," I said as I sat at the table across from Lila and retrieved my own snacks from my bag. I was about to bite down on a carrot stick when Lila gasped.

"Roxy! You didn't seriously bring *healthy* snacks, did you?"

Tilting my head slightly, I looked between the two of them and spoke slowly, "I ... yes. I like carrots. Is something wrong?"

"Ignore her," Jeff said as he rounded the table toward me. I frowned at him and moved over to make more space for him.

"Dad—"

"You packed nothing but sweets, Lila," he said flatly. "And several cans of pop that are now warm." His face remained neutral as she scowled at him.

I tried to hold back a laugh. "You guys are too cute."

She looked at me, her scowl transforming into a suspicious look.

"I like sweets too," I said, and then she finally smiled at me again before ripping open her bag of chocolates.

She paused mid-ripping. "Wait! We have to set up first!"

Jeff and I looked at her, and he spoke first. "Set up what?"

"Let's set up the tiki torches over there, and I'll get the picnic tablecloth and other stuff from the bag."

I turned slowly to look at Jeff. We shared a look that silently spoke something along the lines of *Can you believe this kid?*

And it was ... peculiar. Since when did I ever share a wordless exchange with Jeff that wasn't a glare or a scoff? Never. I didn't even know he possessed other facial expressions.

When I tore my eyes away, he rose and turned to Lila.

"Fine, I'll set them up. Does it have to be right next to that maple?"

"It's not that close. Not nearly close enough to start a fire," I pointed out, trying to be helpful.

He grimaced. "Well, at least there was a reason I hauled four tiki torches on this hike. At least they're short."

"You're the best, Daddy." She smiled with glee as she dug several things out of the large backpack. I eyed her items, which included the tablecloth, more sweets, a fancy metal genie lamp, nail polish, and several card games, including UNO.

"That's an interesting collection," I said as I stood up. "Should I go help your dad?"

She shook her head. "Nah, he's fine."

We sat quietly for a moment as we chewed on our snacks. Then, piercing through the still air was the loudest sneeze I'd ever heard.

Lila and I turned to see Jeff walking back toward us, and Lila burst into laughter. "That was the grossest thing ever, but also the funniest!"

I didn't laugh though, as I studied his face. His nose and his eyelids were a blotchy dark pink as he tensed his jaw. His eyes looked a bit glassy.

"Do you have the sniffles?" I heard myself asking. He just stared at me, and I added, "I mean, obviously you do have the sniffles, but I'm wondering if it's cold virus kind of sniffles or allergy sniffles."

"Stop saying sniffles," he said sharply. "It's just a little allergy, not a big deal."

"It looks like a big deal," I said. "Your nose and eyes are red, and just a minute ago, you looked fine. Normal. Not that I was noticing or looking at you. I mean, you know ..." *Stop! You're rambling.* "Anyway, I'm going to guess an allergy. Ragweed sometimes gets me this time of year. You never know where you'll find it."

He sighed. "Not ragweed. Same effect though. It's tree pollen. The maples and willows."

My mouth was probably hanging open for a long moment before I asked, "You have seasonal allergies?"

He nodded.

"*You*?"

"Yes, me. Why does this matter to you?" he asked with narrowed eyes.

"It—it doesn't. It's just ..."

He was slowly becoming more like a human and not just a robot. And I didn't like it. At all.

"You look confused, Roxy," Lila said. When we didn't answer her, she shrugged. "Let's quit this boring conversation and play Skipbo or UNO!"

We turned to her, and for a moment, I thought Jeff was actually going to laugh. But as usual, he kept his emotions tightly under wraps.

And that was probably a good thing. I didn't need to get to know him better. Today was just an outlier—it wasn't like I'd be spending more time with him and his daughter. Next time, I'd make sure I had an excuse ready to say no.

Then it dawned on me. Why would Jeff take us here?

"Wait, Jeff, you led us here on the hike. You must have known about the place already."

"We went here in the summer," Lila said around a mouthful of food.

"But ... you knew you were allergic to the trees in this clearing, yet you came here anyway?" I looked at his rigid posture in disbelief. "I mean, why are we even hiking in the woods at all if you're basically allergic to the woods?"

"I took an allergy medication."

"Which never helps," Lila whispered loudly.

After a long moment, he said, "My daughter wanted to go hiking."

"The answer is because he's a great daddy," Lila said, coming over to put a lanky arm around his waist. "I mean, at least when he lets me have sweets," she said, bouncing away back to the table.

She convinced us to play UNO after that, and I yawned as I drew six cards.

"I pick ... yellow!" Lila shouted gleefully. "I know you don't have that color, Dad."

He raised an eyebrow. "Oh, really? Were you looking at my cards?"

Hearing no cheeky response from Lila, I lifted my gaze. She was staring at me. "Roxy, you OK?"

I tilted my head in question. "Yes, of course. Why do you ask?"

"You were pretty fired up earlier when we made you draw cards. We got to see your competitive side," Jeff said, his concerned face betraying his light tone.

"You didn't even blink when I just gave you the Draw Two *and* Draw Four together."

"Well, I don't know. I guess I got used to drawing cards?" I covered my mouth to hide the yawn I knew was coming. "I'm a little tired. Just a tiny bit. Anyway, let's play. I'll get you back on my next turn, Lila."

"You'll have to reverse first!" she said with a grin.

Jeff's expression was still serious as he studied me. "You seem more than a little tired. You're not sick, are you?"

"No, no, I've just been busy, lots of late nights recently. And someone's been making me come to the office early several days a week for meetings." I looked at him pointedly.

He didn't respond but merely laid a Skip card down, causing Lila to groan.

I found myself smiling, oddly finding the afternoon somewhat enjoyable despite spending it with my nemesis.

Maybe *nemesis* was too strong a word.

After we finished playing several more games, we decided to head back—even the eight-year-old was getting tired of eating only sweets and wanted a real meal. On the trek back to Jeff's car, I became clumsy with exhaustion. After a few near-falls, he started calling out, "Watch your step," whenever there was anything, even a thin branch, in the path in front of us. I bristled but stayed quiet, as it was hard enough to concentrate on putting one foot in front of the other.

Once we arrived at his house, Lila leaped at my chest and put her surprisingly strong little arms around me. "Thanks for coming, Roxy! I hope we can hang out again soon."

I just smiled at her. I liked the girl. Quite a lot, actually, but I wasn't about to make any promises to spend more time with her and the man who couldn't stand me. And vice versa, of course. I still didn't like him and never would.

As Lila walked off, I heard his abrupt voice as I grabbed my bag out of the SUV. "Roxanne, get some rest this weekend."

"Can't. You wanted me to review those three reports by Monday," I grumbled.

"Take a few extra days," he said quietly.

My jaw dropped, and my eyes bounced back and forth between him and the floor of the garage. "Well, that's ... unexpectedly nice of you."

His eyes betrayed nothing as he stared at me for a moment. Finally, his brisk tone returned as he replied, "We need to be rested to be able to perform well at work."

I narrowed my gaze. "Not so nice then. Got it, sir." I saluted him, knowing it was childish but unable to stop myself as I turned on my heel to head home.

He had a point. I knew it. But would it kill him to be nicer about it?

I shook my head, deciding a nap would be just the thing. As I entered my apartment, I looked around at the clutter piling up. I should tidy up tonight.

I grimaced at the pile of laundry nearly spilling out of a basket as I entered my bedroom. After a long day outdoors, the last thing I wanted to do was clean—or even think about cleaning. Would Danny be online tonight? I hoped so. Sometimes he was around on weekends, sometimes not.

But my brows furrowed as I realized something quite odd: I hadn't thought about Danny or our project today even once, until now.

Chapter 11

I twirled my fountain pen in my hand as I pondered how to answer Danny's question. How was your day? was an innocent question that most people asked to be polite, and I'd answered it awkwardly on more than one occasion. Oh, I'd learned years ago that people asking this question often didn't care but rather were just performing a social nicety—they only expected you to say I'm good, how are you? But that didn't stop me from agonizing over how to respond. Because I wasn't always good, and it felt weird to claim I was.

But this was Danny. I'd told him lots of things I'd never tell anyone else. And he hadn't appeared to think worse of me afterward. I groaned and set the pen down, abandoning my intention to stick to the plan and share my notes on the game design book we'd both spent the last week reading. In what little free time I had, reading the book had been a nice distraction from thinking about the strangely not terrible—but definitely unsettling—hiking experience earlier this month.

SawyerRox4: I'm fine
CastGamer55: Fine can mean a lot of different things, Mindy.
SawyerRox4: You're right.
CastGamer55: I guess that's all I'm going to get tonight, eh?
SawyerRox4: lol, for now anyway
SawyerRox4: It's just a bunch of work stuff, everything piling up, my irritable colleague being irritable, no time

for sleep or self-care ...
CastGamer55: Oh, I'm sorry to hear that.
SawyerRox4: It's no different from any other day, really.
CastGamer55: You're always stressed out and overwhelmed?
SawyerRox4: Pretty much
CastGamer55: That's no way to live.
SawyerRox4: Tell me about it

He didn't reply at first, and I wondered if I was being too negative. People didn't like being around negative people, right?
You should smile more.
You should be optimistic.
You should think positively.
You should be grateful for what you have.
You should stop being so depressing.

I wiped a lone tear about to escape my eye. I was so tired of the voices. The voices from my childhood—parents, friends, teachers, everyone—but also my adulthood. Nowadays, it was just *my* voice. My parents were rarely that blunt anymore, and I avoided most people anyway. Still, that harsh voice was as strong as ever.

SawyerRox4: Sorry to be a Debbie Downer. I'm really fine. How are you doing?
CastGamer55: You're not a Debbie Downer. Don't apologize. You can say whatever you want to me.

A rush of warmth passed through me, followed by goosebumps. No one ever said that to me. Apart from Julia, I couldn't really be myself with anyone. Until now.

CastGamer55: Do you want to try doing a call?

My eyes widened as I scrambled to sit up straight.
What?
We'd never done that, never even discussed it. Why did

he want to call me? I looked down at my old pajamas and remembered the messy ponytail I'd hastily assembled before parking myself on the couch for the night.

No way.

> **CastGamer55:** Hello?
> **SawyerRox4:** Sorry, I wasn't ready for that question. Like a video call?
> **CastGamer55:** We don't have to. The idea just popped in.
> **SawyerRox4:** I don't know …
> **CastGamer55:** You'd asked about my day, and I was thinking it'd be easier to explain in a call rather than doing a ton of typing. And I have an idea for the game. But you can say no.
> **SawyerRox4:** Ah, well I want to hear about your day. What if … maybe an audio call? I'm honestly not camera-ready at the moment
> **CastGamer55:** I don't even know what camera-ready means, but OK. Audio is fine.
> **SawyerRox4:** Typical man, you're probably wearing sweatpants but looking just as good as usual

Why on *earth* did I say that? I had no idea what he looked like. And even if I did, that was so, so inappropriate.

> **SawyerRox4:** Sorry, my usual filter is on a low battery right now.

And then the phone ringing sound came across my computer speakers, and his user avatar appeared large on my screen.

I gulped and accepted the call. "Hello?" I managed to choke out.

I heard chuckling. "Your filter—"

"Sorry—"

I ended the call.

I was ... not ready for this. It was too real. I hadn't planned for this, and we'd never discussed it. We hadn't even shared our real names!

And the worst part? It was too much of a risk.

I couldn't risk our friendship. Because I knew myself, and I'd mess it up.

Then you'd lose him, what little of him you have anyway.

CastGamer55: Are you OK?

SawyerRox4: I'm sorry. Just not ready for that.

CastGamer55: It's OK. Stop apologizing. You didn't do anything wrong.

SawyerRox4: I didn't mean to disappoint you.

CastGamer55: You didn't. I like it when you're honest with me.

SawyerRox4: OK, then the truth is, I am really valuing our friendship ... let's not screw it up, k?

CastGamer55: I don't think a phone call would screw anything up, but sure. I respect your view.

SawyerRox4: Please share though. I really do want to hear how you're doing ... and we have to talk about the book too

CastGamer55: Let's talk about the book tomorrow. I want to reread Part 4, actually, because I think it's related to my idea.

SawyerRox4: You're presumptuous. How do you know I'll be around tomorrow?

CastGamer55: Sorry, I mean the next time we're both online.

SawyerRox4: Don't apologize... it's sweet

CastGamer55: No one's ever accused me of being sweet.

My mouth curved upward. How had I gone from being terrified to talk to him to ... almost flirting?

SawyerRox4: I can't believe that, Danny

CastGamer55: Tell that to, basically, everyone who knows me. Haha.

CastGamer55: But seriously, I understand your hesitation. I don't open up to a lot of people. Not anyone, really.

CastGamer55: Well, except my sister.

SawyerRox4: Baby sister?

CastGamer55: Yes, we practically raised each other.

SawyerRox4: I sense a story there. You don't have to tell me unless you want to.

CastGamer55: Maybe another time.

CastGamer55: I just struggle to connect emotionally with anyone.

SawyerRox4: No, you refuse to

CastGamer55: Well, maybe.

SawyerRox4: You think you don't deserve to.

SawyerRox4: I know bc I'm the same

I felt another tear in the corner of my eye and swiped it away. I might have gone too far here, but it felt so darn good to connect with someone.

CastGamer55: Well, what do you call this, then?

CastGamer55: If this isn't connecting, I don't know what is.

SawyerRox4: *mind blown* You're right

SawyerRox4: Let's talk about the show then

CastGamer55: You're right—you're just as bad at this as I am, Mindy.

SawyerRox4: I'm much worse, Danny

CastGamer55: But you make me laugh.

SawyerRox4: Then it's all worth it

Chapter 12

By October, I'd finally reached my limit in trying to juggle three jobs, so I asked Hazel and Mariana to meet me for coffee.

When I arrived at their table, they both looked up and smiled.

"Hi, sorry I'm late," I mumbled while sliding into the seat opposite them.

They both looked surprised for a moment and then smiled.

"No worries at all," Hazel said. "How are you?"

"Uh, I … I'm good," I heard myself saying, my voice raising as though I'd asked a question.

They glanced at each other and then back at me with creased brows. "Are you, Roxy?" Mari asked.

"Yes, yes, I'm fine," I said, trying to make my voice sound more convincing than my face probably was.

"Roxy," Mari said with a gentle smile. "I know a little about hiding your feelings. I used to do it all the time. Maybe you remember?"

"She did," Hazel said with a vigorous shake of the head. "She even convinced herself she didn't have feelings."

"Oh, I haven't done that at least," I said with a nervous laugh before I realized what I'd just admitted.

That you'd been struggling.

That you wanted to hide the fact that you're struggling.

What was wrong with me lately? I couldn't stop blurting out mortifying things wherever I went lately. I used to be so good at keeping it all under wraps.

"You used to be good at this, right?" Mari said, reading my mind. "Then things start to spin out of control."

My lower lip wobbled as I tried to swallow around the lump in my throat. I needed to change the direction of this conversation. The pity in their eyes was killing me.

"It's OK, you know," said Mari, putting a gentle hand on my forearm.

I forced myself to meet her eyes. "What?"

"It's actually a *good* thing that you're no longer good at denying all your feelings. Because that's bad for you," she said.

"And you know that too," said Hazel in a much softer voice than usual.

I swallowed again with some difficulty as I looked down, hoping a hair curtain would help. I crammed my hands under my legs on the seat to keep them from shaking.

"Agh—" I croaked.

"Here, have a glass of water," Hazel said, sliding a glass toward me.

I accepted it hesitantly and then proceeded to guzzle half of it. Staring at the wooden table separating us, I cleared my throat and then pasted on a small smile. "I'm perfectly fine. Really."

Mari shook her head sadly. "You're not fine. But you're not ready to talk about it. I get it."

My brows scrunched together as I processed this. She didn't believe me. She knew I was lying—she *knew* she was right that I was denying my feelings and hiding it all from others.

And she wasn't ever going to believe me, because she *knew*.

I remembered the old Mariana. She was one of the most controlled people I'd ever met, showing no emotion most of the time or at least believing she wasn't. Some people, including me, had considered her cold and lacking humor. But she'd proved us all wrong. She was anything but cold and unfeeling; the real Mari was warm, deeply sensitive, and one of the kindest people I'd ever known.

Still, I wasn't her. I didn't have a great, wonderful person inside me just waiting to be freed.

"It's just ... I don't do pity," I said, unable to meet their eyes.

Hazel scoffed. "It's not pity, at least not from us."

"It's empathy," Mari said softly. "Maybe you haven't had a lot of that in your life."

I shook my head. "No, it's not—" I stopped to steady my breathing. "I think we should shift gears. I wanted to talk to you both about my workload and—and maybe strategize about how to optimize my time and responsibilities."

Fortunately, I'd rehearsed that line quite a few times before I arrived here. I started breathing a bit easier after having declared my purpose for being here. I tried to look steadily into their eyes, but it was hard.

"You haven't touched the coffee in front of you," Hazel said mildly.

My eyes widened. I hadn't even noticed a waiter bringing it to us. "Oh, uh, you're right. I mean, I don't like it really hot, so I was waiting till it cooled down."

Lying isn't bad if it's for self-preservation, is it? Yet I knew the answer to that. And I think they did too, judging by their expressions of disbelief.

Mariana looked at Hazel before asking me, "Is that why you asked us to meet you?"

"Of course," I said.

Hazel flipped her long, glossy black hair over her shoulder. "Oh, we thought you just wanted to hang out."

I opened my mouth and closed it, unsure what to say. "I mean, it's—hanging out is fine, but I know you're busy. I promise this is just a work thing and won't take too much of your time."

They both frowned, and Mari fiddled with her wallet on the table.

"Did I say something wrong?" I squeaked.

"Not wrong exactly, but we don't consider a coffee date with you to be wasting our time, Roxy," Mari said carefully.

"I was looking forward to just chatting, actually," Hazel

said with a tentative smile.

What?

Ugh, I'd blown this too. They wanted to just hang out like friends? I must be misunderstanding. "Oh. Um, sorry."

Hazel laughed. "*Stop* apologizing, Roxy."

"I like to think we're friends, or at least I'd like to be," Mari said slowly.

Now I knew I must be hearing wrong. She couldn't want to be friends with me. And Hazel ... I looked over to see her nodding along.

"I'm sorry, what's going on?" I heard myself say, like an idiot.

Hazel sighed. "This isn't an intervention, Roxy. We just thought you wanted to spend time with us. It seems you didn't, and that's OK," she said with a touch of impatience.

My heartrate jumped. The last thing I wanted to do was hurt her feelings. Or anyone's. "Oh, I'm sorry—"

Mari frowned and cut me off. "Seriously, no more apologizing," she said gently. "If it makes you more comfortable, let's talk about your work responsibilities, OK?"

The feelings of shame only increased at their responses, but I swallowed and nodded. "Yes, all right. So, as you know, I'm doing three jobs." I looked back and forth between them. "I'm co-managing your new project to set up the counseling center by December 31, Hazel, and still serving as your assistant in your other endeavors, such as book marketing, events, and other outreach. Mariana, I'm also still in charge of event planning at the resort." I paused. "It's a lot of work, and I love doing it all, but —"

"It's way too much," Hazel finished for me, and her brow creased. "Roxy, I feel terrible. I didn't put all the pieces together about how much work we've put on you. I'm really sorry."

"Same," Mari said with a troubled expression. "I knew you were busy, but I didn't realize it was *that* much."

"I mean, it's mostly been manageable, and I like working for you both. Truly, I'm lucky to have these responsibilities." I bit my lower lip. "I shouldn't complain."

Hazel let out a strangled laugh. "No, you're just being polite. We've dumped a ton of stuff on you, and you have every right to complain." When I opened my mouth to object, she shook her head. "No, you absolutely do. Let's figure out how to fix this."

"What can we do to help?" Mari asked.

"Well, I have a few ideas, but ..." I paused and took a deep breath. I'd practiced this part too, but it was still gut-wrenching to say—to admit I couldn't do it all. "Potentially the most impactful change would be to hire another event planner for the resort. Or maybe an existing employee can take on those responsibilities."

They looked at each other, a silent thought passing between them, and I tried to squelch the queasy feeling of regret rising in my stomach.

"Consider it done," Mari said.

"We should've done that months ago," Hazel added.

My jaw dropped. "Oh. That was easy. Are you sure?"

"Absolutely," Mari said with a smile.

"Will that be enough, or do you need me to find a new assistant too?" Hazel paused, putting her long purple fingernail to her lip for a moment. "Or maybe the better question is, what do you see yourself doing in the future, once the new center is open?"

I maintained steady eye contact even though I was still shaky. "I need to think about it some more. Am I ... am I understanding right that you are open to some different possibilities?"

"Of course! There are any number of useful roles—hopefully professionally fulfilling ones—you could take in the new center. I mean, you know that as well as I do, as you and Jeff drafted a list of positions we'll need to hire in the future."

I nodded and pasted on a polite smile. "Yes. I would appreciate some more time to think about it, if you don't mind."

"Sure," she said breezily as she took a bite of the orange

scone in front of her. I realized I was also famished, but eating could wait until I got home.

"Are you hungry? We can order some food," Mari suggested.

Apparently I'm incapable of hiding any feeling on my face now. Ugh, I'd need to work on that. "A little, but it's no big deal."

Mari looked like she was going to object, but Hazel nudged her and spoke instead. "All right, so we'll circle back to this future role discussion in the coming weeks, and Mari will hire a new event planner. I hope this helps, Rox."

I offered a smile that was mostly genuine this time. "Yes, thank you so much. And don't worry, we're still on track to open your center by New Year's Eve, I promise."

Hazel eyed me thoughtfully for a moment. "You know, I was just thinking the other day about the day we met you. You were meant to interview for the position at the resort, and you got lost in the north wing."

My smile was a bit shaky now. "Yes, and you helped me find Mari's office. I was so grateful. Thank you again."

They looked at each other.

"Can I ask you a question, Roxy?" Mari asked.

I blinked rapidly and nodded, dread filling me. "Of course."

"Were you really lost on your way to the interview? Or were you looking for an escape?"

My breath caught in my throat, and my face must have been a sweaty, blotchy mess, so I looked at my nails.

Don't look at them.

Whatever you do, don't cry.

Or stammer or ramble.

Don't give yourself away.

"I—" I heard my choked voice and looked frantically to the side, where I could escape the booth. Just as I started scooting over, I felt a soft, warm hand cover my clammy one.

"Roxy," Mari whispered. "Please don't go."

I froze, my eyes glued to her hand, which slowly pulled back. I didn't trust myself to respond, so I just nodded.

"I'm not asking this as your boss, Roxy. I know it feels like you have to manage everything alone—that you can't be vulnerable with anyone."

"But that's BS," Hazel chimed in. "You can trust us."

My mouth struggled to form words. "I—it's not that I don't trust you." I stopped and took a sip of water. "Don't think that. But you *are* my bosses."

Hazel frowned. "Does that mean we can't be friends? We can't be honest about what's going on in our lives?"

"You say that, but ..." I clenched and unclenched my hands to try to make them stop shaking. "Never mind," I murmured.

"No, keep going," she said.

Seeing my lips clamped shut, Mari sighed. "We're not perfect at this either, you know. Hazel's been my best friend for many years, but we screw up sometimes. We get caught up in life and love and ... it's not always perfect. And that's OK."

"I forgot Mari's birthday one year. I know, who does that? But she spent years never telling me anything, so there's that."

Mari winced. "It's true."

"I forgot to try to call you during that big snowstorm earlier this year," Hazel admitted, "but Mari barely heard from me either. I literally didn't have a working phone and was just trying to survive one moment to the next as I was trapped in the house of the guy I thought hated me. Still, I should've tried to reach you. I was pretty self-absorbed last winter, even more than usual," she added wryly.

"It's fine," I said. "I understand."

As both of them looked at me expectantly with gentle smiles, it hit me.

Maybe it was safe to talk to them.

Maybe I'd never know unless I tried.

Maybe it could even be worth it.

"I—I hear updates from Jeff, not you. Like when Peter was in the hospital, Hazel." I swallowed with difficulty. "But I don't expect anything, so that's OK."

This wretched feeling of vulnerability was killing me, but

I forced myself to maintain eye contact with them.

"It's OK to want more from people," Mari said. "Sometimes it's hard to ask because it's like putting yourself on the line, right? But it can pay off a thousand-fold."

"I know that in theory ... I used to be a therapist."

They both nodded, and I recalled I'd mentioned it once years ago. I guess they paid more attention than I realized.

"Well, I didn't expect this to be a therapy session or intervention," I said with a forced laugh. "I feel like I should pay you."

Mari shook her head, her wavy bob sweeping from side to side. "You're making it seem like no one would ever want to hang out with you unless you're paying them, whether in money or labor. And I get it. I used to feel like that, actually. But it was just ... my anxiety and internalized shame."

My gaze traveled downward briefly and then back up. "My oldest friends." I exhaled slowly, finally feeling my body relax a bit. "Thank you. I—I never talk about this stuff. I have two friends who know, but ... well, one of them I've never met in person, and the other one I haven't seen in years."

"May I suggest something?" Mari asked tentatively.

"Sure," I said, exhaling slowly and giving a half smile that was kind of genuine. "Not as my employer, right?"

She returned the smile. "Soon-to-be ex-employer, you mean. But yes, as your friend."

The rush of warmth that coursed through me caught me off guard, so I just nodded, trying to calm my racing heart.

"Last year, I found an anxiety support group, and it had a huge impact on me and all the stuff I was trying to deal with. Have you ever looked into something like that for your social anxiety?"

My heart caught in my chest, and I must have looked like a deer in the headlights because she added, "Sorry, I am not trying to diagnose you. I have a business degree. I'm far from being a counselor." She chuckled. "It just sounded like social anxiety to me, but maybe I'm wrong."

Unable to do anything else, I forced myself to breathe in and out.

"This is hard, Rox," said Hazel. "I get it. I haven't struggled with that issue myself, but I've had plenty of other challenges in life. And sometimes it's hard talking about things, even for an extrovert like me."

"Thanks," I managed to say. "To answer your question, Mari, no, I haven't. It's weird sometimes when you're a therapist because it feels like all the stuff you tell your clients—all the ways you can help them—like it doesn't apply to you."

They nodded and just looked at me, waiting for me to say more. "Uh, I guess I could look into it."

"Can we help? I have the Meetup app on my phone," Hazel said eagerly.

"I don't ... I guess so," I muttered as she typed away on her screen, not waiting for my answer.

Soon her face lit up even more, her brown eyes sparkling as she looked from the phone to me. "Found one! It's for people with social anxiety. Looks like they have dinners, meet 'n' greets, and even fun outings like mini-golf."

"Right here in Shipsvold?" Mari asked.

"Oh, no. We're too small. The group leader's actually over in Shellington, but they meet in different towns because their members are kind of spread out." She paused, her eyes scanning the screen. "Oh! It looks like they're meeting here in two weeks! A few days after Halloween. Don't worry. It's not Halloween-themed. I'll sign you up."

"Oh, uh ... OK." My head was spinning as I tried but failed to process all this.

"That reminds me! Peter and I are hosting a Halloween party this year. Well, it's mostly me, but he goes along with it. Want to come?"

"You can say no. I know I will be," Mari said dryly.

Hazel's head swiveled toward her best friend. "You are coming."

Mari chuckled. "We'll see. You know I hate Halloween."

"If it wasn't for that Halloween party I dragged you to last year, you wouldn't have reconnected with Pinecone!"

Mari rolled her eyes and turned to me. "Terry was dressed as a pinecone, and Hazel never let go of it."

Hazel just smiled at us both. "It's up to you, Roxy. I hope to see you there."

I wrestled with how to respond. I had to say no—it was bad enough they'd be expecting me to go to the Christmas party in two months. I was usually good at coming up with excuses to avoid social gatherings, but I felt like I'd been laid bare this morning. My self-defenses were lowered, destroyed even.

"Uh, I don't know."

Mari gave me a knowing smile. "Fair enough. Don't pressure her, Haz. Then she definitely won't come."

I forced my lips to curve into a smile. "We'll see. I appreciate the offer."

I'd think of a way out of the party—I always did.

But she signed me up for the social meetup group. Maybe I should actually do that. I didn't want to be lonely forever. What was stopping me?

Chapter 13

The rain pelted against the windows as I ripped open a bag of assorted Halloween candy I'd bought earlier today. Since it was October 31, it was literally the last one sitting on the table at the convenience store. My fragile heart almost cried with joy.

But maybe I wasn't actually fragile. It had been over a week since the exhausting coffee date with my bosses, who were apparently my friends now. My everyday life wasn't any different ... it's not like they were adding me to a group chat or anything. But I'd felt lighter. Freer. Awkward, of course, but a lighter kind that could almost be shrugged off on the better days. Something had shifted, even if it was small. I'd take it.

I had already decided to curl up on the couch and watch a movie tonight since Danny told me he'd be offline tonight. The rain actually made it feel even cozier as I pulled on the fluffy blanket I always used on rainy or cold days. I'd stuffed two mini-size Snickers in my mouth before I heard it.

Ring, ring.

I froze mid-chew.

Had I forgotten to turn off the porch light?

Or, worse, was someone coming to visit?

I lay still as a board on the couch, hoping they'd go away if I made no sound.

But then I heard voices. And another ring of the doorbell. I cursed myself again for not installing a doorbell camera or, better yet, paying a little extra for the apartments above mine without an exterior door. You couldn't even unlock them from the outside, so it wasn't really a convenience in any way. Surely the upstairs tenants didn't have to deal with trick-or-treaters.

Finally, I dragged myself off the couch and ambled over to the door. Sure enough, I'd left the porch light on. I groaned and looked through the peephole.

I nearly fell backward when I saw the familiar face.

What was *he* doing here?

I swung the door open, knowing with his stubbornness, he wasn't likely to go away easily.

"Boo!" Lila jumped out of the shadows to the side, and I nearly jumped with fright in turn.

"Lila! Jeff ..." I trailed off, pausing to catch my breath and put a hand on my chest as I saw Jeff clad in a dark raincoat and Lila holding an umbrella over her witch costume. "Wha-what are you doing here?"

Jeff raised an eyebrow, but before he could speak, Lila held out her pumpkin bucket. "Trick or treat!"

"Oh, right. Um, happy Halloween!" I said, feigning enthusiasm. "Did I leave my porch light on? I'm actually not giving out candy this year."

Lila gasped, her face stricken. "Why not?"

My eyes shifted to her father and then back to her. "It's just not my thing. I tried it a few years ago, but ..."

Finally, Jeff spoke up. "It's fine. I promise we're not stalking you, Roxanne. Lila just likes to be thorough and get as much candy as humanly possible." He paused and looked down at her. "Should we stop at the dentist's house too?"

She looked even more horrified now. "No way!"

"You know, I actually do have some candy. Let me go get some, OK?"

"It's really not necessary—" Jeff started.

"Yay, you're the best, Roxy!" Lila shouted as I turned around to find the candy.

With a few different mini-candy bars in hand, I turned back toward the door, only to find them standing inside on my rug.

"Oh, you're ... inside. Dripping everywhere."

"Sorry," Jeff said, and his wincing actually suggested he meant it.

Guilt crept through the edge of my consciousness. I should've *asked* them to come in and shelter from the rain.

"Here," I said to Lila as I dropped the candy into her bucket.

She immediately dug them out though to inspect and turned to her father. "Dad, can I have one?"

"You had five already," he said sharply. Then his tone softened. "What's one more? Go ahead, sweetie."

Lila proceeded to sit on the floor, hence expanding the amount of rainwater she dripped on my floor.

I bit my tongue lightly and looked back up at Jeff.

He was leaning closer, his hand reaching toward my face, and then we both froze.

His hand went back into his pocket. "You have something on your ... lips."

"My—" I started as my hands flew to my mouth. "Oh, chocolate. I might've had a little candy before you so rudely interrupted me."

His trademark frown returned. "Sorry to bother you."

I shrugged. "Sorry, that was unnecessary for me to say. You just ..." I couldn't finish that sentence: *you just bring out the worst in me*. I wasn't that cold. Actually, I wasn't usually cold at all; I wasn't myself with him though. "It's fine you guys stopped by."

"I didn't know you lived here, Roxanne," Jeff said. "And you *did* leave your outside light on."

"I figured as much. Else you wouldn't have come," I said with a wry smile until I saw his frown transform into something entirely unreadable. Fidgeting with the hair band around my wrist, I looked down at Lila, who was digging through the candy in the bucket.

"Finally, I found it!" she declared to no one in particular. "Mmm, my favorite."

"So, you decided to skip Hazel's party?" he asked.

"Oh, well ... yes," I said. Should I tell him about the social anxiety meetup I had actually put on my calendar as a marker of my commitment to self-improvement?

Are you insane? You can't tell him that. He'll look at you with such disdain, or he'll laugh. Just like anyone would.

I raised my chin. I didn't need to explain myself. "So did you, apparently."

He pointed to Lila on the floor. "Hazel said it was an adults-only party, so it was out for me."

Oh, right, because he had a daughter. This discovery was still hard to grasp.

Next thing I knew, Lila was hopping up and shaking off some more raindrops, much to my dismay. "We should probably go. I want to take some more pictures for Aunt Abby."

"Oh, your mother's family? Do they live out of town?" I asked politely.

Why was it usually so hard for me to ask normal questions in conversations, yet this girl made it easy somehow?

"Oh, no. Mom's family doesn't live around here. We don't see them much. Aunt Abby is Daddy's sister."

"You have a sister?" I asked, my eyes wide and my tone incredulous.

"I do," he replied. "You look shocked. It's hard to believe I have a sister?"

"Yes," I said automatically, realizing too late what his next question would be.

"Why?"

Our eyes locked, and I stared at the warm, amber color of his eyes. His hazel-colored eyes appeared to change color, but I knew it was only an illusion, a trick of light.

Finally, I remembered he was waiting for an answer. "I don't know."

His gaze narrowed ever so slightly until Lila tugged on his arm. "Enough boring talk, let's go."

Jeff's voice sounded oddly lower than usual as he nodded. "OK, we need to stop bothering Roxanne anyway."

"Oh, you're not a bother," I said quickly, flashing a smile at Lila. "It was nice to see you."

"I know, it so was!" Lila said just before throwing her black robe-clad arms around me. I hugged her back, even though I was going to be drenched too as a result.

"All right, I guess I'll see you at work, Jeffrey," I said, walking around them to try to point them toward the door.

Lila giggled. "Nobody calls him Jeffrey, not even Mommy. He hates it."

"Oh? I didn't know that," I said, trying not to smile as I peeked at his glaring face.

"Yeah, his dad's name is Jeffrey." Then she leaned in and whispered, "I'm not allowed to call him Grandpa."

My lips formed an *oh*, but no sound emerged as I shifted my eyes upward to look at him.

What's the story there? I noted his rigid posture as he stared at the floor. Bad blood within his family, perhaps? For some reason, I wanted to know. I tried to think of how to phrase my question.

As I tried to think of how to phrase a question, his head snapped up. "Come on, we need to go, Lila."

Before I knew it, he'd ushered her out the door, and I was just standing there staring at the closed door.

What was *that*?

And why ... why did I feel so disappointed at their abrupt departure?

Chapter 14

Only a few days later, I hadn't seen Jeff at all, as he'd apparently caught a cold. Or so he said in his very terse email. Even Danny had been online less than usual, and I now had only two jobs instead of three. So I'd passed the rare time to myself by watching an earlier season of Cast Afar and emailing Danny all the things I noticed this time that I hadn't caught in prior viewings (yes, plural, because I was obsessed).

Before I knew it, the time had come to get ready for my first meetup with the anxiety group. Cue the nerves, obviously.

I'd changed clothes approximately 8,000 times before finally leaving my apartment, only to panic and head back inside to change. There wasn't much left in my closet to try on. I bit my lip, slumping down onto my bed.

Maybe this was a sign I shouldn't go to the meetup. If I couldn't even decide on an outfit, how on earth was I going to survive this meet and greet?

You won't.

This is a terrible idea. You can cancel, and no one will care.

I stood up and began to pace around the apartment.

"Shut up, stupid inner voice," I muttered, and then my voice rose. "And yes, I know your stupid name because I was a trained therapist. You've been running the show forever, and I'm *sick of it!*"

My blood started pumping faster, and I felt an involuntary smile as I fist-bumped in the air.

Yes, I could do this.

I went on my way, practically skipping down the sidewalk

toward the meetup location, only a few blocks from my apartment, as most things are.

I peered up at the gray sky. Even the cool, gloomy weather couldn't spoil my mood. Was that a cloud shaped like a thumbs up sign?

THUD.

I stopped breathing momentarily as the tremendous force ran through me. Panicked, I looked at the sidewalk as I started to fall backward.

But someone caught me, pulling me upright gently.

As I caught my breath and slowly raised my eyes, they first landed on black leather shoes gleaming beneath dark, well-tailored pants. My eyes lingered on the long cashmere coat and the sleek black gloves that held me firmly. At least I'd run into someone classy!

But I nearly fell out of his solid, steadying arms when my eyes reached his face.

I'd know it anywhere.

Those were the deep brown eyes that once drew me in, the dimple that made his smile so classically handsome, and the mouth that spoke such ugly words.

"Hey, I know you!" he exclaimed, foisting that irresistible smile with unnaturally white teeth on me.

I winced. "Andrew. What are you doing here? Near me."

His solid arms loosened immediately. "I'm just here to visit an old friend. Remember Meegan Thompson from school? Her parents come to the resort here every fall, and they invited me …" Something flickered in his eyes, and then he asked, "Wait, do you actually live here now?"

I stared at him, vaguely aware that I'd stepped back several feet. "Of course I remember my roommate in college," I said coldly. He'd often flirted with her, even in front of me. Were they together now? "Why would her parents invite *you*? You know what, never mind. Doesn't matter."

"Well, sorry for bumping you." He scratched his head and looked around as though searching for an escape. "But wait, *you* barreled into *me*!" He flashed a smile, which I used to find breathtaking. "And then you almost fell."

My blood boiled as I snapped, "Oh, you're such a dashing prince waiting to rescue a naïve princess, aren't you?"

His brows furrowed as he looked me up and down, eyes eventually landing on my face, which was surely flaming. "Excuse me?"

I blinked a few times, realizing what I'd just said. Out loud.

What if someone heard me?

Scanning the area with wide eyes, I didn't see anyone close enough to hear us. "Nothing. I was joking."

He narrowed his eyes, and after a tense moment, his lips twisted into a smirk. "Really? Because it didn't seem like you were joking." One corner of his lips turned upward. "On the other hand, you wouldn't say something smug and sarcastic like that, would you? That's not you, Roxy."

My name on his lips made my stomach turn. "Because I'm the quiet, boring girl you used to date?"

His eyebrows shot up, and he seemed momentarily short of words.

"Not as cocky as you used to be, Andrew?" I said, followed by clamping my mouth shut, reeling from both the horror and humor of the moment.

"You've changed," he said, looking wistful for a brief moment before his eyes hardened with apathy. "But still not enough to interest me," he said with a flip of his hand as he turned on his heel and walked away.

I stood gaping as I stared at the back of his fancy jacket. His unruly mop of hair, which I knew he wore as some kind of stupid statement. His toned form that was visible even through his thick, expensive winter gear, suggesting he was still obsessed with sports. And his shiny shoes that spoke of success. Money. Confidence.

He'd made it.

And look at me—I didn't even know what I wanted to be when I grew up. When would I stop saying that and just figure it out?

Was he right about me?

I started walking rapidly in the opposite direction I'd been heading, barely seeing anything around me as tears pooled in my eyes. I nearly sprinted back to my apartment until I heard a tinny voice calling out my name.

Reluctantly meeting my neighbor's eyes for a brief moment, I looked at my watch and called out, "Jenna, hi, I'm late for a meeting!"

I sped past her as I raised a hand to wave, neither hearing nor seeing her reaction. It wasn't long before I reached the office. Outside, I stood breathing heavily as I held onto the front door to steady myself. After catching my breath, I wiped my eyes on my jacket sleeve and entered the building.

The last thing I wanted to do was work right now, but at least I could escape to my office, pull the shades, and lock the door.

As one does.

I'd nearly made it to my office door when I heard Hazel's voice.

"Rox! I didn't know you'd be in this morning."

I stilled, my hand circling the doorknob now. I turned partially toward her, knowing my face was safely curtained by my messy, damp hair. I was both cold and sweating, desperate to dart into my office and slam the door shut on the world.

"Yeah, I'll talk to you a little later," I mumbled before pushing the door open.

"Wait, wasn't today the anxiety meetup?" she asked, coming closer.

I felt the panic rise, my stomach turning into knots. Hopefully Jeff wasn't around to hear *that*. The last thing I needed was for him to know about any of this. "Oh, it was, but something came up."

Safely inside my office, I started to close the door, offering a wave as I avoided her eyes.

"Wait," Hazel said, putting her palm on the door.

Could this get any worse? Now my boss was here to see me break down.

"Roxy, are you OK? You won't even look at me," she said. "Did I do something wrong?"

"No, no," I murmured. "I just—I have a lot to do. We can catch up later."

"Roxy, please. You can't tell me nothing's wrong. I know you better than that."

Against my will, my fearful eyes met hers for just a second before fiddling with my handbag. "Sorry, I'm being totally unprofessional. It won't happen again. Please—"

"I don't give a crap about professionalism right now, Roxy," she said forcefully. "I thought we were friends. You seem really upset."

I swallowed with great effort. "I—" Choking on the word, I dropped my bag on the table next to us and sank onto the hard metal chair in front of me.

Hazel immediately pulled a chair in front of mine and sat down. "Roxy, dear, it's OK to be upset. I care about you."

I looked up slowly as she edged closer to me and then drew me gently into a warm embrace. Unfortunately, this just turned my quiet tears into heaving sobs.

The more I tried to speak, the more anguished my sobs became, and Hazel hugged me tighter.

She started smoothing her hand over my tangled hair and uttering soothing sounds. Finally, she whispered, "Do you want to talk about it?"

"No, it's—that's OK—I don't—" I hiccupped and pulled back.

"One second," she said, rising to grab the box of tissues from the desk and then handing it to me. She patted me on the back twice and then sat down.

"I can be a great listener, believe it or not," she said with a half-smile. "Is this because of the meetup? Nerves?"

I shook my head, not trusting myself to speak. After going through a large portion of the tissues, I breathed deeply in and out a few times while staring at the red and dark brown pattern of the table I was leaning on. "I bumped into my ex." As Hazel's eyes widened, I added, "Literally. Almost fell on my face."

"Oh, no. Was it a bad breakup? I'm assuming from your reaction that it wasn't good to see them."

"The worst. Andrew, he was … terrible. S-so full of himself. I never proved he was cheating, but there was good reason to suspect it. And when I confronted him, he—he said some really awful things about me."

"Do you want to tell me about it?" asked Hazel quietly. "You don't have to. But I spent many years in the dating scene, so I have seen my share of messy breakups. Was it recent?"

"Oh, no, we were in college. I hadn't seen him since."

"Was he at least polite?"

"No, but neither was I." I exhaled shakily and wiped my eyes with a tissue. "He—he said I was too boring, too quiet … an ice queen. He even said it was creepy that I acted like nothing happened after Grandpa's death. Which wasn't true—I was grieving privately. But he said …"

She waited a moment for me to finish, but I couldn't speak anymore through the sobbing.

"Roxy, it's OK if you don't want to share all the details now. I've heard enough to know that this terrible guy didn't deserve you. I doubt he deserves anyone," Hazel said, shaking her head.

I wiped my face, which surely looked gross with my mascara-laced tears and blotchy, puffy skin. "I know, and I think I already knew that. Julia and I—that's my friend who was also dating *his* friend simultaneously—we talked about it a lot. She helped me heal, or as much as anyone could." I sniffed. "But his words never left me because … they just confirmed what I'd already suspected about myself. And my parents … well, they never came right out and said it, but I know they've always found me lacking. They—they still do."

When I dared look into her eyes, they were filled with kindness and empathy. Not pity. Thank goodness. "I mean, how could I expect anyone to accept me if my own parents don't?"

She grasped both my hands and squeezed. "I get it, Roxy, I really do. It hasn't always been easy with my parents either. I know they love me, but ... Well, I'm not going to ramble about me. I want to help you. What can I do?"

I breathed in and out slowly. "The shocking thing is that I actually said a couple of harsh things to him today, and for a second, I think he was *intrigued*. He said I'd changed ... and then he said—he said it still wasn't enough to interest him." I felt a round of fresh tears fall.

"Oh, honey, you don't want interest from a guy like that," she said in a soothing tone while squeezing my hands again.

"I know. I'd never go out with him again. I–I don't have feelings for Andrew anymore. But it still hurt."

And that's what upset me more than anything. That he *could* still hurt me.

"Of course it did. Because you're human."

I squeezed her hands and then let them go to grab another tissue. "You're here as a friend, aren't you? Not a boss."

Hazel smiled. "Now you're getting it." Then her expression sobered. "But you should get out of here. Take the rest of the day off. Hole up in your apartment with your favorite ice cream and a fluffy blanket and hot cocoa, and what's that show you're into about the island thing?"

"*Cast Afar*," I said. "Some day, when I'm not a blubbering mess, I'll tell you about this board game thing I've been working on with a friend." I looked down. "If you're interested, that is. I mean, it's OK if you're not—"

"I'd love to hear about it! You know, Peter and I actually bonded over Monopoly. You wouldn't believe—"

A throat clearing startled us both, and we turned to look at the source.

I flinched.

No, no, it can't be.

If he's standing there, he probably heard me saying some absolutely mortifying things. And I must look like a bus just ran over me.

Contemplating the possibility of never showing up to work again, I dabbed at my eyes to dry them, trying not to smear whatever remaining makeup I had.

"How long have you been standing there, Jeff?" Hazel asked in the sharpest tone I'd ever heard her use with him.

I chanced a look at him, hoping I was wrong and he hadn't actually heard much.

No such luck.

Jeff's face was white, and his features were arranged in an expression I'd never seen. Shock? Anguish? Horror? Pain?

But those reactions didn't make sense. Well, maybe shock. But the others? No, I must be misreading him. It had happened often enough before.

He stared at us, almost through us, like he'd seen a ghost. "I apologize. I didn't mean to eavesdrop. The door was open, and I just came to ask about the agenda—"

"Jeff." Hazel's lips pressed together as she studied him. "You look terrible. Why don't you go home too? We can all take the day off."

He nodded, his mind seeming to be elsewhere as his eyes still revealed those same intense but confusing emotions. As he turned to go, he collided hard with the door frame. But without so much as a curse or an *ouch*, he was gone before I could blink.

I blew my nose and started to gather my things. "I should go, before he does. I don't really want another run-in with him before I leave." I paused. "Unless you want me to stay and work?"

Hazel stared at the door he'd left open and then back at me. "Did he look pale to you? I mean, paler than usual? He was *so* not himself."

"Yeah, he was acting weird." I sighed. "Your guess is as good as mine. I gave up trying to figure him out a long time ago."

An odd look of regret crossed her face before she nodded. "I know you did. Maybe we all did."

∞∞∞

The following evening, I curled up on the couch and opened my laptop. I had spent more than enough time wallowing—OK, mostly sleeping—and I felt bad about not telling Danny I couldn't chat last night. I just hadn't had the energy or desire to do anything except sleep.

But I was feeling over-rested now and surprisingly clear-headed. Sure, my eyes were still puffy, and my head hurt, but I knew some ibuprofen would fix it.

I quickly navigated to the fan site that Danny and I used to chat. I barely even went to the actual fan forum anymore because, to be honest, I was only interested in chatting with him now. Sure, I had a few other Internet buddies on the site, but I rarely talked to them anymore.

Hmm, that's odd. He didn't message me at all last night.

The chat tool said he was offline and hadn't been online for two days.

Why?

I searched my memory, trying to figure out if I might have offended or annoyed him the last time we chatted. I couldn't think of anything significant.

Then again, maybe it was just a late night at work. I'd just leave the chat window open while I watch some TV. Or maybe I should fold that load of clean towels sitting in a basket on the recliner that was used more often as a table than as a place to sit.

Maybe you'd be less depressed if you weren't such a slob around the house.

I squeezed my eyes shut to block out those thoughts. All thoughts.

Maybe I'd just snooze on the couch for a bit. Sleep was the only guaranteed thought-blocker.

But when I woke with a start at 10 p.m., I still hadn't heard from Danny. He was nearly always online by this time, and his status *still* said he'd been offline since two nights ago.

I frowned as my fingers clasped the remote, but I found myself reluctant to press Play. I wasn't in the mood. I should probably just go to bed.

I'd told Hazel I wanted to take the rest of the week off, and she was fine with it. She applauded me, actually. It was a bizarre conversation, but I was glad to have her approval nonetheless—not to mention relieved that I wouldn't have to face Jeff after that last awkward encounter.

The next day came and went, with still no sign of Danny and no update on his offline status. That night, I couldn't even watch *Cast Afar*. It just made me think of him, and I didn't want to think about the guy who was ghosting me.

Is it really ghosting you though if you were never in a relationship?

He was always bound to get bored with this. With you.

I bit my lip, tasting a salty tear seep through the corner of my mouth.

Maybe he had a good reason. Things came up. We were just friends, and he wasn't obligated to tell me if he was too busy to chat. I wasn't going to be weird about this.

Yet that night, and the next three nights, I watched *Lost* instead of *Cast Afar*.

Chapter 15

After nearly a week of silence from Danny and time away from the office, I'd started to feel stiff after so many hours on the couch—not to mention sluggish and unmotivated—so I'd moved to the desk in the corner of my living room and dusted it off, literally. After over two hours of searching, I finally found the perfect gift for Julia that would actually ship overseas. But then I realized she hadn't told me yet whether she was staying in England for the holidays, so I decided to hold off on the order and call her tomorrow when it wasn't crazy late in her time zone. Yes, it was early for Christmas shopping, but buying for others helped distract me from the persistent ache in my chest reflecting the swirling emotions of sadness, worry, anger, and disappointment within me.

By habit, I switched to the window with game design chat, my eyes lazily wandering across the screen. Then my heart skipped a beat or three.

The chat window showed a green *Available* circle next to CastGamer55.

Calm down. This doesn't necessarily mean he wants to talk to you.

But my eyes widened as I saw the three dots indicating he was typing.

Straightening my back, I forced my hands to stay off the keyboard. I would *not* send him another message. This past week, I'd already sent a few that I wished I could unsend.

CastGamer55: Hi.

Really, that's the best he could do? He spent at least thirty seconds typing two letters? Oh, and don't forget the period. Danny always used correct punctuation—even in chat messages.

Maybe I should ignore his message. He didn't deserve a response, did he?

Or … was I being ridiculous? I shook my head.

I couldn't deny I missed him. Stewing wouldn't solve this problem.

SawyerRox4: Hi
CastGamer55: How was your day?
SawyerRox4: …
CastGamer55: What does that mean?
SawyerRox4: Are you really asking me about my day?
CastGamer55: Yes. Is that a problem?
SawyerRox4: My DAY? How about my week? You just disappear without a trace and then return with no explanation?

I knew how I sounded. I *heard* my tone sounding needy in a very embarrassing way. He probably wondered if I was drunk or, like, in love with him. The latter was, of course, ridiculous. And the former … well, I'd reaffirmed several days ago that alcohol wouldn't solve any problems.

But what could I tell him? Not the truth—that my world had seemed flat and dull without him in it—and that was only when my mind wasn't racing with fear about what could have happened to him.

CastGamer55: I apologize.
CastGamer55: I had a good day except that my elderly neighbor's huge yellow lab jumped me today and ruined my navy suit.
SawyerRox4: Oh, you're a suit, huh? Actually, I know someone with a dog like that too, just a block away, and

those kinds of stains don't come out.

CastGamer55: A minor issue, really. I would ask about your day again, but you seemed angry when I asked before.

So this was it. He really wasn't going to offer even a vague explanation of where he'd been for a whole week. Was he hiding something? If not, why wasn't he offering any explanation?

More likely, he just thought I was overreacting.

Because you are. You're just a casual online buddy he's never met.

Why would you expect anything from him?

After pacing for a few minutes, I decided to let it go. Or at least try. If things got weird, I'd just redirect attention to the game design. Sinking back into my desk chair, I breathed in steadily and set my fingers on the keyboard.

SawyerRox4: My day was OK, apart from the dread I'm feeling because I have so many meetings this coming week
SawyerRox4: But hey, let's talk about the game! I have been working on a map
CastGamer55: You have skill in drawing?
SawyerRox4: I wouldn't call it skill. It's more just for putting my own mental map on paper...
CastGamer55: I can appreciate that.

In the coming days, we talked about the intricacies of the game more than ever, and I finally felt like we were making progress ... on the game. Not between us. He showed up every night and seemed engaged. But something about him was different.

He seemed a bit more guarded. Distant but not in a rude way. If anything, overly polite.

Were we not friends anymore?

Now we were just board game design partners?

Chapter 16

After an entire week off, I returned to work and went straight to Hazel's newly selected office. Immediately after I knocked on the partially open door, she rose from her new modern-style desk and smiled. We exchanged greetings, and she nodded when I told her I was feeling refreshed and ready for work. The truth was, I was not feeling anything like refreshed, but I was ready to bury myself in work and start feeling useful again.

When she said Jeff had taken the week off too, my eyes widened.

"Why?"

It was *unheard of* for Jeff to take more than one day off, ever.

"I told him to," Hazel said as we both sat down in folding chairs in front of her desk. The rest of the office furniture and decor were scheduled to come next week. Finally. "I think you were both under a lot of stress."

"Yes, I was. And maybe he was too." I nodded slowly. "Well, I guess that was a good decision."

"Of course it was," Hazel said with a twinkle in her eye. "As if I'd ever make a bad decision."

I frowned. "Oh, of course not. I didn't mean to imply—"

She laughed. "Relax, Roxy. I'm joking. Friends, remember?"

"But we're at work, so …" I trailed off. "You know what, I'm being weird again. I'll stop."

"I like your weird, Roxy."

I felt tears well up in my eyes. I was so lucky to work for such a compassionate, lively woman—and even luckier that she was choosing to call me a friend, for some unknown reason.

I impulsively threw my arms around her for a quick hug. "I'm not a hugger, Hazel. So don't get used to it."

She burst into laughter and was still clutching her side when a throat cleared.

Jeff walked in, saying, "Hazel, are you—"

He stopped short when our eyes met. Something in my chest seized.

"You're here," he said quietly, his lids heavy over his hazel eyes.

How was I supposed to interpret that? Was he upset I was here? Was he surprised? Was he spooked by something again?

Was he glad to see me?

I almost burst into laughter at that question. Yeah, no.

"In the flesh," Hazel said, waving an arm in my direction. "Now, what did you want to talk about?"

"Oh, I can just—" He paused, his eyes lingering on me as he spoke to Hazel. "It can wait until you're done with Roxy."

Why was he looking at me like that?

I wondered if I had toothpaste on my face or smeared eye makeup.

Probably both.

But his expression was still odd. Impossible to read, but definitely not normal.

"I'll go," I said, rising abruptly.

As I passed by, he wasn't looking at me, but the muscles in his neck tensed as his Adam's apple bobbed.

"I'll see you in an hour or two, Rox," Hazel said. "Peter's coming to pick me up for lunch, but otherwise, I should be here all day..." She was saying something else, but I lost track.

My head was still spinning with confusion as I headed out of her office. I'd barely taken a step out of the room when I heard the shrill voice.

"Hello? *Hello?*"

I took a deep breath as my eyes landed on Jeff's ex-wife. Of all the people to be forced to deal with right now. "Hello. May I help you?"

Aileen spun around, and her bright red lips curled in distaste as she looked me up and down. "Rhonda, was it? Can you find my husband and daughter? They're supposed to be here."

"My name is Roxy. If you're looking for Jeff, he's with the boss at the moment." I paused, my voice shaky. "Can I leave a message for him?"

Her eyes narrowed to slits as she sauntered over. "*Where* is he?"

"I told you, he's meeting with—"

She scowled as she interrupted, "I don't have the patience for this, Rhonda." She cupped her hands together like a megaphone and started calling Jeff's and Lila's names.

In a matter of seconds, Jeff bounded out of the office where I'd left them, and Hazel followed.

"Aileen, what are you doing here?" he said, exasperated.

"Where's Lila?" she demanded, hands on her hips. "By the way, you should fire the receptionist. Very rude and unhelpful," she said as she jerked her thumb at me.

I gasped. "Excuse me?"

Before she could rant about me, Hazel stepped in. "Roxy is not a receptionist. She's a project manager."

"Whatever," Aileen said, rolling her eyes.

"Why would she be here? You're supposed to be picking her up this afternoon." Jeff glanced down at his watch. "In less than an hour. Did you forget?"

The woman had the nerve to snort. "I remember our schedule. Maybe you don't. You have her on Fridays, remember?"

We all stared at her in disbelief until Hazel finally spoke up. "It's Thursday."

"What, no, tonight is—" She halted and then laughed airily. "Oh, usually I go out on Fridays, but this was Carlton's only free night. I forgot it wasn't Friday."

"You have a date tonight?" Jeff's face was rigid. Was

he *jealous*? Did he still love his wife? I mean, his ex?

Not that it mattered, of course.

"I do. He's taking me to this high-end restaurant in St. Paul. And then we're—"

"I don't care what you're doing on your date. Did you arrange a sitter for Lila?"

"A sitter?" She shook her head. "No, I thought you … well, you can watch her tonight, right?"

He nodded. "What are you even doing here then?"

"I was coming to say goodbye to my child before I leave. I thought she'd be with you."

Jeff shook his head, his entire body radiating anger. "Why? Don't you know what time the school day ends?"

She stuck out her bottom lip. "Now I remember why I divorced you," she snapped.

He just glared at her, shaking his head and then looking away.

So she probably wasn't the one who'd asked for the divorce.

Leaning back against the reception desk, Hazel swept a hand out dramatically, her voice abnormally cheerful. "So, what's everyone's holiday plans? I just love turkey, don't you?"

"My family hosts every year in Cancun. It's one of our little traditions." Aileen's voice was dripping with condescension. "Isn't it, Jeff?"

His lips were pressed together as he nodded once, and she smirked.

"I'm just staying home, going to relax and do some online shopping," I said flatly, realizing how boring that would sound to most people, especially people who were used to celebrating a U.S. holiday outside the country.

Hazel looked surprised. "Don't you usually fly home to your parents' house in Nashville?"

It was Chattanooga actually, but I shrugged. "Sometimes. It's no big deal."

Hazel smoothed her long hair behind her shoulders, and

her eyes lit up. "Oh, Roxy, you're welcome to come to our house! Peter's a surprisingly good cook, and Mari and Terry are coming over too."

I winced. "Oh, don't worry about me. I'd just be a fifth wheel at your house. But I do appreciate the offer." I schooled my features into calm acceptance. "I'll be fine, seriously. I've been alone on Thanksgiving before."

"How sad," Aileen said, fluttering her eyelashes with mock sympathy.

The ensuing silence had us all shifting our feet, wishing to be anywhere else.

Suddenly, Jeff spoke quietly, facing me, "Do you want to join us?"

Mine weren't the only eyes that widened at that question.

"Oh, I couldn't intrude—"

"You wouldn't be intruding," he said firmly. "Lila would love it."

I blinked a few times, and my mouth opened for an awkwardly long moment before any words came out. "Um, OK," I managed to say, shocking myself.

"You'll come?" he said while Hazel mouthed "Oh."

"Yes?" I swallowed the lump in my throat and shrugged as if I hadn't given the most bizarre answer ever. "Sure."

I would later wonder why on earth I accepted his invitation and would conclude it was Aileen's presence. She was not a nice person, I'd realized, and my acceptance would probably irk her. It was petty, but I couldn't think of any other reason. None that made sense, anyway. It couldn't be that I *wanted* to spend a holiday with my work nemesis.

"What?" Aileen screeched. "You're inviting *her*, your co-worker?" She pointed at me rudely and then narrowed her eyes toward him and then back to me. "Is something going on between you two?"

I tried to stifle a giggle. "No! That's not something you *ever* need to worry about, trust me," I said, avoiding Jeff's eyes.

Jeff was silent for a moment, and I heard him breathe out slowly. "Aileen, we agreed to let Lila decide where she spent the holiday. And she chose my house over Cancun, remember?" he reminded her.

She bristled. "Well, I can change my mind—"

"No, you can't. And you won't."

She glared at him and then at me. "Whatever. I'm going to go pick up *my* daughter. Be ready at six tonight."

"Bye," Hazel said, a little louder than necessary.

When Aileen stomped off, Jeff rolled his eyes. His shoulders lowered, and he immediately looked less tense. Just his normal level of tense.

"Sorry about that," he muttered.

"I still wonder how you ended up with that woman," Hazel said with a laugh. "And stayed with her for seven long years ... I don't get it. Was it because of Lila?"

As he nodded once, I shook my head in astonishment. Seven years of *that* must have been challenging, even for a robot like him. For the first time, I felt some sympathy for him. "Wow. That couldn't have been easy. She's ... a lot."

"Honestly, this was nothing. She's much tamer now, actually." He shook his head, looking down and shifting from one foot to another. "Wasted years," he murmured.

My eyebrows traveled up my forehead. "Oh ... wow. I'm sorry."

When his eyes met mine, his expression spoke of pain and, oddly enough, uncertainty. I almost gasped, shocked at the raw feelings I'd never seen him show, subtle though they were. He exhaled slowly, lightly shaking as if to clear out the feelings.

I looked to my left and suddenly noticed Hazel had gone. Had she not said goodbye? Had I missed it? My cheeks colored as I realized I'd been staring. For who knows how long.

"Well, I guess—"

"I should—"

We both stopped talking for a moment and then spoke simultaneously again.

"I need to get—"

"We should—"

I pressed my lips together but felt a grin tugging at my lips.

Why was I grinning? I had no idea.

Why was *he* grinning?

Wait, what? *He* was grinning?

I stared at his mouth, the corners upturned slightly, revealing a small dimple on his left cheek. He was …

Hot.

Jeff Chamberlain was gorgeous.

How had I been deprived of this smile for these last few years without even knowing it?

Get a hold of yourself.

His smile faded, and his brows scrunched together. "Are you all right, Roxanne?"

I blinked quickly and nodded. At least I think I did.

Roxanne. You're only Roxanne to him.

He called me Roxanne to denote how little acquainted we were. We were not even friends.

So why on *earth* was I still thinking about those upturned lips and the unexpected dimple as I headed back to the office?

Chapter 17

Oddly, I didn't spend the next week trying to come up with excuses not to attend Thanksgiving.

No, I spent the week trying to figure out *why* I wasn't trying to get out of it.

On the big day, when I rang the doorbell after a pleasant, slow stroll in the short distance to Jeff's house, Lila opened the door. She was wearing a very messy pink apron over her orange and yellow striped pajamas.

I smiled and greeted her. "How are you?"

She backed up and ushered me in. "I'm great! Do you like my jammies with Thanksgiving colors?" Before I could reply, she frowned. "I just wish we had snow for turkey day!"

I wrinkled my nose. "Snow? No, thanks. I love a warm, colorful autumn. It's rarely this nice for Thanksgiving. We're more likely to get snowed in during a blizzard, you know?"

She eyed me oddly and then shrugged. "I don't know."

I chuckled, suddenly remembering most kids didn't care that much—or notice—weather trends. She led me to a seat at the kitchen table, a few feet away from where Jeff was cooking.

Clueless about what I should say or do, I just said the first dumb thing that came to mind. "You can cook, Jeff?"

He looked up, the steam from the stove creating tiny sweat beads on his face. "Yes. Most adults can."

"I don't know if that's true."

He shrugged. "Well then, yes, Roxy. I can cook."

"Can I help?"

"No. Just relax," he said firmly.

"Roxy, get out of here! I'm helping Daddy. You're the guest!" Lila exclaimed.

I laughed. "You don't know what mad cooking skills you're missing out on. But sure, I'll just sit and wait." My eyes immediately shot to the floor. I couldn't believe I just said that. It's, like, something sassy that Hazel would say. Not me.

But Jeff and Lila nudged each other, and I could almost swear I heard a masculine chuckle as he turned around to retrieve something from the refrigerator.

OK, maybe I hadn't sounded totally awkward. Or had I?

I was examining a still-life painting hanging near the table where I sat when suddenly he was there, sitting next to me on a kitchen chair just a foot away.

I gazed at him and then back at the painting, not really seeing it this time. Awkwardness hung in the air for what seemed like hours but was probably only a minute. Why did he come over here? Did he have something to say? Why wasn't he saying it?

I snuck a few glances at him, but he was silent, apart from asking Lila to stir something on the stove.

"She said she was pregnant."

I turned to him, surprised. "Who?"

"Aileen. Nine years ago." He paused, dragging a hand down the side of his clean-shaven face. "She was lying, but I didn't know that until I finally realized she couldn't have been pregnant for eleven months. After we married."

I nodded sympathetically. "And you stayed for Lila?"

"Yes."

"Ah, that explains a lot."

He nodded. "So now you know. Lila doesn't know any of that though."

"No, of course not. I won't breathe a word." Ironically, my voice got slightly breathy at the end.

We locked eyes for a moment. "I just wanted to clear that up." He abruptly stood up and strode away.

It wasn't until a moment later when it dawned on me. As they'd shooed me out of the kitchen, he'd called me Roxy. Not Roxanne. Why?

And why was he telling such personal details about his previous marriage? Had something changed between us?

I tried to take a quick mental inventory as Jeff and Lila bustled around the kitchen. My thoughts weren't cooperating though. I just ... well, I was at his house for a major holiday. Maybe we were almost friends.

And that meant ...

Maybe we didn't hate each other.

Dinner was delicious but uneventful. Lila carried most of the conversation and actually blushed when Jeff told me she'd painted the beautiful still-life. In the quiet moments, I realized this was one of the more peaceful, relaxing Thanksgiving dinners I'd experienced. Usually I could barely taste my food because of all the loud, distracting voices around me, not to mention the tension and resentment that rear their ugly heads at least a few times every year. My parents invite way too many people and serve way too much alcohol, and it's all I can do to politely sit there for the full meal and then devise an excuse to head to my old bedroom.

"Daddy, when we finish cleaning up, can we watch a movie with Roxy?"

"That's up to her," he said, glancing at me quickly before draining his glass and looking back at his daughter.

She turned to me as I stacked the dirty dishes and brought them over to the sink. "Have you ever seen *The Princess Diaries*, Roxy?"

I smiled. "I have. But it was a long time ago."

"Will you stay and watch with us? *Please*?" she pleaded.

"Well, I ..." I glanced at Jeff, who was loading the dishwasher. "I suppose I could. If your dad doesn't mind"

"Yes! This will be so fun. Of course it'll be fine with Daddy," she said with a giggle. "I'm going to change into my pajamas, be right back?"

I wanted to tell her not to be so sure about her father's preferences in the matter, but I decided it would ruin the mood. Instead, I asked, "Wait, aren't you already wearing pajamas?"

She giggled. "These are last night's jammies. Dad said I could wear them all day if I change tonight."

"Oh, that's ..." *Unexpectedly sweet*, I wanted to say.

Jeff wasn't wearing pajamas, but he wasn't wearing a suit or tie either. With his dark jeans and maroon fitted sweater, he looked so different. Like a normal person, not a robot. A normal person that was also effortlessly handsome.

Wait, what?

I shook my head to clear out the odd thoughts.

When Lila raced out of the room, Jeff turned to me. "You can say no if you'd rather go home."

I shrugged, trying not to think about whether he was implying he'd rather I leave. "It's fine. I don't have any other plans."

"Good. You're welcome to join us then," he said, his tone polite but not in the stiff way he usually spoke.

Before I could thank him, he walked out of the room to a hallway closet and retrieved a broom, handing it to Lila as she bounded back into the room with a neon pink and green nightgown and fluffy orange socks.

When I finished wiping down the table, I asked what else I could do to help.

"Nothing! You're our esteemed guest. Go rest on the couch," Lila said with a smile.

I smiled back. "Well, I like the sound of that."

A few minutes later, she reappeared. "Would you like some champagne, Roxy?"

My eyes widened. "Oh, I ... is your dad OK with that?"

"I think he's having some." Then, as though it should be obvious, she added, "I mean, he told me to ask you."

"Oh. Then yes, please." I wouldn't turn down good champagne. Jeff didn't seem like the type to buy the cheap stuff. "Tell your dad thank you."

Drinking with Jeff was weird. I'd never seen him drink before, but then again, I usually skipped the office parties.

We were almost done with *Princess Diaries* when I glanced over to ask Lila how she thought the movie would end. Her head was resting on Jeff's lap as her chest rose and fell rhythmically.

My eyes rose to Jeff's, and he was smiling faintly. "I knew she wouldn't make it through the whole movie. She never finishes movies this close to bedtime."

I returned the smile tentatively and then pretended to keep watching the movie. But the tension was driving me crazy, so after refilling our glasses, I ventured to ask, "So, Lila chose this over Cancun with her mother?"

"Yes," he said after taking a sip.

"I'm honored to be here then," I replied, trying not to sound sarcastic as I usually would.

He didn't speak for a while as he swirled the champagne in his glass slowly.

"It was a whole ordeal. I asked if Lila could come here for once, and Aileen didn't take that well. And she took it even worse when Lila freely *chose* to come here."

I nodded. "I can imagine. It seems like she's used to getting her way."

After a brief moment of thoughtfulness, he sighed. "I guess you're right. She is."

"May I offer some advice?" I heard myself asking. And that's when I realized I was a bit tipsy, because everything seemed upside down: Jeff and I were hanging out basically alone. We were talking about something personal, and I was offering advice. In no sober world would that make sense.

He glanced at me with the corners of his eyes crinkled and then put his feet up on the coffee table, careful not to disturb Lila. "Sure, let's hear it."

I wondered if I'd regret what I was about to say. Or this whole conversation. "Don't be so passive with Aileen." I paused and continued a bit shakily, "You shouldn't let her walk all over you."

His jaw tensed as he looked at me steadily. Finally, he said, "Go on."

Inhaling slowly, I continued, "You should set boundaries, for starters. And some routines so that all three of you have more predictability, which is especially important for children with divorced parents. The word *no* will be your best friend." I laughed. "To her, that is. Don't you dare tell *me no*."

Realizing what I'd just said, I immediately plunged into panic mode. I sounded *flirty*. I set my glass down, knowing I should've stopped at one glass. Or less.

But then the miracle of all miracles ... he smiled. It wasn't a full-on smile where your cheeks hurt, but it was more than a slight quirk of the mouth and lasted for almost two seconds. "Your ability to gauge all that from only a couple of meetings with Aileen is impressive."

"Ah, I've met her type before."

He rubbed his jaw a bit. "Right, you were a therapist. Sometimes I forget."

"Yes."

He didn't say anything, perhaps waiting for me to elaborate. But that was the last thing I wanted to talk about. It wasn't easy admitting I'd just *quit*. I try my best to avoid thinking about that whenever possible.

Finally, I cleared my throat. "Are you from Shipsvold originally?"

"No, I grew up in Superior," he said flatly. "I had a friend here years ago, and he helped me get the job with Mariana."

"Oh, does your friend still live here? Would I know him?"

Jeff's mouth was set in a thin line as he shook his head.

"Sorry to hear that," I said, unsure why I was apologizing.

"It's nothing to be sorry about. The town is better without him in it."

My brow was creased as I considered this. "Did you have a falling out?"

He nodded, crossing his arms over his chest as he stared at some distant object across the room.

I mirrored his crossed arms. "You can just say, 'I don't want to talk about it,' you know."

He glanced over at me, his face softer. "I know." He sighed. "Bart and I had been close friends forever. At times, he was my only friend." He exhaled even more slowly this time. "I caught him dating my sister behind my back. He convinced her not to tell me, but she eventually did. After I cooled off, I tried to be accepting of the awkward situation."

"Sure you did," I said with a chuckle.

"I know, it's hard to believe," he said wryly. "But that's not the worst of it. He cheated on her."

My jaw dropped as my eyes widened considerably. "No! He's scum. What kind of person does that to their *best friend's sister*?"

"The kind of friend I didn't want."

"Of course, yeah." I added softly, "Still, it can't have been easy losing the best friend you'd ever had. That's huge, Jeff."

He touched the sleeve of his sweater over his forearm. "It was. But nowadays, I don't need close friends or have time for them anyway. I don't miss it."

"I'm kind of the same," I lied. Because it was actually my social anxiety that kept me from making many friends—not a lack of time. And not a lack of need.

Before he could ask any questions I wouldn't want to answer, I searched my brain quickly for a new subject. "Lila is great, you know. And I have to admit, you're a great dad to her," I blurted out, feeling my cheeks heat up.

His eyes met mine for a long moment before he spoke softly. "Thank you."

"You're welcome," I replied, offering what I hoped was a friendly smile.

His warm gaze stayed on me for a few more seconds before he looked down at Lila, sleeping with her head on his lap and snoring softly. He gently ran his fingers over the strands of hair that escaped from her ponytail. "I should probably go carry her to her room."

"Oh, I should—it's probably time to go home anyway," I said while hastily rising to my feet and nearly cursing at the numbness in one foot. I wiggled my toes and bent my feet as I waited for the feeling in my foot to return.

"That's fine," he said, a note of *something* in his tone. Was it reluctance or relief? He rose to stand in front of me. "Thank you for coming."

I offered a warm smile. "Thank *you* for inviting me and cooking and … all of this. It was really generous."

His brows furrowed. "Generous?"

"I mean, you know. Everyone felt bad for poor Roxy, so …" I trailed off and shrugged.

"That's not—"

"It's OK, really."

"Listen, it's really—"

"Let's not end a nice holiday with arguing. Deal?" I smiled wistfully.

He stared at me and shifted one foot in front of the other. "Deal. Goodbye, Roxy."

For some reason, my preferred name sounded different on his lips. Different how? I couldn't decide, but it wasn't different *bad*. But I had to get out of there because I was obviously tipsier than I realized.

"Bye, Jeff."

After walking the short distance home in a daze and just barely dodging the neighbor Jenna going into the elevator, I entered my apartment and threw my keys and purse on the kitchen counter. As I removed my coat and shoes, I tried to resist the urge to go open my laptop and check to see if Danny was around. I'd already learned it wasn't a good idea to talk to him while under the influence.

But after changing into my pajamas, I found myself opening the chat on the computer. He was offline but had left a message.

CastGamer55: I hope you had a nice Thanksgiving, Mindy.

I smiled like an idiot and typed back a similar response. He was thinking of me today! Even though he said he'd be busy all day with family.

Still smiling, I went to brush my teeth and wash my face. When my phone buzzed, I hurried to my bedside table where I'd left it. Scanning the text message, I found myself smiling again, but I was too tired to think about why.

Jeff: You forgot to bring home leftovers.

Roxy: You forgot to offer.

Jeff: Fair enough. Have a good night, Roxy.

Chapter 18

"Anything else you'd like us to know? Or any more questions about the marketing role?" Jeff asked as the last interview of the day was concluding.

The short, curvy woman with fiery hair and lipstick nodded. "I'm a stubborn redhead, obviously, but you should know that makes me the perfect candidate for the job because I am tenacious and determined."

Surprised, I grinned. "That's a great closing argument."

"So I've been told."

I chuckled and offered my hand into her warm, solid grip as I said, "Thank you, Laney."

"No, thank you! It was so nice meeting you."

Jeff shook her hand. "We'll be in touch next week, probably around December 5th so we can get you onboarded before Christmas."

As she left our newly designated conference room, I plopped back down in the new comfy swivel chairs we'd purchased recently. Jeff glanced at me and sat down as well, crossing one leg over another.

"I like her."

"She's perfect."

We spoke at the same time and then laughed together.

And I was struck by how much a simple laugh and lingering smile *transformed* his face, lending levity to his features and showing his perfect white teeth. I might have stared a bit too long though because his smile faded.

Jeff's dark eyebrows rose. "What?"

"I just … I'm happy we found our marketing and events coordinator." Right, *that's* the reason. Not that I was checking him out.

"Did we? I don't remember agreeing to that," he said, but his tone was light.

I hesitated before saying, "It's important to me to find the right person so I don't feel compelled to take on all of that work myself. Laney's right for us. I just know it."

"Great," he said with a shrug. "Let's hire her."

I stared at him, dumbfounded. Who was this guy being agreeable?

"Thanks."

"Save your thanks for the new hire," he said. "I do think she'll do great things here."

"I feel like we should get some champagne or something." When his eyebrows rose, I added, "We are hiring the first employee! That's big."

He rubbed his jaw. "True. Sadly, I have no alcohol in the office."

"That's probably for the best," I said with a laugh.

He didn't smile but rather just looked at me intently and nodded slowly. After a long moment, he said, "You have the bluest eyes I've ever seen."

My breath caught in my throat, and I struggled with producing any words. "I … why are you telling me this, Jeff?"

He cleared his throat. "I don't know."

Before I could even think of how to respond or what to feel, Hazel strode into the room through the open door, followed by Peter.

Reflexively, Jeff and I took a step back from one another and turned our gazes to them. "Hazel, hi," I said, my voice higher than usual.

She looked at me in amusement. "Did you go for a run? You sound out of breath."

I'm sure my cheeks turned deep pink then because I felt the heat all over my face. "No, I … well—"

"We're just excited because we found our first employee to hire," Jeff cut in, glancing at me briefly before turning back to Hazel.

Her eyes lit up. "That *is* exciting! Darling, did you hear that?"

"Yes, I'm right here, *darling*," Peter said with a queasy expression. For someone who rarely showed emotion, that was a curious sight. "Congratulations on the new hire."

I looked between them, a smile playing on my lips.

Peter nudged her, and she sighed. "He lost a bet, and now we get to call each other *darling* for a whole week!" She smiled gleefully and squeezed his hand. "Though I think by the end of the week, we'll just want to keep doing it forever, won't we, darling?"

"We'll see." His nose wrinkled. "Darling."

She stretched up to plant a kiss on his chin, and I saw his slight grin.

I looked away, surprised how much the affection between them had grown in less than a year. I felt like even more of an outsider than I ever had before. Almost all my friends and even acquaintances had a partner. Realistically, I knew I'd probably be alone forever, other than maybe a couple dates here and there. I wouldn't ever have a husband or even a long-term boyfriend. And I didn't want that.

I didn't want that.

I really didn't.

Except lately, I wondered.

I snapped out of my reverie when I felt a hand gently touch my arm and linger for a moment. As my eyes began to refocus, I saw Jeff stepping back.

He looked confused, perhaps concerned.

And now I was confused.

Turning to look at Hazel, I cleared my throat. "Sorry, what?"

She narrowed her eyes first, but then a laugh erupted from her mouth. "I asked if you'd have any objections to planning my launch party."

My brows furrowed as I tried to remember when such a party was ever discussed. Nothing turned up. "I didn't know you wanted a party. It makes sense though."

"So you can do the planning?"

Hazel's eyes were so eager that I couldn't say no.

Still, I should say no.

"Sure, OK," I said with as much enthusiasm as I could muster. I'd hoped to get away from event planning, but she was my boss, after all.

Her eyes lit up. "Wonderful! And of course, you both need to attend."

I inhaled sharply and looked at Jeff with panic. He just nodded.

My head bobbed up and down quickly. "Sure, OK."

A huge holiday party? Not a chance.

I'd get out of it. I'd figure out a way.

"Don't even think about trying to make a last-minute excuse, Roxy," Hazel said in an unusually sharp tone.

My eyes went wide, but then she winked as she strode past me to the window. I stood there awkwardly with Peter and Jeff, two men who were also kind of high on the awkward scale. Well, maybe not Jeff. He was generally decent at polite communication; it was mainly around me that he made a point of being curt and condescending. Only ... not as much lately.

Hazel came back over to us after looking out the window for a moment.

"Just don't skip out, please? This is important to me."

People always said that: *Don't miss my party because it's important to me.* Yeah, everyone's party is important to someone. Why does their version of important have to trump mine? Most people had no idea what they were asking of me, the level of distress I'd feel. Even people pleasers had our limits.

"We wouldn't dream of missing your party," Jeff assured her, stepping closer and tensing the hand closest to me as it rose. For a moment, I thought he was going to place an arm around me.

As if.

Crazy thoughts. I must have been more tired than I realized.

He continued, "Roxy and I will be the first ones to arrive." At Hazel's widened eyes, he hastily added, "I mean, separately."

My own eyes must have been huge because Hazel gave me an oddly curious look before giving him the same one. "Good. Oh, I forgot to mention, I want the launch party on New Year's Eve."

"New—New Year's Eve?" I squeaked.

"Her birthday," Peter added.

"Oh," I said with a forced smile. I usually looked forward to celebrating New Year's Eve with myself and my new resolutions, but I guess not this year. "Good to know. Can we meet to discuss your requirements sometime this week? I think your schedule is clear for Friday."

Hazel checked her phone. "Yeah, fine. Just put it on my calendar." She stuffed her phone in her purse. "Actually, Jeff, you might as well come too. You can manage the budget."

Before either of us could object, she smiled and grabbed Peter's hand. "We've got to go! Thanks, you guys. You're really the best."

I slumped onto the nearest chair and then noticed Hazel was closing the door.

Frowning, I swiveled around in a circle until I became slightly dizzy.

Jeff stood watching me. "Are you all right?"

"I'm great. How'd you know?" I said, my voice laced with sarcasm.

"You could have said no."

"Everyone always says that to me. It's not so easy, you know," I said, crossing my arms over my chest before thinking better of it, given the deep V-necked sweater I was wearing today.

"I don't know. I probably say no *too* easily."

My brows traveled up my forehead. "Wow. I can't believe you admitted that."

He shrugged, putting his hands in his pockets. "Why? I have flaws, and I know that. Just like anyone."

I started to nod and then shook my head. "I thought you were only aware of the flaws in others." Then, I muttered, "Especially me."

He tilted his head, his face a mask as he studied me. "You make a lot of assumptions about people, don't you?"

My defenses rose. "No, I don't."

"Hmm."

"Fine. Maybe I do. But my assumptions are based on tons of evidence. People usually live up to expectations, don't you think?"

"I used to think that," he said quietly. "Now I'm not so sure."

Chapter 19

Even after finding and training a new event manager for the resort, I was still feeling stressed every day trying to manage all the things. This morning, it was the business development project, this afternoon was mostly spent in emails and calls with Hazel's agent and potential publisher, and then I spent the evening at home brainstorming some ideas and assembling them into an agenda for tomorrow's meeting with Hazel and Jeff. I was barely sleeping, so I was exhausted, today even more than usual.

So instead of going to bed early as any sane person would do, I chose to pour a glass of wine, sink into the couch with my Santa Claus slippers and fleece Christmas blanket, and surf the web for a while. Did people still say "surf the web," or was that outdated? I had no idea. I laughed out loud, reminding myself to ask Lila next time I saw her.

But the web was not surfed, as I found myself instead opening the gaming site chat window.

> **SawyerRox4:** Danny! You're there. Thank goodness.
> **CastGamer55:** I'm flattered.
> **SawyerRox4:** Oh, I didn't mean ... that
> **CastGamer55:** I'm just joking. Apparently I'm terrible at it.
> **SawyerRox4:** No, you're not ;)
> **CastGamer55:** Oh, I have a lot of faults, and bad humor is near the top.

I chuckled. Hadn't Jeff said something similar earlier this

week? It was still weird to even think about that interaction. I'd always assumed he had such a big ego, but it seemed there was more to him. Maybe.

Why are you thinking about your co-worker now?

Shaking my head, I set my fingers on the keyboard and inhaled slowly.

SawyerRox4: Can I ask you a question?
CastGamer55: Sure.
SawyerRox4: You couldn't be actually flattered, like in that way, because that would not be cool with your wife. Or husband, or whatever.
CastGamer55: LOL. That was the most awkward way anyone's ever asked me if I'm single.
SawyerRox4: Dying inside
CastGamer55: Hey, I've been wanting to ask you that for months. At least you *did* ask.
SawyerRox4: True. So I'm the idiot and you're the coward?
CastGamer55: Haha, something like that.
CastGamer55: To answer your question, I've just come out of a long-term relationship. With a woman.
SawyerRox4: Ah, sorry, I hope it wasn't too brutal.
CastGamer55: Oh, it was and it is.
SawyerRox4: Kids?
CastGamer55: One.
SawyerRox4: Grown up?
CastGamer55: How old do you think I am? LOL
SawyerRox4: Uh … 55? or maybe older, since you've had that handle for a while
CastGamer55: You assumed I was 55? All this time, you thought you were talking to a 55-year-old who was potentially married with grown-up kids?
SawyerRox4: Well, I didn't know. We never talked about personal stuff before…
CastGamer55: I'd argue many of our discussions are very

personal, more personal than I've ever had in some cases.
SawyerRox4: Now I'm flattered. ;) But you're probably right
CastGamer55: Your turn.
SawyerRox4: For what?
CastGamer55: Married with a dozen kids? Or in your 70s? Please tell me you're not a teenager, at least.
SawyerRox4: Oh. I'm 28. Single, obviously
CastGamer55: Why obviously?

If I truly answered that question, he'd just be dismissive like everyone else and say it's all in my head.

And I didn't want him to be dismissive. Because ... maybe there was something between us. Or there could be in the future. He wasn't old enough to be my father, after all. Not that I'd ever really believed that.

SawyerRox4: I don't know. So hey, we supposedly have a blizzard coming tomorrow, so there's always a chance I won't get online tomorrow night. I can still work on the game design stuff though. Just so you know

Was that weird? I didn't need to report my whereabouts or forewarn him that I might not be here to chat, so ... I don't know why I did.

Or maybe I did.

After a long pause, he continued the conversation.

CastGamer55: We have a blizzard warning here too. Curious, where are you at? I heard Minnesota was going to have the worst of it.
SawyerRox4: Oh, are we really doing that?
CastGamer55: ?
SawyerRox4: More personal details?
SawyerRox4: OK, fine. I'm in southern Minnesota. Rural, less than two hours southwest of the Twin Cities

CastGamer55: Wow, I'm kind of in that region too.

My heart started pounding in my chest.
He ... he lived near me?
I didn't know if my sudden perspiration was excitement or anxiety about this prospect, but I kicked off the blanket and tried to calm my shaking hands to type a response.

SawyerRox4: Seriously? That would be crazy
CastGamer55: Yes. And yes.
SawyerRox4: I'm going to be honest, because I've had a teeny bit of wine...
CastGamer55: OK.
SawyerRox4: Knowing you're in the same neck of the woods feels kind of surreal. I can't even ... Do you know what I mean?
CastGamer55: I do. I had a situation like that a month or so ago.
SawyerRox4: OK, so you get it
SawyerRox4: Now it just feels like ... we could maybe meet in person sometime, just for the heck of it. But then, it feels like our online friendship would never be the same.
CastGamer55: Is that necessarily a bad thing?
SawyerRox4: You want to meet in person??

Was that question presumptuous? I hope he didn't take it to mean that I wanted to meet him in person. I mean, I didn't *not* want to meet him in person. I'd just never seriously considered it. Well, except for maybe a few dreams causing me to blush from head to toe the next morning.

CastGamer55: Yes. How about New Year's Eve?

What? I checked my wine glass, and I'd barely touched my second glass yet. I couldn't be drunk. Was he *really* asking me that?

SawyerRox4: Really?

CastGamer55: Well, I'm out of town for Christmas and pretty busy before that. But I could do New Year's.

SawyerRox4: Wow, you're serious?

CastGamer55: ...

SawyerRox4: I have to go to a work party, well, kind of a work party. The boss is kind of my friend too. I think. I'm not good at recognizing when someone is a friend. Until a few minutes ago, I wasn't even sure if *you* considered me a friend.

I couldn't believe I had the courage to say all this, even online. I couldn't believe I was even considering this. And I couldn't believe what I typed next:

SawyerRox4: You could meet me at the party if you want.

CastGamer55: I was just going to suggest that.

SawyerRox4: Oh. You want to?

CastGamer55: Why else would I suggest it?

SawyerRox4: Fair point

CastGamer55: Mindy, will you dance with me on New Year's Eve?

Chapter 20

What was that sound? Why did my head weigh a million pounds? Had I tried to swallow sandpaper? Why was my nose not working? And why did every part of my body feel achy?

These questions dug their way into my consciousness as I tried to sit up in bed.

Too hard.

I'll go back to sleep. Yes, sleep is good.

Ding-ding-ding.

That sound! Not again. Who the heck was at my door? My eyes fell shut again.

Ding-ding. Ding-ding-ding.

Growling, I somehow managed to get into a sitting position and then slowly lumbered to my feet. I located my slippers by my bedroom door alongside a large pile of laundry—clean or dirty, who knew?—and stepped into them as I struggled to keep my balance amid the swirling headache.

Ding-ding.

Ugh, this better be extremely important. It'd better not be a social call from the chatty neighbor, Jenna. Or anyone else. Hazel knew I'd called off sick, so it wouldn't be her, surely.

I pulled the door half-open with great effort, wishing for the hundredth time that I had a peephole.

Was I seeing things? It looked like Jeff. I squinted and moved a bit closer. Yeah, that looked like Jeff, standing there with a large, hunter-green messenger bag over his shoulder.

"Oh, it's you." I yawned. "Nobody ever visits me. Hardly

anyone knows where I live. I thought you were my annoying neighbor. Her name is Jenna. Best to avoid her."

I thought he was going to laugh for a moment, but his face became more serious. "Roxy, are you OK?"

"Uh, sure," I said, knowing and not caring how obvious my lie was. I probably looked like death, but I was too tired to be self-conscious. "What are you doing here, Jeffrey?"

"Can I come in?"

"Uh … I'm sick. You don't want my germs."

"I do, actually," he said. At least that's what it sounded like, but I must have heard wrong over the pounding in my head.

"Sorry about canceling this morning. Or yesterday morning, sorry," I said slowly. "Hazel made me take a sick day."

"She sent me over with some files."

"What? What files?"

Jeff stepped toward me, and I stepped aside. He took the opportunity to walk into my apartment. Awareness zinged through me. Why was he in my apartment?

"First, let's get you some medicine. You look like you haven't had any, at least not for a while."

I scratched my head, feeling my tangled hair. "I think … maybe yesterday?"

"We have to know for sure, not maybe. Otherwise, you could overdose."

I laughed weakly. "You're kinda cute, Jeffrey."

Did I actually say that? I was too tired to care. I thought I detected a tiny wisp of a smile from him, but I very well could've imagined it.

"Thank you. But I'm serious. Are you sure you don't remember?" The frown was back.

"Don't be mad," I pleaded.

"I'm not mad, Roxy. I just—"

"Wait, I have an idea. I'll be right back." I padded to my room and over to the nightstand. I picked up the box of NyQuil, realizing it was unopened.

"Jeff, good news!" I said as I turned to go find him in the

other room.

But I nearly slammed into his chest before putting my hands out, landing on his chest, which was ... firmer than I thought it would be. Not that I'd ever thought about it.

Liar.

I bounced back, letting my hands fall to my sides. "Oh, I didn't know you'd followed me in there." I frowned, my hands tingling for some reason.

"What were you doing?" he asked, and then he touched my forehead with the back of his hand before moving to my cheek.

And I couldn't talk. What I suspect was a mild fever before was now burning up. "I ... what?"

He removed his hand from my face and watched me closely before his lips twitched. "I was checking for fever. It's probably mild. But are you all right?"

"I'm ... you're baiting me, aren't you? Sometimes you're so mean."

"Only sometimes?"

My eyes flashed. "See, you're doing it again!"

He sighed. "If you say so."

I rolled my eyes. "That's code for *I disagree but don't want to deal with this argument.*" When his eyebrows rose, I realized I'd said that out loud. Or I'd slurred it aloud. For some reason, this seemed hilarious, so I burst out laughing.

He shook his head, but with a hint of a smile. "Listen, Roxy, I do need to know if you've had any medicine recently. Was there a reason you came in here?"

"Oh yeah, I forgot to tell you ... uh, last night, I took the last one. See, there's the empty one on the floor. And *this* box here on the nightstand is not open."

He nodded slowly. "OK, I see. That's some pretty advanced logic for someone who is so unlike herself that she said I was cute." And then he smiled.

He smiled!

And I completely forgot what he said, but my face felt like

it was on fire. I think I just did something embarrassing, but I don't care because *that smile*.

He was never unattractive before. But he usually looked about ten years older than he actually was because of the constant frown and creases between his brows, the always buttoned-up business attire, the perfectly groomed hair and face, and the no-nonsense tone he always took.

But outside of work, he was different. He not only acted different but also looked different. Better in both ways. Come to think of it, he'd been acting somewhat different at work too. He was a lot more complicated than I ever would've guessed.

And that smile.

"What?" I asked, unsure if he'd even asked me anything.

His face was full of concern again. "Why don't you lie down, and I'll get you some things. You don't even have water in here."

"I can take care of myself, Jeff," I said, stifling a yawn. "You don't need to be here."

He winced, and then his face softened. "How often do you let people take care of you, Roxy?"

"What are you …" I trailed off. Why was he asking me that?

"It's not a sinister question. I'm just sensing you have a tough time accepting help."

"I don't—" At his raised eyebrows, I sighed. "Well, doesn't everyone?"

"Some people don't find it hard to accept help. Apparently. Not that I'd know." He rubbed his jaw. Did he have the faintest hint of stubble? I squinted and leaned forward to get a better look, but he moved back. "Roxy, I just want to help. Let's not argue over this too. We can have this argument tomorrow, OK? Or any other time you want. Please just get lie down, get comfortable, and wait for me to return."

I stared at him with half-open eyes. Who was this man?

"Please?" he asked as one hand absently rubbed his sleeve.

"Hey, you don't have to ask me twice," I said, as though

he wasn't being extremely confusing and weird (and, in turn, so was I).

"I did ask twice," he muttered under his breath. But I heard him because he was inches from my face as he leaned over to pull the covers that were bunched up on the other side of the bed, gently tugging them up to my neck.

Had I ever been this close to him before? I could see the curve of his jaw, the rich swirls of color and shape in his eyes, the muscles in his ... well, everything.

I could lean forward and ...

My heart pounded in my chest.

No!

No, no, no.

Suddenly, Jeff reared back.

I bit my lip. At least, I think it was my lip. "What's wrong? Do I smell gross?"

"No, you ... you just had a look of horror all the sudden. I assumed I was the offender."

"No, you don't smell gross. Quite the opposite, actually." I could still smell his faint woodsy cologne, kind of surprising for a guy like him but definitely not a bad thing.

He eyed me for a moment as the corners of his mouth lifted. "OK. Why the—you know what? It doesn't matter. I'll be back in a bit with a glass of water so you can take the medicine."

"But—" I started and then stopped, realizing he wasn't going to hear me. Or if he did, he'd ignore me.

What was he even doing here? This was so embarrassing. Probably much worse than I even realized because I was more than a little stuffy-headed and exhausted.

A minute later—or who knows, since I couldn't trust my judgment of time now—Jeff returned with a cup of water and a separate cup of ice. When I raised my eyebrows, he set the cups on the nightstand and started to open the medicine package. "I know you like ice water, so I brought ice."

He knew I liked ice water? I tried to remember; we'd rarely shared meals. Other than that recent one, at his house.

I swallowed painfully, realizing most people liked ice water, so this didn't signify. "Uh, why not just, I don't know, put the ice in the water then?"

"Because I didn't know if you'd want it now or if you'd get chills or something," he said while handing me the cold medicine. "So, ice or no?"

"Uh, no?"

When had anyone ever been so thoughtful to me? Other than maybe Julia. I *must be hallucinating.*

"Hallucinating?" Jeff asked. "It's that bad?"

I said that out loud? Was I?

"Oh, I—no. I'm fine. I said *hungry*."

"You did not," he said under his breath. "OK, what do you want to eat? Soup? Crackers?"

"Boring food, you mean," I said with a laugh.

"Yes, sick woman food."

"Sick *woman* food? Are you saying that men don't eat the same kinds of things when they're sick?"

He shrugged, putting his hands in his pockets. "No. I just haven't been around a lot of men when they're sick."

In an accusing tone that would probably embarrass me later when I remembered it, I asked, "Oh, but you've taken care of a lot of other sick women?"

His eyebrows rose a bit. "No, only my mother and sister."

"Oh. Right."

What an absolute idiot I was. I was never going to be able to show my face at the office again after today.

"I'll go find you something to eat that isn't too boring," he said, about to turn around.

"Oh, hey, wait!" I called, probably louder than I thought. "Why did you say Hazel sent you over?"

"She said it was really urgent that we finish reviewing the legal resource list by Monday at the latest." His shoulders lifted briefly. "I don't know why it's so urgent. But here I am."

"I don't think I'll be able to look at work stuff yet. I'm not —"

"No, no, don't worry about it. Just get better and rest, Roxy. After you eat, you can go to sleep for as long as you want." He darted out of the room, and I stared after him.

What on *earth* was going on? And why was I *this* tired?

Chapter 21

As my eyes fluttered open, I was assaulted by a piercing yellow light and immediately squeezed them shut. I grasped blindly at the covers to pull them over my face, feeling something oddly warm and firm that must have been part of my body I wasn't yet registering.

Because thinking was hard.

I groaned and decided to stay under the blanket until that blasted sun went down—or at least until it stopped streaming through my window.

As I tried to get comfortable, my elbow connected with something solid, and I yelped.

What hard object did I leave on the bed? Maybe a hardcover book. It wouldn't be the first time.

I stuck my hand out again to push the object away, but it was surprisingly heavy, weighing the blanket down.

A throat cleared.

A throat ... not my throat. Not raspy enough. My throat was killing me.

Wait, what or *who* made that sound?

I threw the blanket off my face and arms and screamed.

A *man* was sitting on the bed, less than a foot away. A fully clothed man holding a book, with a face like ...

"Jeff?" I croaked out.

"Good morning, sunshine," he said, setting the book down next to him. "I probably have a bruise on my leg now, thanks."

"I'm sorry. But what are you *doing* here? I—" I stopped to cough into my elbow.

"You're sick. I'm taking care of you."

Before I could unpack that crazy sentence, I started to push the hair out of my face until I thought better of it. As bad as my hair felt, it probably looked nowhere near as bad as my face. I propped my upper body on my elbow. "Um, sorry for screaming at you."

He chuckled. "Well, it wasn't exactly a scream, to be fair. More like a frightened whispery croak."

I winced.

"Sorry, that came out wrong."

I stared at him. First he'd chuckled, then he'd apologized. And he was *here*, in my *bedroom*. "Is this some kind of alternate universe? Or—I know—it's a fever dream, isn't it?" My head sank back into the foam pillow, and I closed my eyes. "I should go back to sleep then."

"You can sleep again if you want, but you're not dreaming now. You slept for a long time." I felt a gentle nudge on my arm. "You seem a little bit more lucid now than you were yesterday."

My eyes flew open. "You've been here since yesterday?" I couldn't comprehend.

"Don't worry, I slept on the couch," he said. "Or I tried. It's a little soft for my taste."

"It's lovingly broken in," I said, "because I sit there a lot. I mean, not like … I'm not a couch potato. I don't watch that much TV, only a few shows I'm really dedicated to. But I like to be comfortable, so sue me."

He looked at me with raised eyebrows and then chuckled again. "You don't have to explain why your couch is soft. I wasn't criticizing you. I just happen to like sleeping on firm beds."

I couldn't seriously be having a conversation about what kind of *bed* he preferred *while he was in my bed*. This was beyond inappropriate. We were colleagues!

And yet there was something about him relaxed and leaning against the headboard that looked … not wrong.

I shook my head. My brain must still be waking up from the sedating cold meds.

"Are you feeling a little better?"

"Eh, a little." I glanced over at him again. "I mean, yes. A lot better. You can go now. You're released from sick duty. Did Hazel tell you to stay with me? I thought she only told you to bring the files."

He scratched his head, a frown appearing on his face. "You don't have to lie about how you're feeling, Roxy. I'm not in a hurry to get out of here."

I stared ahead at my half-open closet on the opposite wall while trying to process all this. "What about Lila?"

"What about her?"

"Didn't your ex ask you to take Lila this weekend?"

"She did, yes." He paused. "But I said no. I've had Lila every weekend lately, and I love it, but she also needs to spend time with her mother. Both of them actually agreed it would be nice. Besides, you are the one who told me to put my foot down with Aileen."

"I did?" My brows furrowed. "Wait, now I remember. I can't believe you actually took my advice." I laughed. "You still haven't told me why you stayed though. It's a bit above and beyond the call of duty for a co-worker, is it not? Especially a co-worker you hate."

He frowned and remained silent for a bit. "You might not believe me, but I don't hate you. I actually never have."

"You could've fooled me. Well, actually, you did fool me."

"Not intentionally." He let out a long breath that spoke of mild frustration and something else I couldn't identify. "Anyway, I didn't mind staying. I'd already said no to Aileen about having Lila stay over again, and you really seemed like you needed help last night."

I'm sure my puffy, snot-stained face turned pink then. "I ... I don't actually remember it all that well. Hopefully I wasn't acting too weird or inappropriate."

"Only a little." When my eyes flew to his though, he was trying to suppress a smile. "It's fine, Roxy. I need you healthy for the big week ahead, when the decorators are finally coming.

Besides, you've endured spending time with me twice for the sake of my daughter. Staying to take care of you was the very least I could do."

"Oh, I see." I turned away so he couldn't see my frown.

He'd stayed because he was trying to repay a favor or something?

So what if he did? That shouldn't bother me.

I tried to shove away the thoughts. "I rarely get sick, you know. But it's been kind of stressful these past few months. Wearing so many hats." I snuck a glance at him again. "You know what that's like, right?"

He nodded. "Stress can definitely make us more susceptible to illness."

I propped myself up on my elbow again and looked more closely at him. "You have morning stubble," I murmured. "I've never seen that before. You're usually so …"

"Buttoned up? I think that's what you said last night."

"I said that?" I remembered thinking it, but I couldn't believe I *said* it. What else did I say out loud that I didn't remember now?

"You did," Jeff confirmed.

I inhaled sharply, trying to remember last night. "Did I say anything about … anything?"

He pressed his lips together as if to suppress a smile. "Sure. You told me to call and order a Christmas tree from Terry." I winced. Terry owned a tree farm, but I didn't usually decorate since I lived alone and it just felt weird.

"I don't remember that at all," I muttered. "Did you actually call him?"

"No, I figured I'd check with you today when you were lucid. After that, you said you had no decorations and asked if I wanted to go shopping with you in the Christmas Village." He'd spoken casually as though this wasn't a bizarre and embarrassing thing to ask.

"Oh my gosh, no. Please erase that from your memory," I said as I dropped my face into my palms.

He chuckled. "If you say so."

"What about ... did I mention, um, the party?"

"The annual Christmas party? Or the New Year's one?" he asked.

"Well, either one."

"You said you were skipping the Christmas party as usual. And you're bringing a date on New Year's Eve." His eyes were intent, and I didn't know what to make of it. At all.

"Oh ... I don't remember that at all." I winced and looked down at my hands. "Did I say anything else?"

"You said that you always get excited about making resolutions for the new year. And that you were nervous. About the New Year's party." His face was unreadable when I gazed up at him again. "That's it. It was during the night when your fever spiked."

"Oh," I said quietly.

We sat there in silence for a long minute or two, and finally, he sat up straighter and then swung his long legs down to stand up. "I'm going to make you some food. Last night, you were asleep before I could feed you."

"Oh, you don't have to ..." I trailed off, remembering what he'd said last night about how I never let people take care of me. "Actually, food is good. Thank you. I'm just going to get cleaned up. I look a fright, I know."

He shook his head, a ghost of a smile crossing his face before he turned and strolled out of the room in a relaxed manner, as if this were a totally normal situation.

As I dragged myself out of bed and ambled over to the bathroom, my mind reeled with all the events recently and the words exchanged just now.

I couldn't help but wonder if I actually didn't hate him either.

Maybe I might even like him.

But only a tiny bit.

Chapter 22

Ugh, a dreaded dinner party. I hated them almost as much as big cocktail parties because at least you could be a little more anonymous at a huge party or, you know, escape to the bathroom or the deck outside.

But surprisingly, I wasn't hating this Christmas-themed dinner party so far. Danny had given me a pep talk last night after I told him about Hazel's impromptu party, and I think it was helping. Even though Hazel had given up drinking almost a year ago, she served wine for guests, and I'd had one glass. I was limiting myself to one glass, but I still felt a little more relaxed than usual.

Of course, with my luck, I ended up being seated next to Jeff.

And I didn't hate it. But it was awkward that we kept brushing forearms together when we'd reach for a utensil or glass at the same time. He seemed quieter than usual but not exactly his usual standoffish self either. I didn't know what to make of him—as per usual the last few weeks. We'd never really talked about the weekend I was sick. I sometimes wondered if I'd imagined it.

Hazel cleared her throat loudly. "It will surprise no one that I'm going to give a little speech." She smiled along with everyone else at the table. "As you all know, we are now on track to open Yours Truly Wellness next week! Of course, we won't start seeing patients until January, but the week after Christmas will be a key time for appointment setting and publicity. Terry has an info table set up all week at the Christmas Village. We are set. *We did it!*" This was followed by smiles and congratulations around the table.

"I'm so proud of you, Hazel. Every single one of us is," Mariana said, biting her lip as if trying to control her emotion. "You're going to make me cry, and that is *so* not my thing," she said with a small laugh.

Hazel beamed and then turned to where Jeff and I were sitting. "Roxy and Jeff, I couldn't have done it without you. Both of you have done an amazing job. I know you were both a little hesitant about managing this project, but you've done a phenomenal job." When we both nodded awkwardly, she laughed and added, "I also know you both prefer not to have a big show of gratitude, so I'll stop now."

Laughter filled the room, even from Jeff and me. My Christmas jingle bell earrings shook, making a tinny noise, and I caught Jeff looking toward me for a moment.

"We should make this an annual holiday tradition! I'll host, or we could take turns hosting. We can eat tons of festive food, have a gift exchange next year, watch some cheesy Christmas movies, the whole works." Her smile was infectious to everyone but me. When she noticed, her smile faltered, but only briefly. Her eyes were warm as she added, "Remember, family is not just blood. I love you all."

"Haz, seriously, is it your goal to make me cry tonight?" Mari crossed her arms and tried to scowl but only ended up laughing.

As more conversation about everyone's Christmas plans ensued around me, I focused on eating my food slowly and trying not to bump elbows with Jeff. If I seemed really absorbed in eating, people might not bother me or notice that I wasn't conversing. It was not a great strategy, but it was often the only one I had in these forced casual parties that I couldn't avoid.

Still, my anxiety continued rising, and I nearly spilled my glass on myself when Jeff leaned over and bumped shoulders with me.

"Can you pass the butter?" he asked.

I tried to breathe as I set my glass down carefully and then reached for the butter in front of me. Suddenly, his hand was under my forearm, and I gasped as I turned to him and nearly threw the butter at him.

"It looked like your sleeve was going to land in the pasta," he said, pointing at my plate.

I gaped at him, unsure of his meaning at first. Then it dawned on me, and I blinked rapidly. "Oh, you were just—OK, thank you." I tried to flash a smile, but it probably looked more like a grimace.

"Sorry, I didn't mean to alarm you."

"No, you didn't ... I'm just ..." I couldn't continue the sentence: a hyper-sensitive weirdo who misinterprets social cues and wishes she were anywhere but here.

His eyes met mine as he swallowed a bite of food and then veered back to his plate.

Why can't you just act normal? Ever?
This is not that hard, Roxy.
Just socialize. It's easy.
I couldn't take it.
Must.
Leave.
Now.

Rising abruptly, I bumped the table slightly as I pushed my chair back with my legs. "Restroom," I mumbled to anyone who might be listening, avoiding eye contact with everyone.

Once safely in the bathroom further down the hall, I splashed some water on my face and then flipped the toilet lid down and sat, my hands covering my face.

The usual mix of shame and relief coursed through me as I tried to breathe normally and waited for my heart rate to eventually calm down. Ten minutes later, I was still shaky but feeling less light-headed, so I washed my hands and face and left. I didn't feel ready to return to the party yet, so I sat in a small sitting room and started doing a modified body scan meditation. Sometimes it helped me calm down, and sometimes it was useless, but it was worth a shot.

The room was sparsely decorated because Hazel, when she'd given me a brief tour, said this was Peter's space. I mean, it was his house, but she'd taken over the decoration of much of the house since she'd sold her own next door, and nearly every square inch was covered in Christmas decorations. I marveled at their unlikely success as a couple, given how wildly different they were.

It was a massive old house, and this part was far enough away from the formal dining room that I couldn't hear them. But as I stared at the plain wood-paneled walls, adorned only by a winter holiday landscape painting, a figure walked into the room and startled me.

Immediately sitting up straight, I said, "Oh, hi, Peter. I … I'm sorry, I know this is your private space. I didn't mean to—"

"Roxy, it's fine. You're welcome to relax here. I actually wanted to talk to you about something." He paused, hesitation on his face. "But first, are you OK?"

"I'm—yes. I am now." I bit my lip and sighed. "Was it that obvious when I left?"

"No."

"Oh …" I remembered Peter was a man of few words. The sooner I changed the subject, the better. "So, what's up?" I asked, aiming for a normal tone.

He sat down on a chair across from mine. "I have a surprise planned for Hazel, and I was hoping you could help me."

My eyes widened. "Oh, of course. It's my job to support her."

"No, that's not what I meant. Just … as our friend."

My heart leaped into my throat. Peter considered me a friend too? I couldn't believe it, and I surely hadn't done anything to deserve it.

"Oh, right."

He eyed me for a moment, not breaking a smile. His stoicism reminded me of Jeff in that way, but they were different too, in ways I couldn't quite articulate. "I want to arrange for her parents to surprise her on her birthday. At the New Year's Eve party."

My jaw dropped. "That's ... wow. How incredibly thoughtful." I remembered then that she didn't have the best relationship with her parents, though it certainly sounded better than mine. "Do you think they'll agree to it though? I mean, her dad's in Japan, and her mom is ... I forget, somewhere in Europe. That's quite a trip for a birthday party, especially with holiday travel costs."

He nodded. "That's why I think it'll mean a lot to her. She thinks they're not interested in her life, but they are. I could tell instantly from one conversation with them. So I've already reached out to them, and they're excited."

I smiled. "That's truly wonderful. I am so happy for her that she'll get to see them—and that she has you."

His lips turned up at one corner. "That's kind of you, Roxy."

"How can I help?"

"Could you arrange their travel and lodging? They could stay at the house if they want, but I'd rather not just assume they'd want to. So we can book hotel rooms and cancel if needed."

"Of course, I'm happy to do that." *Happy* was a stretch, as I was a bit tired of coordinating events and logistics for others. But this seemed like a worthy cause. "What about Hazel's sister?"

"Halley can't come, unfortunately. And maybe it's for the best, so this visit is truly about Hazel, you know?"

"Makes sense. Well, this is such a wonderful gift. It's last minute, only ten days away, right? But it's definitely doable."

"Eleven days, but yes. Let me give you my phone number so we can chat about this tomorrow some more."

I handed him my phone so he could type in his number. "I'll start working on this tomorrow, along with the final party details."

For a moment, Peter looked conflicted. "Is that too much? Sorry, I don't want to overload you."

"Not at all!" I smiled brightly, maybe too brightly.

He looked hesitant but then nodded. "All right. Well, we should probably get back to the table, right?"

"Yeah, before they send out a search party," I heard myself saying, followed by instant regret. What a stupid thing to say.

But then Peter chuckled. "It's a very Hazel-like thing to do."

I relaxed my shoulders as we walked back.

OK, he found it amusing, maybe not so stupid after all.

As we walked back, he turned to me. "We'll see you at the annual resort Christmas party, right?"

"Uh, no. I'm traveling home for the holiday, so …"

Of course, my flight out would be the day *after* Mari's party, but they didn't need to know that.

"Oh, I see. A big family holiday? That's probably more important than a party at work."

More important, maybe, but definitely not more appealing. And something told me he knew that. Something in his voice sounded … off. Not convinced of his own words.

Chapter 23

SawyerRox4: Hi!! I didn't know if you'd make it online this morning

CastGamer55: And miss a chance to talk to you? Not a chance. I told you I'd pop on a bit.

SawyerRox4: *blush*

CastGamer55: How's your holiday going?

SawyerRox4: Christmas is OK so far.

CastGamer55: Just OK?

SawyerRox4: Christmas Eve lunch at my grandma's house has never been the same since we lost my grandpa. He was the only one who understood me.

CastGamer55: I'm sorry for your loss. I can't imagine. I've never known my grandparents very well.

SawyerRox4: Well, that's kind of sad too. Who do you celebrate with?

CastGamer55: My mom, sister, a couple of aunts. It's nice to see them, but it's also nice when it's over. If that makes any sense.

SawyerRox4: TONS of sense

CastGamer55: So, not a great night then?

SawyerRox4: It wasn't terrible. One of my many cousins is pretty awkward too, so we hung out with the little kids, our other cousins' kids. It's actually better than hanging out with the other adults.

CastGamer55: Well, that's good then. We had a low-key dinner and gift exchange last night, and today we'll be cooking all morning.

SawyerRox4: Sounds nice. Much the same here, except my grandma can't come today, so it's just me and my parents. Sooo excited about that.

CastGamer55: I think that means you're not excited.

SawyerRox4: You're a smart one

CastGamer55: Haha. You can tell me all about it later. I'll be online tonight.

SawyerRox4: Oh good. I suppose I should go see if Mom and Dad are awake yet.

CastGamer55: Before you go, I wanted to check in ... are we still cool to meet at the New Year's party? No pressure. Just checking.

SawyerRox4: ... yes? Not gonna lie, I'm kind of nervous. But I'll send you a message with my address the day before, as we talked about, OK?

CastGamer55: Perfect.

As soon as I put the phone down, I realized I'd forgotten to ask Danny if he was having a white Christmas, wherever he was visiting his family. I still couldn't believe he lived in southern Minnesota too. What were the odds?

When I walked to the kitchen, I found my mother cooking already and came to a stop near her. "Morning, Mom."

"Morning," she said, quickly looking at me and then back at the gas stove, which was a recent upgrade. Hardly anything in my childhood home was the same anymore.

"Can I help with anything?"

"No."

"You don't have to make that much food, really, since it's just the three of us."

That got her attention. "Roxanne, 'just the three of us' is your family. And it's still Christmas."

She turned back to the stove, stirred for a moment, and then put on her cutting gloves and retrieved the cutting board from a lower cabinet.

I tried to think of something to say. "I wish we had a white Christmas."

She didn't answer.

"Mom? Just wondering, do you think this dress would be OK for a work party I'm attending next week?"

She finished cutting the onions and then turned to me, eyeing me up and down. "Is it a fancy party?"

"Kind of? Not the most formal ever, but definitely not casual."

My mother eyed me and then turned back to the stove. "Well, if you want my honest opinion, that dress doesn't do you any favors."

"Why?" I asked, afraid to hear the answer.

Her eyes assessed me again. "I don't think the designer had a pear shape in mind when they created that dress."

I looked down at the dress and felt the snugness at the hips. I thought it was supposed to fit this way. Emotion welled up in my chest, and I wanted to kick myself. I *asked* for her opinion. *Why?*

"OK, Mom."

"How's your love life these days? Are you bringing home a man one of these days?"

I looked at her blankly. "No, what gave you that idea?"

"I mean, you're heading toward thirty, and you've barely had any boyfriends. Only two or three, right?"

Actually, it was only one. I'd dated a bit, but I'd only called one a boyfriend. But I just nodded to her.

She added the onions to a pan on the stove and started stirring. "Well, are you trying, at least?"

"What do you mean by *trying*?" I asked quietly.

"I can't hear you! You always talk so darn soft."

I repeated myself, my voice starting to shake.

"I mean, putting yourself out there. Being social. Letting guys know you're interested. Have mutual friends set you up." She spoke so casually, as though it was as easy as tying my shoes.

"I thought about trying a dating app once, but—"

"Oh, don't bother with those things. You're better off meeting a man in person."

"How am I better off doing that? That's really hard for me, Mom."

Dad walked into the room then and made eye contact with me briefly before going to the fridge.

Mom eyed me for a moment, her disappointment evident on her face. "It's time you outgrew this shy thing, Roxy. I can't understand why it's so hard. Sometimes you just got to try. That's not so hard." She turned to my dad. "Right?" But he just shrugged, as usual, preferring to not get involved. To not defend me. Story of my life.

I tried to breathe in slowly, but my breath caught in my throat. There was no use trying to explain anything to her. She'd never accepted me, and she never would. She wouldn't even try.

"Do you even want to find someone?" she asked, sounding exasperated as she stirred faster and faster.

"Well, I don't *not* want to. But—"

"You've got to make up your mind and just do it. Simple. Quit overthinking everything."

"OK." Tears pooled in my eyes, and I walked backward slowly and then turned, walking as casually as I could so they wouldn't suspect I was upset.

Dad glanced at me briefly but then went back to peeling an apple.

I tripped and nearly fell down the steps leading to my old bedroom, but I managed to stay upright by palming the wall.

I rushed into the room and closed the door softly so they wouldn't hear.

After sobbing quietly for a few minutes, I wiped my eyes and opened up my laptop again.

I felt numb as I turned it on, even as I opened the chat window.

Danny wasn't online.

I started browsing random sites, starting with a quirky gift website to look for a birthday gift for Hazel. I eventually found myself on a news site when my eyes landed on the scrolling red banner near the top: Winter Storm Warning for central Tennessee and Kentucky.

What?

I blinked a few times and refreshed the page, certain it couldn't be right. But it was. The storm was expected to roll in tomorrow and potentially last a few days. It had originally been expected to head further east, but now it was heading straight for middle Tennessee.

I'd lived here long enough as a child to know that snow was taken very seriously. Schools closed whenever there was even a slight dusting of the white stuff. I couldn't imagine what would happen if a blizzard blew through here, especially in the mountains.

But something stirred in me. Maybe this wasn't so bad, I thought while navigating to a travel website. I could go home early. I could leave this place where I was constantly criticized and my feelings dismissed. Before long, I'd found a new flight to replace the old one, which was two days from now.

I was about to click the PURCHASE button when the door suddenly opened.

Mom walked in and sat on the bed, trying to see what was on the computer screen, but I pushed it aside.

Guilt set in. Mom was coming in here to see how I was doing because she cared, and meanwhile, I was trying to get the earliest flight out of here.

And then she spoke. "What are you doing hiding in here?"

My spirits deflated once more. "I wasn't hiding—"

She rolled her eyes. "Oh, come on, I know you better than that."

"Do you, though?" I asked bitterly. But she didn't hear me because she was moving my suitcase off the treadmill. "Oh, are you … you're here to work out?"

She gave me a strange look. "Obviously."

My old room had been turned into an exercise room. At least it had a futon that I could sleep in when visiting. But now, I felt like an intruder in my own room.

I pulled my laptop back over to me and saw the pop-up message stating that I had only fifty more seconds to decide before the airfare deal expired.

I glanced at my mother, who was grimacing as she moved some of my clothes out of the way.

I clicked PURCHASE.

∞∞∞

I let guilt eat me up for much of the quiet plane ride. Despite the obvious drawbacks (literally, the danger) of staying here with my family and hence flying out in a storm a few days later—or worse yet, stuck here because flights were cancelled—the news that I was leaving early hadn't gone over well. My spirits sank after seeing the sadness on my dad's face and the agitation in my mom's tone when I'd held firm and asked for a ride to the airport.

But now, walking into the baggage claim area after the uneventful flight, I felt a strange sense of calm and anticipation. I'd made it through a difficult, albeit short holiday visit with my family, and I was coming home to the place I loved and the people I loved. Maybe someday, they'd even love me back. I actually had a few friends in Shipsvold now. Maybe even something more ...

No, there wasn't anything more. It didn't bear thinking about. Did it?

Undeniably, things felt different between Jeff and me lately. His sharp edges had softened, and he was a lot more complex and interesting and even *kind* than I would've guessed. And he gazed at me almost as if ...

As if he wanted more.

I had to be hallucinating. Or wishful thinking, because I

couldn't deny he was attractive. And interesting. My heart beat faster when he was near, and not just from irritation anymore. I didn't hate working with him now, and I even felt a little dismayed that our close collaboration was at an end.

But then there was Danny. It definitely felt like *something* could develop once we met. Why else would he want to meet up? And why else would I have said *yes*?

Surely I couldn't have feelings for *both* men, could I? I was not that kind of woman.

It didn't matter anyway because both Jeff and Danny probably saw me only as a friend. That awkward friend they occasionally found funny or smart.

After pondering the situation throughout the entire flight, I'd then rambled on about it to Julia over the phone for the past half hour, ever since we were allowed to turn our phones back on after landing.

"Rox, I know this is hard for you because it's, like, your *life*, but I am loving this diversion. I want to live vicariously through you!"

I laughed. "Diversion?"

"It's just nice to get my mind off everything."

"Uh-oh. Is it the neighbor again?"

"He is a pain in the butt, Rox. I can't even—no, I'm not going to waste this phone call talking about him. So not worth it."

"Aww, that's not fair. I just blabbered on about my stuff for ages—"

I stopped short, drawing in a quick breath.

There he was, on the other side of the baggage carousel. Looking tired and annoyed but still just as effortlessly handsome as always, Jeff was scanning the area, his eyes slowing when they reached the crowd I was standing in. I averted my eyes quickly, but the damage was probably done.

"I think he spotted me!"

"Who?" Julia asked.

"Him!"

"Which him?"

"Jeff," I mumbled, hoping he couldn't read lips. "Oh crap, he's walking straight toward me. Julia, I've got to go. So sorry—"

"Go on and talk to him. And text me later, or else!"

I ended the call and stuffed my phone in my purse.

"Hello," he said, stopping in front of me with uncertainty on his face.

"Hi," I said, shifting from one foot to the other and back again. "What are you doing here?"

His lips curved upward into a small smile, which was not a little distracting. "Flying home, just as I imagine you're doing."

"Of course, yeah." I licked my lips, a bad habit when I was nervous.

"Isn't it early? I thought you said you'd be staying another day or two," he said, curiosity in his tone.

I didn't remember telling him when I'd be back, but I nodded. "Yeah, there's a big snowstorm heading to middle Tennessee today, so I wanted to get ahead of the weather."

He nodded. "I heard about that storm. Unusual."

"And you? Flying home early too?"

"No, I'd only booked a short trip because work has been so busy." He looked over at me. "Do you want to share a ride home?"

I looked into his rich hazel eyes. "Uh, OK?"

He chuckled. "That sounds like a question, not an answer."

"I mean, yes, we can ride home together. I guess."

He raised an eyebrow but looked back to the carousel. "Finally," he said as the suitcases began rolling onto the carousel. His was one of the first, so he grabbed it on the first pass.

"I'm surprised you bothered to check luggage for such a short trip."

He shrugged. "I brought a lot of gifts for my sister and my mom. And they have gifts for me to give to Lila, of course. They wouldn't have fit in a carry-on."

"Ah, I don't have that excuse. I'm just a heavy packer. Just call me Madam Heavy Packer," I said with a self-deprecating laugh.

His eyes traveled over my face, searching for ... I don't know what. "I'll call you Roxy," he said quietly.

I sucked in my cheeks. "I noticed you'd started calling me that a while ago. Thank you."

"You're welcome," he said, his eyes still roaming over my face.

Trying to ignore the butterflies making a ruckus in my stomach, I put on a smile. "So, how was your family thing?"

His expression darkened. "It was fine."

"Really? Your face says otherwise."

I clamped my mouth tightly, thinking I'd gone too far, but he just sighed. "Some parts were fine. Others, not so much."

"Care to vent a little?"

"No," he said sharply.

I turned away then, looking for my own luggage on the other carousel next to us. Of course he wouldn't want to share personal things with me. Why would he? I felt my cheeks heat up as I considered how he must see me.

He sighed behind me, and I could feel his breath on the side of my face. "It's not you."

I nodded and tried to smile. I'd heard that more times than I could count.

The ride home was quiet and awkward for the first twenty minutes as he drove our rented car.

"If it helps at all, I had a rough time with my family too," I finally said quietly.

He frowned. "It doesn't help."

"Oh, I'm sorry," I said, averting my eyes to look out the passenger window.

"It's almost as though you're *trying* to misunderstand me sometimes. I meant that I don't like that you had a rough time," he said, staring straight ahead.

Before I could process that, my phone buzzed in my pocket.

Hazel: Hey, I saw a big storm over Nashville. Are you OK??

Roxy: I'm fine. Came home early.

Hazel: I don't remember if I ever told you this, but I'm really sorry I didn't call you during that epic snowstorm in February. It was a rough time being stuck with Peter when we were *not* getting along at all, and I had no reception.
Hazel: Still, not an excuse though.
Roxy: It's fine! Don't worry about it, seriously.
Hazel: I want to do better.
Roxy: Thanks, but it's all good! :)

"That was Hazel," I said as I put my phone down. "Just checking to see if I was stuck in the snowstorm." I didn't mention the part where Hazel still didn't even remember I wasn't from Nashville. I was fairly sure I'd corrected her before, but it wasn't worth doing again.

I saw him nod briefly and then grimace. "My deadbeat father called at Christmas."

My eyebrows shot up my forehead. "Oh?"

"Yeah. And my mother actually *let* him." His frown deepened. "So that's why I had a bad holiday. You?"

"I'm sorry to hear that. I guess you don't like your father, eh?"

"Not liking him is an understatement. He destroyed our family when I was young."

"That's ... I wish I could help." I reached out with my free hand and rubbed his upper right arm gently.

For a moment, I thought he was going to shake off my hand, but instead, he briefly placed his left hand over mine before returning it to the steering wheel. I pulled my hand back as though burned ... because I was.

Heat swept over me, and I wished I could open the window. But he'd wonder what was going on with me, given that it was wintertime.

I wondered myself, actually. Touching him was completely spontaneous. Bold. Risky, even. All the things that I never was.

He cleared his throat. "I'm really looking forward to New

Year's. The party, I mean."

This statement did nothing to calm the swirling emotions threatening to overtake me. I tried to laugh a bit. "I didn't see you as a party animal."

"I'm not." He eyed me briefly before turning back to the road.

I swallowed hard. "Oh. Me neither. But I guess I'm looking forward to it."

He glanced over at me again, his eyes somehow piercing my skin, before once again looking straight ahead. "Good."

Good? What did that mean?

And what was I going to do? Never in my life would I have imagined being torn between two men. Granted, I didn't even know if either of them felt *that* way about me.

But what if they *both* did?

Chapter 24

The party was tomorrow. Cue the panic.

It was New Year's Eve *Eve*. I'd spent hours each day this week checking over and finalizing details for Hazel's big birthday/holiday bash. Basically, she was inviting the whole town and several others beyond Shipsvold.

And at night, I spent hours talking to Danny. The more we talked, the more comfortable I felt with him and the idea of meeting him.

Granted, I was still terrified to meet him. Just … a little less terrified.

Despite being extremely busy, I found Jeff popping into my mind at odd moments. I hadn't seen him in days, and it felt odd. Bittersweet, sort of. But more bitter than sweet.

I missed him. Jeff. The sometimes surly, sometimes sweet and generous guy I'd worked with and therefore talked to nearly every day for the last eight months.

A dull pain pierced my chest, and I wondered every single day if this whole New Year's meetup thing had been a mistake.

But then I logged on, and talking to Danny made me remember how much I liked him. I really liked him, in truth.

Even when we were arguing … which we did often lately.

CastGamer55: It was your idea to add a romantic element to the game. Now you want to cut it?
SawyerRox4: No, I don't want to cut it. I just think we should leave it open-ended

CastGamer55: Open, how?

SawyerRox4: The outcome. The game could end with either an HEA or not...

CastGamer55: What's an HEA?

SawyerRox4: Happily Ever After. It's a romance thing. Why are you even advocating for this if you don't know basic romance terminology?

CastGamer55: Well, excuse me. I'll be sure to do my homework next time.

CastGamer55: You don't think the game should conclude on a happy note?

SawyerRox4: Not necessarily. Real life isn't like that.

CastGamer55: This is fantasy though. Or sci-fi.

SawyerRox4: I can tell you're not into genre fiction

CastGamer55: You're right about that. But I do think it's pointless to include a romantic relationship as even an option in the game if there won't be a happy ending.

SawyerRox4: Why does it matter?

CastGamer55: Because we want players to feel happy after they finish the game. Right? Seems like good business sense.

SawyerRox4: Oh, um, are you an accountant? Just realized I never asked...

CastGamer55: No.

SawyerRox4: ... ok then

SawyerRox4: Do we want them to feel happy? That implies satisfied, but don't we want them to be excited and maybe a little unfulfilled so that they want to play again and again?

CastGamer55: Can't they be all of the above?

SawyerRox4: That would depend on the individual temperament and personality

CastGamer55: Let me guess: psych major?

SawyerRox4: lol, yeah

SawyerRox4: So, players could choose their path. Like in the game of Life. You could choose the kind of relationship you want to have with other players

CastGamer55: OK, tell me more.

SawyerRox4: Maybe some players want to pursue romance, but others want to make friends, and then others who don't want to pursue any relationships other than as project teammates or even as enemies, which could be interesting ...

CastGamer55: I admit that would be good because it better reflects the actual show. Some people connect as friends, others as lovers, etc. And some actually wish to do others harm.

SawyerRox4: Right! So you see, players on the romance path don't need an HEA necessarily.

CastGamer55: Wait, that doesn't follow logically from what you said. It isn't even relevant. It's a poor attempt at syllogism.

SawyerRox4: Let me guess – logic major?

CastGamer55: Haha. That doesn't exist.

SawyerRox4: Too bad, right? Must be philosophy then

CastGamer55: You're feisty today.

SawyerRox4: Well, you're a bit argumentive today!

CastGamer55: I still like you though.

SawyerRox4: You mean, like ...

CastGamer55: We should give the players an HEA, Mindy.

SawyerRox4: When a reader finishes a romance novel, they actually find the happy ending *so* satisfying that they want to start a new one. So they can have the HEA and still leave them wanting more.

CastGamer55: Isn't that what I said?

SawyerRox4: What? No. You're confusing me. They will be wanting more regardless of whether they have the HEA. You see?

CastGamer55: I'm calling it a night, Mindy. Goodnight.

SawyerRox4: That was abrupt

CastGamer55: Sorry, just tired and maybe a bit irritable. Long week. I'll see you tomorrow!

Tomorrow.

I took a deep breath in and exhaled slowly, several times.

Was I really going through with this?

Chapter 25

To say I was a bundle of nerves in the school gym, which had been transformed into a glitzy ballroom, was a massive understatement. But it was a kind of nervous excitement, not just the dread I usually felt at events like this.

I'd talked to Peter quietly while Hazel was occupied with guests arriving, and we confirmed the plan to have her parents arrive later. I'd also confirmed all the party details and setup numerous times, so I had little to worry about in terms of logistics. Theoretically.

I talked to Mari for a while before Terry came and stole her away for a dance. I was standing awkwardly (my default pose, really) when I realized I'd erred in not installing potted plants around the perimeter of the space. In romance novels, the ballrooms always featured huge plants for wallflowers to hide behind when the need arose.

Instead, I patted my long hair trailing down my back in a loose, silvery hair tie, wishing I hadn't let Hazel convince me to put it up tonight. If there was ever a time I needed that security blanket, it was tonight.

And then all thoughts vanished.

A man appeared from the crowd, impeccably dressed in a sleek black suit and bowtie. I resisted the urge to wipe my damp hands on my dress.

Jeff was gorgeous. Why had it taken me so long to notice?

You noticed. You just chose to hate him instead.

Did I? Or did his brusque personality just overshadow everything else?

Then again, he made it clear from the start that he disliked me. He might as well have been Mr. Darcy, who famously said, "My good opinion once lost is lost forever."

The moment he spotted me, Jeff's eyes went wide, his pupils growing as he strolled toward me.

Why was he looking at me that way? Did I have lipstick on my teeth?

Or maybe it's that dress. You know you can't pull off a strapless dress. It's even worse than the one your mom saw you wear.

I looked away, my heart sinking as I wished I'd worn the older navy blue dress purchased the last time I was forced to attend a cocktail party. Instead, I'd chosen a strapless, knee-length teal dress that glittered under the soft lighting overhead and swished around my legs as I walked.

Jeff stepped forward, and his mouth moved but produced no sound at first. Finally, he spoke slowly, "You are beautiful."

My eyes widened as I tried to form words. He didn't say I *look* beautiful; he said I *am*. There was a difference.

Stunned, I started to feel a bit dizzy and wobbled in my uncomfortable heels.

"I'll be right back," he said as he pivoted abruptly.

I scanned the area, bewildered as he got lost in the crowd. I decided to stay put; it's not like I had anywhere else to be. Danny was planning to text me when he was almost here in town, and I hadn't heard from him yet. I'd even checked my spam a few times, as I didn't have his number yet. I'd merely given him my address and phone number yesterday, forgetting that I didn't have his, since we'd always chatted in the gaming site chat rather than through SMS. We hadn't even exchanged real names yet! I wasn't even sure why. In any case, he'd warned me this morning that he might be late.

Within a minute, Jeff returned with a glass of ice water and handed it to me.

Conscious of his eyes locked on me, I drank quickly and then handed the empty glass back to him. "Thanks. That was thoughtful of you."

"You're welcome."

OK, time for small talk. Quite possibly the worst invention ever. "So, what do you think of the venue? I know it's not as fancy as the resort ballroom, but you know Hazel *insisted* we find a different venue so we could make it her own. And I quite like it, actually."

"It looks nice. Elegant but also whimsical. Like Hazel."

I nodded as my eyes swept the room, which we'd decorated with hundreds of hanging candelabra and floating lanterns above us. "I agree."

He looked out at the crowd and then turned to me and stuck out his hand. "Dance with me, Roxy?"

With my lips parted in shock, I stared into his deep, expressive hazel eyes. *Expressive?* My heart skipped a beat. I'd never seen such feeling in him—a softness and even vulnerability. I swallowed and nodded, placing my hand in his. I felt a surge of electricity as the room narrowed to just him and me. Our eyes were locked as he led me onto the dance floor, and suddenly, only he and I were in the room.

"Oh, uh, it seems they've put on a slow dance now. We don't have to …"

He simply spun me around and wrapped his hand around my shoulder. He left a respectable distance between us, but it still felt too close.

And not close enough.

I hadn't even drunk any champagne yet, but my head felt like it weighed nothing as he whirled me around with ease.

"You're a good dancer, Jeffrey," I said, aiming for a light tone.

His hand noticeably tightened on my waist. "Thanks. So are you."

"You are a man of few words, aren't you?" I said when the music slowed down even more.

His eyes looked darker than usual, and he leaned in to speak softly into my ear. "Maybe talking is overrated."

I gasped and pulled back to see his face. His lips were

parted slightly, and his eyes hooded. I breathed in his woodsy cologne lightly. "What would you prefer then?"

His eyes danced in the lower ballroom lighting as he squeezed our joined hands lightly. "Do you really want to know?"

Mesmerized, I felt my head bob up and down. "Yes, please."

"So polite," he said, dipping his head a bit. "May I confess something, Roxy?" He watched intently as I nodded again and took several shallow breaths while forcing my feet to keep moving. "My thoughts right now aren't so polite," he said, his voice barely above a whisper.

I swallowed hard as I felt him tug me closer, ever so slowly. "Well, that's … I guess that's OK."

He chuckled softly. "So it won't surprise you if I kiss you at midnight?"

I stared up at this man, shock coursing through me along with … something else. My field of vision had narrowed to him. Him alone. "Yes," I heard myself say in a breathy tone that sounded nothing like me. "I mean, no. It won't surprise me."

His eyes were nearly as dark as his suit now as he smiled briefly and looked down at my mouth. "Or how about now?"

"Now? In front of—people?" I had a fleeting thought about Danny arriving and seeing me with Jeff. *But he was running late anyway*, I reminded myself as my heart pounded in my chest.

Jeff's shoulders lifted as he smiled faintly. "It's only me and you. Let the rest fall away."

All thought suspended, I felt my mouth form a smile. "I already have—" I started to whisper. And then he was leaning forward, and I forgot whatever I wanted to say.

His lips lightly brushed my forehead first and then my temple before descending to my lips. His mouth moved over mine, feather-light at first. The flutter gave way to a soft, warm pressure that I hoped would never end.

It was probably half a minute at most, but it felt like half a lifetime. *I was meant to kiss this man,* I thought hazily.

But far too quickly, he pulled back, his hands slowly falling away from my cheeks and landing on my shoulders for a moment before resuming their former position as his feet started sweeping the floor again.

I hadn't even realized we'd stopped dancing.

As he whirled me around the room again, I realized the song was no longer a slow one, but we still danced close, taking slow steps around the other dancers.

Still buzzing with sensation from head to toe, I murmured, "That was ... I don't even have words."

He flashed a wide smile that looked so odd on him but also so *right*. Our eyes remained locked. "I like you too, Roxy."

I swallowed and struggled to regain my senses. "I—I always thought you hated me. But lately, everything I thought I knew ..." I shook my head. "Who *are* you?"

The lingering smile faded, and I watched his Adam's apple bob as he swallowed hard. "It's the opposite of hate, Roxy." And then he pulled me close and whispered into my ear, "I'm already half in love with you, Mindy."

My heart raced at his words. The kind of words I never thought I'd hear from a man. The words I never thought a man would *want* to say to me. I held my breath, studying his earnest face.

Wait.

I froze, the room suddenly starting to spin.

Had he called me *Mindy*?

I retreated and looked up, searching his face for answers. I might have imagined it. I must have. "Wha–what did you call me, Jeff?"

His eyes were unreadable but never veered from mine. "Mindy," he said softly.

My body was immobile except for my hands falling away from his shoulders. My mouth moved but refused to produce any words as my pulse jumped and breathing became more difficult.

I knew the answer already.

I *knew*.

But I heard myself asking, "Why—why are you calling me that?"

He breathed deeply, still staring into my eyes but not smiling. "Mindy, it's me."

"Danny?" I whispered so softly he couldn't have heard me, but he could read it on my lips.

He nodded once and reached out to take my hand.

"But ... how could this be?"

It couldn't be.

Could it?

"You're Danny?"

"Also known as CastGamer55," he said, squeezing my hand.

"*You* are the guy I've been talking to almost every day for *months*? *You*?"

Uncertainty clouded his face. "Are you disappointed?"

I shook my head. "None of this makes sense. You can't be—you can't. And yet here you are, and he's not." My voice reached a higher pitch. "I don't understand how this is possible. If you're Danny, that would mean ..." I trailed off, staring into his handsome face and seeing it anew. A cold shiver ran down my spine as I glanced down at our joined hands. "You knew."

He nodded and squeezed my hand again.

"Why didn't you tell me?" I asked, anguish seeping into my tone. I dropped his hand as if scalded and stepped back. "Is this some kind of trick? Oh, look, Roxy's such a fool as usual."

His eyebrows lifted as he shook his head rapidly. "No, it's not like that. I wanted to ... I wasn't sure how I felt until a couple of months ago and then—"

My eyes flashed. "You've known for *months*? Or did you somehow plan this? Have you known all along?"

His jaw tensed. "Only since November."

I gasped. "Before Thanksgiving?"

"Yes."

My mouth hung open for a long moment before I pressed my lips together and asked in a low voice, "Why didn't you tell me?"

"Initially, I was in shock." He rubbed his jaw. "I wasn't sure what I felt or what to do about it."

My lips were set in a thin line. "But you ultimately decided the best decision was to *lie to me*."

He frowned. "I wouldn't say that. It was—"

"Just stop," I said, shaking my head as my body raged with mortification and fury. "What an idiot you must think I am. An utter fool."

He placed his hand on my arm, but I shook it off. The frown lines on his face deepened. "Not at all. I thought I made my feelings clear earlier—"

I scoffed. "For all I know, you like to date girls who are stupid fools. How would I know? I don't know you at all, do I?" My voice was shaking as I spoke, but for once, I didn't care.

His eyes shuttered as his jaw tensed, but he said nothing.

Despite the humiliation coming in stronger waves now, I mustered as much anger and scorn as I could while glaring at him and then turned on my heel and speed-walked away. Jeff didn't deserve to see the devastation setting fire within me and the betrayal threatening to consume me.

I heard my name once or twice as he followed, but he lost me in the crowd as I found my way outside, just before the hot, angry tears started to fall.

Chapter 26

I'd dealt with a lot of mortification, shame, sadness, and a host of other negative emotions in my life, more than my fair share. But nothing had prepared me for this level of devastation and heartbreak—not even the wretched guy from college who'd broken my heart. I hadn't loved him. Maybe, in hindsight, I hadn't even liked him that much. But Jeff ... Danny ... the pain was unbearable.

I had trusted them. Him.

When Hazel and then Mari called me on New Year's Day, I put on the best performance of my life. I assured them I was fine. Better than fine. After all, I reminded them, I usually loved spending the holiday setting New Year's resolutions—at least that wasn't a lie. And then I turned my phone off for the rest of the hazy week that I spent mostly in bed, with tears and makeup residue streaked on the pillow and hair matted to my face. After eating my weight in corn chips one night while furiously swatting at the tears still pooling in my eyes, I thought about cutting my hair off, but I was too lazy to go find scissors. Being the cliché I was, I returned to bed and tried to shut out the voices in my head replaying all my interactions with CastGamer55, especially since November.

I'd actually made it to the couch today and just finished spooning the last bit of Nutella out of the jar when the doorbell rang.

Instinctively, I pulled the covers over my head. Whoever it was could go away.

What if ...

No, he wouldn't come here, would he?

I shook my head, knowing I wouldn't answer the door anyway.

But the ringing turned into light knocking and then heavier knocking.

And because the walls were not thick in this building, I heard, "Roxy, we know you're in there! Open up!"

Relief flooded my body, along with something I didn't want to identify.

It wasn't Jeff.

I threw off the blanket and tried to sit up, my limbs achy from lack of use lately. If I knew Hazel, she wouldn't give up easily.

"Roxy, please!" another voice called out, accompanied by more knocking.

Neither would Mariana.

I groaned, rising to my feet as I pushed the hair out of my face. I headed a bit closer to the door. "Hold on," I said, my voice slightly hoarse.

"We brought cheesecake! Just let us in," Hazel pleaded. "Roxy, please."

I closed my eyes, willing myself to be calm as I walked over to the door.

After unlocking it, I opened it just an inch, wincing when I saw their worried faces. "I need to freshen up. Can you wait a bit?"

Hazel scoffed. "Just open up."

My lips rounded in horror. "No, I'm ... not presentable."

She shook her head in exasperation. "We don't care."

"Well, I do," I said irritably.

Mari leaned closer to the door. "Roxy, maybe you could let us in, and we'll wait while you freshen up?"

Everything in me wanted to say no and slam the door. I closed the door and leaned my forehead against it briefly before pulling it open fully and then dashing away before they could see what I mess I was.

"Roxy?" Hazel called out.

"I'll be back in a minute," I said right before closing the bathroom door.

I placed my hands on the counter, avoiding the mirror, and counted to ten.

I could do this.

I could.

I picked up my hairbrush and started combing through the tangles before my eyes finally met my own in the mirror. I nearly dropped the brush when I saw the ghastly reflection. It was even worse than I thought. My cheeks were pale except for the messy dark stains, likely the remnants of my eye makeup from the party that I'd never washed off and instead just half-rubbed off on my pillow. I put the brush down immediately and dipped my face down toward the sink to scrub it off as quickly as I could. My face had pink blotchy spots when I finished, but at least it was better than week-old makeup. My hair was still a knotted mess, and I briefly considered pulling it into a ponytail or bun. But my hair was a security blanket—a poor one, but one of the few I had. I sprayed in some dry shampoo before it ran out because, of course, I'd forgotten to buy more, and then I brushed as best I could. After spritzing myself with rose-scented body spray and brushing my teeth in record time, I took a deep breath, ready to face these women whose opinions I cared about far too much.

Well, as ready as I'd ever be.

I stepped out of the bathroom hesitantly, feeling a bit more alert. But the sinking feeling returned as I took in the messes very visible in the kitchen and living room.

"Sorry to make you wait," I said with a faux cheerful tone that wasn't going to fool anyone. "How are you doing?"

"We're worried about you," Hazel said plainly. "Obviously."

"Oh, me?" I forced a laugh. "I'm fine. I was slacking a bit on cleaning, but you know, um, I was getting ready to start before I heard you knocking."

Hazel narrowed her eyes. "Right. Just slacking a bit."

"I'm not the best when it comes to cleaning."

"Or showering?" she asked with a raised eyebrow.

My jaw clenched as I tried to think of how to respond to her bluntness. "It's nothing."

The long silence was tense as I tried to breathe in and out normally.

"Roxy, you haven't been taking care of yourself. Your phone has been off all week. We're here because we care about you," Mari said firmly.

I exhaled slowly. "I just—it's not as bad as it looks."

"We've all been there, Rox," Hazel said, gentler this time. "Everyone has had rough weeks. Or terrible ones. You're not alone."

I swallowed with some effort. "I know."

"Do you?"

Nodding slowly, I replied, "I guess in theory." I let out a long exhale. "I'm sorry I lied to you. I wasn't fine, like I told you earlier this week. Or was it last week? I can't even keep track."

"Oh, we knew you weren't fine," Hazel said.

My eyebrows rose. "You did? How?"

"Maybe you're not as good an actor as you think," Hazel said, and then she bit her lip. "That was blunt, sorry." She proceeded to clear some of the clutter from my dining table and chairs before ushering us over to sit down. Mortification sunk in again as I realized the couch was probably too messy—too far gone, just like I was.

"The point is," Mari added, "you don't need to act at all. You can just be yourself."

I scoffed and then laughed weakly.

"I say this from experience," Mari said quietly. "The idea seemed so crazy to me at first too. Why would anyone want to know the real me? The real Mariana was a poor, heartbroken little girl who lived in squalor and was ridiculed for her poverty, who lost her father and then struggled through foster care, who stupidly gave her heart to a boy who didn't seem to deserve it.

Who in their right mind would want *that*?"

I blinked several times, trying to process this. "Mariana, I knew you had a hard childhood, but I never knew about all of that. What incredible strength and—and *bravery* you have had." I felt my eyes start to sting, threatening tears.

Hazel looked at Mariana for a moment and then turned to me. "Listen to me, Roxy. You have to believe me, all right?" I stared at her blankly. "You promise?"

"Fine," I mumbled.

She took my hand. "You have that too. The strength. The courage. It's there inside you."

"Probably more than me," Mari admitted with a soft smile. "You just don't know it."

My eyes searched the floor. "If you really knew me …"

"We do know you, Roxy. We know you're an amazing person who battles some difficult things, and yet you get up and try again every day. You never give up."

"Isn't avoidance, like running away from parties, a means of giving up?" I asked.

Hazel shook her head. "I don't think so. I think it's a means of coping and self-preservation. And what's more important than that? Not much. Despite what society would have us believe."

I started shaking my head but then nodded. "I would argue with you, but … it's exactly what I used to tell my clients. I know, intellectually, that you're right."

"Rox, can I ask … you rarely talk about your original career in mental health. What's that about?" Hazel's expression was friendly, even though her question felt threatening.

I took a deep breath and hoped my face wasn't beet red.

One word.

"Shame."

Mari nodded, and Hazel widened her eyes in understanding.

"Before you urge me to seek counseling, you know I already know what a counselor would say. And I know, I know, knowing isn't the same as doing. But it's just not ... for me." I winced, knowing this made no sense.

"Can we just ask you to think about it? You can decide against it," Mari said hesitantly. "But just give it some thought."

I fought against the urge to immediately say no and make up an excuse for them to leave. "I guess so."

Suddenly, both of them were coming closer to give me a hug.

I froze and fought the urge to slip out of their embraces or push them away.

Hazel stepped back and laughed. "Not a fan of hugs, huh?"

"Sorry, I've just never been into hugs. Yet ... this didn't feel terrible." They eyed each other briefly. "And by the way, I don't know where my filter is today. I guess I lost it in this mess of a nightmare week," I looked up and tried to smile.

"Or maybe, deep down, you're realizing we are your friends, and we want to know *you*." Hazel tilted her head. "Could that be it?"

My brow furrowed as I tried to process this. "I'm confused, but—"

I gasped as I looked down at Hazel's hand. I pointed to her ring finger. "Is that what it looks like?"

Hazel beamed as she held out her hand to examine. "It is. Peter asked me to marry him at the party."

I smiled, but only briefly. "Wait, the New Year's party? Oh no, did my argument with—uh, did I ruin it? I'm so sorry I missed it."

Hazel was still smiling. "Do I look like someone whose engagement was ruined? No, I'm deliriously happy. I thought it would take Peter a lot longer to work up the nerve."

Mari pointed a thumb at Hazel. "It's true. She's been talking about it nonstop." She paused a moment and then looked me square in the eye. "Are you going to tell us what's going on with you and Jeff?"

"*Nothing!*" I cried. At their surprised faces, I lowered my voice. "Sorry. Nothing is going on."

Mari leaned in. "But something *was* going on, right?"

"I mean, we all saw you kiss him," Hazel said with a grin.

I scoffed. "No, *he* kissed *me*—you know what? It doesn't matter. It was nothing."

"Remember the whole we're-your-friends thing?" Hazel prodded.

I let my face fall into my hands for a long moment.

"Fine, there might have been something. But it won't become anything."

"Because it's nothing?" Mari asked.

"Right."

"You're here exhibiting a classic case of rom-com heartbreak, looking as though you spent an entire week in your bedroom. All for nothing?"

I sighed. "That's not—it's not about romance. It's just—he lied. I'm an idiot. And I can't ever face him again."

Both women frowned as they studied me, and I fought the urge to look away. Finally, Mari said, "I don't think you can avoid each other forever. Even if you didn't both work for us, you know how small this town is."

I inhaled sharply. "You said 'avoid each other'—do you mean *he's* avoiding *me* too?"

Hazel threw up her hands. "I don't know. He's impossible to read and obviously didn't tell us a darn thing. But he's been working from home all week. And when we asked him to pass along a message to you, he made up some weird excuses."

"Not like him at all," Mari said with a shrug. "But you know that, Roxy."

What did that mean?

Was he angry with me for some reason? Was he embarrassed? Was he—

You need to stop.

I took a few steadying breaths. "Well, speaking of work, thank you for giving me the time off. What's next week's schedule look like? I'm sorry I haven't checked my phone or computer for a few days." This was kind of a lie—I hadn't checked it all week, since their last call.

"Don't worry about it. I can manage my own schedule for a week or two." Hazel smiled but then looked down at her nails. "I'm actually thinking of hiring an assistant."

My heart thudded in my chest. "What? *My job?*"

She shrugged. "You don't really want to be my assistant."

"I—I do. I ... enjoy the job," I sputtered. "It's a privilege."

Hazel rolled her eyes. "You don't love it. I can tell. Everyone can."

Was it true? Was I doing a job I didn't enjoy?

I bit my lip. "Well, even if that's true ... not everyone loves their job. Many people don't. But they're fine with that."

"Sure, plenty of people find fulfillment in things other than their job, Roxy. But I see ... there's a longing I sometimes see in your eyes. The closer we came to opening the new wellness center, the more I saw it. You want to be involved but aren't sure how."

My lips wobbled as I tried to speak. "Oh, I don't know. You might be reading into things."

Mari chimed in, "Hazel's usually a pretty good judge of people, actually. Well, except her fiancé when they first met, but love makes idiots of us all." She smirked in Hazel's direction.

"Can I share an idea I had?" Hazel asked carefully. "You don't have to say yes, of course."

Hesitation was probably written all over my face and tightly clasped hands at that point, but I nodded.

"I've been thinking I'd like to hire an expert advisor. A staff psychologist, if you will. As you know, I'm working toward my master's and licensed counselor credentials. I could really use someone like you to serve as the on-staff psychologist. You wouldn't have to see patients at all. I would just consult with you as needed, and you'd give professional input when I need to make important decisions about a patient or even about the business." She grinned. "I can't think of anyone more perfect for this role."

My voice shook. "I—I am flattered. I fear I would

disappoint you though."

"You wouldn't. You *can* say no, but please don't decline because you think you'd disappoint me. That's not possible."

I didn't think I had much emotion left to feel or tears to spill at that point, but once again, I was wrong. My heart started pounding in my chest as I tried to wrestle with everything she'd said—everything both of them had said. "I'm—this is—"

"Roxy, you look overwhelmed," Mari said, stopping when she saw me flinch. "That's understandable! You don't need to give an answer immediately, right, Hazel?"

Hazel shook her head. "Of course not."

"OK, so I can think about it?"

"Of course. Sorry if I made you feel otherwise. I get overly excited sometimes," Hazel said with a smile. "Take all the time you need!

Mari smiled widely too. "And if you decide you're not interested in this offer, you can use us to bounce ideas off."

Before I could try to process this dizzying conversation, Hazel suddenly sat up straighter with a twinkle in her eye. "Should we go get the cheesecake I put in the freezer?"

I raised my eyebrows. "The freezer?"

"Everyone knows that cheesecake is best frozen. Like ice cream."

Mari shook her head and smiled. "Not everyone knows that, Haz. But I think we should maybe cook some lunch first."

"Oh, no, I'm not hungry," I protested.

"Have you eaten any meals at all this week?" she asked.

I opened my mouth to respond, but the words didn't come. Fritos and chocolate probably didn't count as meals—nor did cups of white and brown sugar mixed with butter, when I'd run out of packaged sweets. Now I was almost out of sugar too.

Mari nodded and rose to her feet. "That's what I thought. I'll go see if you have any scraps of real food in your kitchen and whip something up."

Before I could protest further though, she'd walked away, and Hazel placed a gentle hand on my shoulder. "Friends take care of each other, Rox. If you want to have an epic sob-fest, we'll sob with you. If you want to forget all this and watch movies all day, we'll be here."

"That's ... I don't know what to say," I managed.

"Let us see you, Roxy."

I looked up through a veil of tears. "I haven't had ... this is going to sound pathetic, but I haven't had many close friends in my life. Well, other than Julia, but we've rarely seen each other since college. She's in England right now."

Hazel nodded sympathetically. "It's not easy to keep up a close friendship from such a long distance."

"It's not."

"It's easier to maintain the facade that you're mostly fine, right? Have you even talked to her this week?"

I hung my head in shame. "No."

"Hey, chin up," she said. "Friends don't let friends mope alone. Deal?"

Chapter 27

Although Hazel and Mari convinced me to shower and rejoin the world, I still felt stuck and numb and lost and a host of other emotions I'd never been good at handling.

What would I do now? I'd reluctantly agreed to let Hazel hire a new assistant. So the very next day, after an excessively long night of sleep, I turned on my phone. I cleared all my notifications without reading them—I didn't need to heap on more guilt—and proceeded to write my job description on my phone. This productivity provided a momentary boost in my mood, but by evening, I was restless again.

My computer beckoned, but I was determined to resist any chance of seeing Jeff online. Or even being reminded of our shared interests, the game we'd spent hundreds of hours planning and talking about, our many personal conversations, and ... all the feelings. Attraction. Hope. Betrayal. Disappointment. Humiliation.

I tried to imagine what I'd tell a therapy client in my situation. I might tell them to look into hobbies, reading, yoga, exercise, journaling ... all the things I had zero interest in right now.

After another full day of twiddling my thumbs, I finally decided to get out of the house. My fridge and pantry were nearly empty, I was sick of ordering crappy delivery food, and a walk to the store would be good for my body and my mind. Or so they always said.

But the problem was ... Jeff lived a block away. I couldn't face him, knowing what a complete fool I'd been. I probably couldn't avoid him forever, but I'd try as long as I could. As a disguise, I wore large sunglasses and stuffed my telltale long, dark hair under a thick hat and coat.

The first time I ventured out, I didn't see him. And I realized the fresh air and movement were exactly what I needed. Granted, it was *freezing* fresh air, but nevertheless, this was the best I'd felt all week. So I resolved to start a daily walking ritual, which I'd attempted before but never in the dead of winter. I was motivated.

It was only day two of my new walking regimen when I spotted him across the street.

My pleasantly heightened heart rate turned into a stampede pounding into my chest as I dashed the last twenty steps to my apartment building. I pulled open the heavy door that led inside.

I stood inside, staring through the fogged-up window between the front door and the mailboxes. He was now facing my apartment building and—

Oh, no. *No.*

He was starting to cross the street!

I fled, panic flooding my veins as I rushed out of the entryway and into the hallway leading to my apartment. Halfway down the hall, I was out of breath and didn't see my neighbor Jenna until she was right in front of me.

"Roxy! I haven't seen you in forever. We should catch up. I have to—"

"Sorry, Jenna, I have to go," I rushed out the words as I pushed past her down the hallway and then unlocked my apartment with shaky hands.

Before opening the door, I glanced backward and saw Jenna still standing and watching me, looking crestfallen. I opened my mouth to apologize, but she turned on her heel and walked away.

Swallowing the bitter taste in my throat, I squeezed my eyes shut to block out the shame as I pushed the door open and took heavy steps inside. I quickly slammed the door shut and put the deadbolt on.

I leaned against the door for a moment, panting, and then threw off my winter coat and gear. I was still hot, my heart still racing, my breaths still coming short, so I removed most of my clothing and ambled over to the bathroom.

Throwing off the rest of my clothes, I avoided the mirror and climbed into the bathtub. The heat in my body turned to a bone-chilling cold as I wrapped my arms around my shaking knees and finally turned on the tub faucet.

What a coward I was.

Even worse, I was a jerk.

Being a coward was nothing new for me, but I genuinely tried not to *ever* be a jerk. My empathy had initially drawn me to the mental health profession, but eventually, it became a hindrance. I couldn't cope. I hated the thought that I couldn't always help someone. And I never, ever wanted to be the cause of someone else's pain. But Jenna's face ...

And Jeff. Had he planned to approach me? Was he, even now, pounding on the door? I couldn't hear anything beyond the rushing hot water filling the tub.

That's when I noticed the water was about to spill over the edges. I quickly switched off the faucet and pulled out the drain plug.

When the water returned to a normal level, I replaced the plug and leaned back.

I waited to hear the sound of him knocking or ringing the doorbell, but all I heard was blissful silence.

Except ... it wasn't that blissful.

Especially when the heat in the water dissipated.

And then I was left with cold water, and a heart that was anything but.

I gripped the edges of the tub, the loneliness becoming a physical ache.

Was *this* really my life?

My one life. The only one I had.

And here I was, hiding in a bathtub, shivering and fighting

back tears from eyes that burned from sobbing every day for the last ten days.

I pushed everyone away. Everyone. Even the people who, for some reason, were determined to be in my life—they would eventually give up. Because I'd keep pushing them away too. Because that's what I did.

I breathed in and out unsteadily, rocking back and forth as I hugged my knees again.

You're being overly dramatic.
You don't need other people.
"No," I whispered.
You can just set another silly New Year's resolution.
"No."
You're better off staying—
I screamed, over and over again, "No!"
There you go again, being too dramatic. As if your life is so hard.
"Shut up."

And that internal voice—the one that had always reminded me I was worthless—didn't stop.

At first.

But I kept shouting back. Again and again until …

All was quiet.

Inside and out.

Peace.

With my limbs shaking but feeling lighter, I stood up slowly and grabbed a towel.

"Finally," I whispered.

Chapter 28

I sighed while spinning around in the cushy black leather chair I'd hand-selected for the individual offices. "I really am sorry. I didn't think."

Julia was silent for a moment on the other end of the phone line. "I know you are, Roxy. Just don't disappear again without a little warning. Just a 'hey, I need some time to just sulk and pine for my lost love while foregoing all life tasks, including communicating with my best friend'—that would be enough. I just want to know you're OK."

The hurt in her voice gutted me. "You're right. I'm so sorry. I never meant to hurt you. And if I'm ever in that awful state again, I promise I'll do my best to reach out," I promised her. "Thank you for listening to my literal sob story. Wait, actually ... there is one more thing. I've finally decided ... I made a belated New Year's resolution to ... Oh, Julia, I don't know why this is so hard to say." I paused and cleared my throat. "I–I'm going to get help. I already called this morning and set up an appointment with a therapist, and I'm going to try that meetup group again. I'm tired of living like this."

Again, she was silent. "Wow. I'm so proud of you, Roxy."

"Thank you. It was honestly pretty scary making that call."

"Of course it was. I hope it helps," she said quietly. "I wish ..."

"What do you wish?"

"I wish I could do the same. Therapy just doesn't work for me."

"Or maybe you've just never been truly ready," I suggested. "And that's OK."

After a long pause, she spoke in a more cheerful tone. "Thanks. Yeah, I'm too busy right now anyway. My eyes are so sore every night from studying constantly. Hey, speaking of exhaustion, I should probably let you go soon. It's getting late here."

"Sure, you go get some rest. And thanks for being the best friend a shy girl could ever have." I smiled, even though she couldn't see me. "I'm so lucky."

"Right back at you. Love you, Rox."

"You too." I ended the call and looked around the room for at least the twentieth time today.

As soon as I accepted her job offer this morning in person, Hazel had been generous and offered me the second-best office, right next to hers. This was the first day of the rest of my life, and I felt both nervous and excited. I honestly wasn't sure if I could cope with working in this field again, but Hazel reminded me I would never know if I didn't try.

My eyes drifted toward the open window from this office into the rest of the suite and landed on a curious sight. A woman was standing at the front desk with something wriggling in her arms. Was that a *puppy*?

I rose and walked over to the closed door. Opening it hesitantly, I immediately heard panting, and the woman laughed as she leaned on the reception desk.

"Hi, may I help you? I think our receptionist is at lunch. Do you have an appointment with Hazel?" I stared at her adorable little gray and white puppy, whose eyes were round as they stared up at me. "He is adorable."

The woman smiled as she smoothed her dark, wavy hair behind her ear. Her eyes were a rich hazel, which caused a sharp pang in my chest that I was not prepared for. I inhaled and exhaled deeply and focused on smiling politely.

"I'm looking for Roxy, actually. Do you know where I can find her?"

"Oh!" I exclaimed, my eyes widening. "You've found her. I mean, I'm her. I'm me. Ah …"

Her smile brightened as she rubbed the dog's floppy ears. "It is so amazing to meet you, Roxy! I heard I could find you here."

My brows scrunched together. "You did? That's … interesting. I only joined the permanent staff today."

Her eyes twinkled as she stuck out her hand to shake mine. "I'm Abby." She paused and watched me closely, but I only smiled politely. "Chamberlain."

My jaw dropped as I let go of her hand. "You're …"

"Jeff's my big brother."

I stood speechless, eyeing her more intently. Those eyes. They were exactly like Jeff's. And the hair, the facial features …

"I can't believe I didn't see the resemblance immediately," I said softly. "Wow. You're here visiting him, I guess? I mean, yes, of course you must be."

She nodded. "Can we go sit down? Or can you go have coffee?"

"Um, I'm not sure the nearest coffee shop allows dogs." I bit my lip. "Do you want to come chat in my office?"

Why was I inviting her into my office? I should be immediately inventing an excuse—somewhere I had to be, an appointment I was late to, a conference call.

I forced myself to stop that train of thought in its tracks.

Breathing in steadily and then exhaling slowly, I reminded myself that I didn't need to invent excuses anymore. I could just … be me. As crazy as that sounded.

Abby nodded, still smiling. "Yeah, it's totally not fair that adorable puppies aren't allowed everywhere. We have that same problem in Duluth."

"Oh, you're from Duluth?" I asked while leading her into my office and pulling up a chair for her.

"We're from Superior, but I live in Duluth now."

"Oh, I'm jealous. I went there once on a business trip, and it was so beautiful. Then again, those massive hills must be treacherous in the winter."

She laughed. "Seriously. You can't even imagine. I wish I could fly south for the winter."

"But it's worth it to live there, right? I would just love living so close to the lake. Any lake."

She frowned. "Isn't there a nice big lake over by that resort where Jeff works?"

"There is. Obviously nothing comparable to Lake Superior, but still gorgeous in the summer and even in winter. Don't even get me started on the fall." I smiled.

Her beautiful eyes were round as she asked, "Why don't you find a house or apartment on the lake?"

I tapped my chin with my finger as I pondered this. The thought had never crossed my mind, probably because I wasn't a big fan of change. "I don't know, actually. That's a good question. I do know there are some cozy little houses to rent on one side."

She smiled and nodded.

"But you're not here to talk about lakeside homes, are you?" I asked wryly.

She grinned. "Obviously not." After placing the eager puppy on the floor to explore the room, she leaned forward in her seat. "So, let's get to it. Why don't you want to live happily ever after with my amazing brother?"

My eyebrows rose, and I nearly laughed. "He didn't tell me you were so, um, direct."

"I think he believes that I reserve my bluntness just for him. But he's wrong, as is often the case." She laughed and sat back. "Are you going to forgive him or not?"

My lips parted to speak, but the words died in my throat. I couldn't tell this woman I'd never forgive Jeff. Though it was probably true, I didn't want to hurt her. She obviously adored him.

"You're trying to find a nice way to say no, aren't you?" she asked with one raised eyebrow.

I couldn't help smiling. "I like your directness, actually. I've spent so much of my life trying to guess what other people were thinking, usually assuming they were judging me. But with you ..."

"With me, you *know* I'm judging you?" She laughed. "Well, I am."

"Abby ..." I cleared my throat, reminding myself to be honest. Be *me*. "I don't know if I could forgive him even if I want to. I'm sorry it's not what you want to hear."

Her expression was skeptical. "What's not to love? He's the best." Her face sobered. "Growing up, he was everything. I looked up to him, and he took care of me. And he's still everything I could ever want in a big brother and so much more. There's no one better, you know." Before I could interject, she added, "And it's not just because he's my brother. He's a wonderful person with a big heart, even though he tries so hard to hide it. And he would hate that I'm here."

My jaw dropped again. "He doesn't know? I thought ..."

"No, he didn't send me." Seeing my frown, she added, "But only because he has too much pride. He's over the moon for you, Roxy. You know that, right?"

My brow furrowed. "Well, I don't know about that. We might have had something, but it was never—you know what, it doesn't matter now."

"I know he hurt you," Abby said quietly. "And I can imagine how you felt as a result. I've been hurt before too." She stopped to pick up the puppy again as he started to yelp at her feet. "But the difference is that the guy who hurt *me* was never worth my time. He wasn't a good guy, but he was good at fooling people, including me and my friend Annalise, who he was also seeing. With my brother, it's the opposite."

"You dated a guy who was also dating your friend? How—"

"No, no. Annalise and I met and became friends *after* we both realized what he was doing. She's great. You'd love her."

I laughed. "You don't even know me, but you know I'd love her?" I bit my lip. "That sounded terrible. I didn't mean to be rude—"

"No, it's cool. I like blunt people. But I feel like I do know you because of how much he's talked about you for months now. Actually, probably a few years," she said casually, looking around the room. A giggle slipped out. "Oops, I probably wasn't supposed to say that. Or be here at all. But Jeff's helped me so much in my life that I owe him so much. The least I can do is fix his love life."

I swiveled around slowly in my chair. "I'm not sure if it can be fixed. But I appreciate that you're a loving sister trying to take care of a big brother who's always looked out for her. I love that you two are so close. He—he needs someone he can be close to."

"I agree, he does." Abby raised her eyebrows and tilted her head forward.

I sighed. "Well, at least we agree on that."

"Do you love him?" she asked while slowly petting the sleepy puppy in her arms.

My breath caught, and I folded and unfolded my hands. I'd tried not to think about that as I attempted to come to terms with the lost chances we had. "I—I don't know."

She studied me intently and then finally nodded. "Fair enough. When you realize he's worth giving another chance, you know where to find us."

As she stood up, I struggled with words. "I don't know if he wants ... he and I just ... the night we—" I groaned and shook my head. "I don't know what to say."

"It's OK, Roxy. Take some time to think. A good relationship is worth waiting for."

I tried to smile but probably failed miserably. "How long are you in town?"

"Just until Saturday. I wish I could stay through Sunday so Lila and I can have more adventures, but my roommate needs me back so we—never mind. It's not important. Lila and I had a great day yesterday at that indoor water park just east of here. I couldn't believe she'd never been there before."

"Ah, well I'm glad she got the opportunity." I cleared my throat and forced a smile. "All right, I'm sure you have ... a lot to do. I hope you enjoy your vacation!"

"I'd enjoy it a lot more if you forgave Jeff," she said, nudging me in the elbow. "I'm joking, mostly. You have to figure out what you want. If that's not my brother, fine. But if it *is*, don't let him slip away. We all make mistakes. Constantly. And people hurt each other sometimes. But occasionally, people are worth all of it."

"Why?" I asked shakily. "Why are they worth it?"

"Because that person might be the one."

"As in ... *the* one?"

Abby smiled. "You understand now, don't you?"

As soon as she left, I slumped in the chair as my mind turned over the words over and over again.

The one.

Chapter 29

The sun was starting to set in the sky as I walked home from work the next day. I stared upward at the layers of pink, purple, and orange that celebrated the brilliance of nature, the last breaths of the day. It was the perfect time to walk home, actually.

"Roxanne."

I stiffened and nearly slipped on the icy sidewalk as Jeff rounded the corner toward me. After some momentary thoughts about running away (and probably falling on my face), I breathed in the cold air and let it out slowly.

"Hi," I said as we studied each other, a few feet away. He looked handsome as always, but there was something different about his expression and his stance. Uncertainty wasn't something he wore easily.

"Hi."

"So we're back to Roxanne." And even though I wasn't even speaking to him anymore, somehow that hurt. Deeply.

He tilted his head and squinted as if confused. "I just think the name Roxanne is beautiful." Then he added, "So is Roxy." Shaking his head, he actually smiled briefly. "What I mean is, hello. How have you been?"

My eyes were glued to his face while attempting to process his words. He called me Roxanne because he thought it was a beautiful name? My knees suddenly felt weak, and I thought for a moment I was in real danger of falling into the massive snowbank next to us. It wouldn't be a soft landing either, as this wasn't fresh, pillowy snow but rather hard and coated in ice.

"Fine," I whispered. "Well, that's not quite true. But you knew that."

He nodded, a flash of pain crossing his face. After making a visible effort to swallow, he pulled something out of his messenger bag and handed it to me. His hand was shaking slightly, but it might've just been the frigid air.

In my hands was a stack of paper stapled together with the words **Sibling Chat** centered at the top. The rest of the page was the text of a chat. "What's this?"

"This is three months' worth of Messenger chats between me and Abby." He looked at the papers and then back up at me, his eyes full of hesitation. "I'm truly sorry. More than you know. I know you're angry that I didn't tell you, and maybe you felt uncomfortable about having shared things with me under somewhat false premises."

"Uncomfortable? Try foolish. Humiliated."

He nodded as his brows lowered further. "Let me be the fool. These chats are yours to read if you want to. You can see who the real fool was."

I quickly wiped away the tear that threatened to escape my lower eyelid. "Jeff, I don't know what to say."

He squeezed my hand. "Remember, this is just a few months of texts. Roxy, I have been in love with you far longer than that. Maybe since the day we met, though I didn't realize it then. You were the woman who rejected a handshake from me when we first met and glared at me every moment since." What he didn't know was that I'd rejected the handshake because my palms were slippery with sweat. The curse of social anxiety. "You never liked me. And I still … I was still intrigued. When Hazel told us we'd have to work together closely, I was actually afraid. I—" He stopped to clear his throat. "I didn't want to fall for you."

I flinched. "Why not?"

"Because I knew …" He trailed off, scratching his neck as he stared at the floor. Finally, he met my eyes, clear and focused. "I knew I'd never get over you."

My heart was about to burst right out of my chest, and I closed my eyes briefly.

When my eyes locked to his again, I said, "I know it too now."

His faint smile disappeared. "You know I'd never get over you?"

"No," I said, a little breathless. "The other way around."

Hope bloomed in his eyes—possibly the most beautiful sight I'd ever witnessed—and he hesitantly reached for my hand. "Can you forgive me, Roxanne?"

I didn't pull my hand away. "Jeffrey ..."

"If you say yes, I promise I'll let you make most of the major decisions in our new board game." He squeezed my hand lightly.

"Hmm. Even the one about the romance arc between players?"

"Even that one," he said with a rare full smile, dimples on full display. "So, what will it be—the mandatory happy ending or not?"

My eyes were surely shining by then as I grinned up at him. "I choose ... the happily ever after."

He stepped toward me and slowly reached up to cup my cheeks. "Roxy, I love you. Will you give us another chance?"

My lips were curved upward as I reached up on tiptoes to kiss him.

Yes, I, Roxy Swan, kissed a man. In public. I *initiated* that.

I began with an awkward peck and then another and another. I pulled back just a couple of inches to look into his eyes. And then I leaned in to kiss him again, or maybe he leaned in first. I didn't know, and I didn't care.

When his lips were fully melded to mine and his hands ran through my hair, I lost the ability to think. There were only his soft, warm lips and mine, meshed together in a fiery dance that starkly contrasted with the freezing winterscape around us.

He pulled back first, holding my upper arms gently. "Roxy, thank you."

"I had no idea you were into me all along," I said in wonder. "None. You hid it very well. Too well."

We both laughed.

Then I took a deep breath and said, "Jeff, thank you for making me want to try again. I … I should have forgiven you immediately. Or maybe I did, but I was so afraid of getting hurt again. Because that seemed inevitable. But I'm trying to trust. Not just you but myself."

He leaned forward to kiss me again and then wrapped me in a long, warm hug that was so amazing it would later make me want to reevaluate whether I liked hugs or not.

I pulled back slowly, placing my hands on the soft fabric of his jacket over his chest. "I was just thinking. My friend Julia would love our game. I bet she'd even have some good ideas. Maybe this grand gesture of yours could include flying her out to me this weekend to celebrate?"

Suddenly, a woman's voice startled me. "That wouldn't be great timing. We already told Lila you'd come to our slumber party on Friday night."

I turned to see Abby grinning ear to ear.

"Were you eavesdropping on us?" Jeff asked, his hands on his hips.

"Hardly at all," she said breezily as she pulled us together into an awkward group hug. "I mean, the outcome was obvious. Both of you lovesick fools."

I turned to the man at my side, touching his shoulder gently as my heart was ready to burst in my chest. "That's a serious accusation. She's calling you a lovesick fool."

He pretended to think about it. "Fine. I'll be a lovesick fool for you, Roxy. Only for you."

Epilogue

Nearly one year later

"I can't handle this, Jeff!" I whispered, gripping his shoulder tightly. "I hate waiting. Just tell me what it is!"

He peered down at me with a quirk of his lips. "They say good things come to those who wait, right?"

"They also say you should create your own destiny," I said with a frown, "and being patient is not part of my destiny."

A laugh erupted from Jeff's smiling lips, and I found myself returning his smile.

He spun me out with his arm outstretched, my shimmery red dress flaring as I twirled out and back toward him, laughter dancing in my eyes. Back in his arms, I gazed up at him and wrapped my hands around the back of his neck.

"Fine, I'll wait a little longer, on one condition."

His right eyebrow rose. "Demanding now, are you?"

"You know I am," I said, a shiver running down my spine as I realized how much more confident I was than the Roxy of one year ago.

Jeff stepped in closer as our feet still moved in time with the slow tune playing distantly, outside our bubble. "I know just what you need," he murmured just a breath away from my ear.

Before I could utter some saucy reply I'd never imagined I was capable of, his lips captured mine as his palms cradled my face. As his lips moved over mine, I let out a sigh of happiness, and I felt his lips form a smile as he continued kissing me gently. When I parted my lips, he accepted the invitation to deepen the kiss.

But before I lost all sense of where we were and why we were here, I gently pulled back. "You know how to stall with me—I'll give you that."

He laughed once again as our feet resumed the rhythm we'd apparently lost during the kiss. As I gazed into his deep hazel eyes, I started to speak but then noticed his eyes veering left.

I shot him a questioning look and swung my head around before nearly tripping on his feet.

My eyes flew back to his in question. He was biting his lip to suppress a smile.

"What—Jeff, did you see her? Is that Julia?"

Before I knew it, my best friend was by our side, enveloping me in a tight hug as I still held Jeff's hand. "Julia, it's been so long. It is so, so good to see you."

Julia laughed and released me. She smiled and nodded at Jeff, who returned the smile.

I glanced up at him in awe. His eyes were sparkling in the dim party lighting, and I gasped. "You invited her ... you arranged for her to be here?"

"I did," he said, his voice low. "A few others too."

I scanned the perimeter of the dance floor, seeing my other friends, Hazel, Peter, Mariana, and Terry, whose arm was supporting his grandmother, Nora. I knew Nora's partner was currently in the hospital, so I hadn't expected her—or Terry for that matter—to show up to the New Year's Eve party tonight. I was startled to see his sister Abby too, with a friend I hadn't met.

My widened eyes softened as they landed on the striking blonde woman on the end.

Jenna.

I swallowed with some difficulty as I bit my lip and looked back at Jeff nervously.

"Julia," I said as my gaze swung to her. "We have so much to catch up on. But can you excuse me for just a moment?"

My best friend nodded, her face shining as she gave Jeff a

conspiratorial glance.

I let go of Jeff's hand and turned to him briefly. "Give me a moment, Jeff. I need to do this alone."

Inhaling deeply, I took careful steps toward my former neighbor. We hadn't spoken since summer. I'd attempted to make amends in the spring, but she had brushed me off—and rightly so. I'd been rude and dismissive to her every time we'd spoken prior to that.

"Jenna, hello," I said with a tentative smile.

She wasn't smiling. "Hi."

I swallowed again, my throat scratchy as I said, "Thank you for—for coming. I … I don't know how Jeff convinced you. But I'm grateful."

She put a well-manicured hand on her hip. "He didn't."

I raised my eyebrows. "Oh. Well, thank you—"

Jenna sighed. "I'm not really into grudges. Such a waste of energy."

I inhaled and exhaled slowly. "Thank you. I need to apologize—"

"Roxy, it's fine."

"I was a jerk to you. You were just trying to be nice and befriend a lonely, anxious woman, and I was totally ungrateful—"

"You don't need to be grateful if someone pays attention to you, Roxy." Her mask of indifference was softening now. "But, yes, you gave me the brush-off a lot. And I didn't understand why, back then."

My mouth opened and then closed.

"When you moved out of our building in the summer, I figured I'd never hear from you again." She paused. "But you kept trying. I got texts, calls, apology notes on my door. That long email telling me about your anxiety. You didn't give up. The thing is … *I'd* given up. I went through some personal stuff with my parents deciding to move into assisted living but then deciding not to, and back and forth. Plus the usual dating drama, which I thought I'd be long done with by the time I hit 45." She shook her head with a rueful smile.

"Oh, I had no idea. I'm so sorry."

"Well, you couldn't have known because I didn't tell you." She offered a half-smile. "Because I was being stubborn and hormonal and, well ... stubborn, mostly."

I nodded, still shocked. "I understand family drama." I took a deep breath, realizing it would probably be a good time to actually open up to show her I'd changed. "My parents and I ... well, it hasn't been smooth sailing for a long time. Maybe ever. But I've been doing therapy to help manage my feelings and reactions. Realizing I didn't need their approval but still trying to find better ways to communicate with them has actually helped, even if we'll never really see eye to eye." I shook my head. "Sorry to go on and on—just trying to say that I can emphasize. Just like friendship, family is important but not always easy. I'm sure your parents are lucky to have you as a daughter helping them out." I offered a shy smile. "And I'd be lucky if you wanted to give this friendship thing another try."

Jenna pursed her lips. "Even though you won't have to see me anymore, since you're living in some cozy little cottage on the lake now and I'm still stuck downtown?"

"Yes, even then. And even if one of us moves away." I looked out of the corner of my eye to see Julia coming to stand beside me.

"Roxy's actually pretty good at long-distance friendship. If you don't mind the occasional ghosting." Julia laughed. "I'm joking. She doesn't do it anymore."

Eyebrows raised, Jenna stuck out her hand. "I'm Jenna. And you are?"

"I'm Julia. Roxy and I go way back, but I've been studying in England so we haven't seen each other." I saw Julia tense her hand after it dropped to her side. It was one of the subtle signs of social anxiety for Julia, who hid her nerves much better than I. "So, Jenna, you're the extroverted neighbor?"

Jenna flashed her perfect white teeth in a smile. "Loud and proud."

We all laughed as Jeff appeared and pulled me into his side.

"You two are adorable, almost nauseously so," Jenna said with a teasing smile, and then her expression became more serious. "Fresh start, Roxy?"

Putting my finger to my lips, I pretended to think about it for a moment. "Um, absolutely. Yes. I am, after all, making a list of New Year's resolutions in my head already." Jenna laughed, while Julia rolled her eyes.

And Jeff ... he planted his warm lips on my temple before asking for another dance.

A Humble Request

Thank you for taking the time to read and review! Even brief reviews mean so much to independent authors.

If you loved this book, please consider leaving a review or rating:
- Amazon
- Goodreads
- BookBub

If you want to get in touch, please email me at *alana@alanahighbury.com*. I'd love to hear from you!

I also love connecting with readers through my newsletter. If you subscribe, you'll get bonus chapters, exclusive access to major news and great deals, and a chance to find out more about author life. Sign up at *https://alanahighbury.com/newsletter*.

Readers, you are my favorite kind of people. Thank you.

Acknowledgements

As my first published romance series comes to a close, I have so many people to thank, but I need to start first with my readers who know what it's like to let anxiety run your life. The character of Roxy is, in so many ways, my most authentic protagonist yet. I drew heavily on my own experiences coping with anxiety and shyness when writing from her perspective, but in the end, this is still fiction. I hope readers who've struggled with anxiety can relate and can feel seen. Anxiety—especially social anxiety—is underrepresented in romance and fiction in general, so my aim was to write a story of love and hope for a woman living with one of the least talked about but most difficult mental health issues I've faced.

I have to thank my supportive team of experts, who always come through for me even when the timeline is bonkers! The all-star team includes my cover designer, Stefanie Fontecha of Beetiful Designs; my PR advisor, Amanda Kerr; my social media marketer, Kristyn Fortner; and my web designer, Emily Rusu. I'm also grateful to the many reviewers, street team members, editors, and other bookish people who've supported me; there are far too many to list, but I appreciate each and every one of you.

I can't forget my fellow indie authors, who are nothing short of brilliant. I love how much we all support and raise each other up instead of competing. I want to give a shout-out especially to indie authors Sara Breaker, Alana Oxford, Amanda Darcy, Harriet Ashford, and Ginny Sterling for inspiring and supporting me and making me laugh (and they're fantastic writers, so please go read ALL their books).

Readers, where to begin? Thanks to you, I've just finished publishing my first romance series. Your support and interest have inspired me in more ways than you can imagine. Being an indie author is basically a full-time job, on top of which many of us (me!) also work full time, raise children, etc. Every kind word from every reader has touched my heart in profound ways.

To my family and friends, thanks for continuing to support me as a writer. I'm still amazed that so many people I know have actually read my books. Thank you, truly. And for my own little family, Mr. Highbury and our beautiful children, you are my everything.

Books In This Series

Love & Holidays

Meet Me On Christmas Eve

A cozy but angsty second-chance romance set at Christmas in a snowy small town

Snowed In On Valentine's Day

An enemies-to-lovers romance with two neighbors stranded together in a snowstorm

Dance With Me On New Year's Eve

An enemies-to-lovers, secret-identity romance where our shy protagonist finds love and a fresh start

About the Author

Alana Highbury is the bestselling author of the holiday romances *Meet Me on Christmas Eve*, *Snowed In on Valentine's Day*, and *Dance with Me on New Year's Eve*. She's also the author of the Austen Inspired series, releasing in 2025. Her novels blend rom-com, contemporary romance, and women's fiction, and she brings two decades of professional experience and a master's in English. When not writing, she's usually found reading, cross stitching, board gaming, or hanging out with her family, which includes a writerly husband, two children, two beautiful, lazy cats, and a feisty cockatiel.

Check out Alana's website at https://alanahighbury.com, or follow her on social media:

https://www.facebook.com/alanahighbury.author

https://www.instagram.com/alanahighbury_author

https://www.goodreads.com/alanahighbury

https://amazon.com/author/alanahighbury

https://www.bookbub.com/authors/alana-highbury

What's Next?

*Stay tuned for the first book in my brand new **Austen Inspired** series, releasing in February 2025.*

Working from home with her best friend Jack down the hall, Viviana Cantwell leads a comfortable life, yet she can't ignore the low hum of anxiety and whispers of self-doubt: *You're in your 30s now. Working a boring job. Still single, living alone in a drab apartment. Your parents and sister have it all—why can't you?*

When a gorgeous, arrogant publishing executive comes to town with his wealthy, charming friend, Viviana sees the answer to all her problems. She can date her dream man and embark upon her dream career: a novel featuring her very own Mr. Darcy should write itself, right?

But falling for her best friend instead doesn't fit into her plan—or her book plot. Plagued with confusing feelings about Jack, heaps of self-doubt, and constantly flawed assumptions about everyone, she clings to the one thing that's always been right in her life, her friendship with Jack—she can't risk losing him too.

Made in the USA
Coppell, TX
09 April 2025